Rain by Rachel Ann

To Corinne, while after I struggled with a title for book 2 the entire writing process, you didn't even see it yet and it rolled off your tongue like you wrote it yourself. Love ya!

To Jim, I love you.

I0665105

Preface

It had been months since the bar had legally become mine. Tony was a bit taken back by how it all played out. Ty thought it was the coolest thing ever. But, as family does, they both spent countless hours getting it ready for business. Lisa has been nothing short of a fairy godmother in getting me up and running. Using her connections to book gigs, get distributors aligned and all the inner workings. Even Doug has helped. Lisa has come to visit me the most over the months, with Doug making a few trips and even Tony came out once. We would never have crossed paths if not for Nick, but nonetheless have formed quite a bond. Lisa is probably my best friend, second to Rob.

Rob and I had a lot to overcome after Nick and I broke up as I pretty much ditched him most the entire relationship. Nothing was intentional, I explained over and over. He always seemed to have his suspicions about what went on before I flew home but has always known to leave it alone. He has really taken to helping with the bar as well. He has his regular day job, but seems to hang with me helping as well.

I am finally hitting a groove with my life again after all that drama. I work in the office for my brother a lot less. I help him with what I can, usually spending half the day on

Monday and Tuesdays there. Melissa was helping out a bit more with Bella in pre-school, but she is expecting again and will probably become a full-time mommy soon enough. The bar is taking off. We open normally Wednesday through Sunday. I try to have live shows every Friday and Saturday. With Lisa's connections, I've been able to have giant names stop in. That has gone a long way to making the place so popular.

Chapter 1

Just getting settled into my home office on Monday morning after getting home at 3am from closing the bar, my desk phone rings. Caller ID says its Lisa. "Hey Lady, what's up?" I answer.

"I have a question for you and you can think about it if you want and I won't be offended if you say no." she sounds so nervous. "Tony finally proposed to me and we are getting married in Vegas in 3 weeks. I would love it if you were my maid of honor." She finished.

"Oh my god!! Congratulations, Lisa. I would be honored, are you kidding me?" I reply instantly.

"Rain, I'm so happy you said that, but I have to be completely honest. Tony is having Nick as his best man. They are band mates and have been best friends since high school. I'm not sure how this would work for you." I could hear the sadness in her voice.

"Oh, well, that's something to mull over." I have not seen Nick since everything went down on his birthday at the Storm. I handed him back his rings and never mentioned him again to Lisa, Doug or Tony. I can't. I realize that they all interact with him on a daily basis, but we somehow keep it all separate and it's working. "Well, Lisa, it's your wedding, what do you want?" I ask.

"I want you there, but I don't want you to deal with something that will upset you. I know its awkward and I....uggh." I can hear the frustration in her voice.

"I'll do it. I will be your maid of honor. Of course." I reply feeling a million thoughts begin to form in the back of my mind.

"Are you sure?" I can hear the happiness in her voice.

"Yes, it will be fine. What do I have to do? I've never done this before." I laugh, secretly thinking I probably got myself way in over my head.

"Well, the wedding will be on a Saturday night but we are planning things to begin about Tuesday or Wednesday. Would that be ok?" she asks.

"Whatever I need to do. It's your big day" I say. "Send me a text with the date and details and I will make sure I am there, I don't need a date, do I?" I ask.

"Uhhh, that's all up to you. Doug is really helping coordinate a lot of this for us. I will tell him to send the details to you, ok?" she asks.

"That will be fine, but hey. Not to cut this short, but I really got a lot of work to get done, can I call you later?" I ask.

"Sure thing, I have a bunch more calls to make. I will talk to you soon, love ya, take care." she says sounding excited.

"OK, bye." I say as I hang up the phone. I am so happy for her, not sure what a maid of honor entails, but I send a quick text to Melissa to ask. I begin to look at my calendar and attempt to figure out how a week in Vegas will work, and with 3 weeks' notice? I send Rob a text to see what his plans are that week as well.

I begin to go thru my emails and see if there is anything urgent that needs my attention. Nope. I open up my trading software and work on some accounts. I have quite the cash flow right now, between the bar and the market. I keep stuffing money away into an account so I can be prepared to reimburse the cost of the bar.

I sit back in my chair and think about how many sharp turns my life has taken. I keep myself completely busy these days. No more relationships. Just throw myself into work. Stay busy and in control. Last time I let my guard down, I ended up an unconscious Jane Doe in a hospital. Nope. Never again. Not even a single dinner date since. But I guess, looking at a silver lining, I met Lisa and Doug and Tony. And now Lisa and Tony, tying the knot. I may not particularly want any sort of relationship, but those two belong together. A ying to the yang.

The phone rings again on my desk. Caller ID says Rob. "Hi Rob, you at work?" I ask.

"Yeah, meetings in a bit, what's up?" he asks.

"Lisa is getting married in Vegas in 3 weeks, I am the maid of honor." I say.

"So, I'm the honorary date for this shin dig?" I can hear his smile thru the phone.

"I was actually seeing if you wanted to babysit the bar?" I eek out.

"Uhh, you know I have my own job, right?" He asks.

"I don't want you to quit your job, but just kinda hang out and play boss for a few nights? Maybe?"

"Ahhh, what are the dates?" I knew he would.

"Not set in stone, but it would be Wednesday thru Saturday, 3 weeks from now." I say.

"So, who are you getting paired up with for the wedding?" he asks.

"What do you mean? Paired up with?" I ask.

"Who is the best man? You will be matched with them for the week" he says.

"Oh, my god." I say flatly. Lisa tried to warn me. It did not even sink in.

"What, hello? Rain, ya there?" Rob asks.

"Shit, its Nick." I say, almost whispering as my mind wanders.

"Are you ok with this?" He asks.
"Uhhh, I did not think about it enough before insisting it was ok. I was just so happy for Lisa." I reply honestly. "Hey, I gotta let you go. I got things to do, and apparently think about, stop by for dinner?"

"Sure, see you later" Rob replies and hangs up.

What the hell did I sign up for? A million more things go thru my head. Will he be drunk the entire time? Is he completely sober now? Will he bring a date, do I bring a date? How bad will this be? Enough. I am going for Lisa, I can hold my head up high and be there for her. This is not about him, this is not about me. This is Lisa and Tony's wedding and I will do whatever I can do to see it go off without a hitch.

My desk phone rings again. Caller ID: Doug. "Hi Doug, how are we this morning?" I ask.

"Good, just got off the phone with Lisa, I sent you an email with dates and the hotel info. Plane ticket info and times. Rain. Are you good with this?" He asks, taking a serious tone.

"Haha." I laugh nervously. "This all just played out in my head right before you called. I am good with it. I am there as Lisa's maid of honor, nothing more, nothing less." I say matter of factly.

"OK. I trust your judgement." He replies.

"Ok, I trust yours, Doug. What do you think?" I ask.

"Ahhh, it's irrelevant what I think."

"Doug, answer me!" I reply back.

"Well, I think everyone is an adult and should act as such. To be honest, I don't think there will be any issues. Hey, will you bring a date or are you coming solo? I am ordering the plane tickets now." he says.

"I'm coming alone." I say. "I think I should be focused on Lisa, so no reason to go find someone to play my date all week."

"That sounds legit, OK. Ticket is ordered, check." He says.

"Are you bringing a date?" I ask.

"Uhh, I think I have enough to keep track of, playing wedding coordinator." He says, sounding a bit annoyed.

"Well, when everyone is paired off on the dance floor, I will be at the bar, meet me for a drink and I will dance with you." I say sincerely.

"I'm gonna hold you to that, Rain. But for now, I've got 100 more things to get done in the next hour. I will be in touch." And we hang up.

Chapter 2

After speaking with Melissa about what a maid of honor does, I'm still happy for Lisa, but wished I wasn't her closest friend, I thought sarcastically to myself. I had to throw a bachelorette party for someone who lives life like she is constantly at one. I need to throw a bridal shower, I also needed to co-host some sort of dinner for the wedding party and brunch for the bride and groom and parents of them. This all seems like a cakewalk until you add the name of my co-host. Nick. Will I ever be free? I come to the conclusion that he will have Doug do his dirty work for him anyways and Doug will probably do mine for me, so I just don't stress about it. I will get there. Doug is getting me from the airport to the hotel and we will figure out the details in the car.

It's spring here in the east and temperatures are starting to be pleasant. Vegas is not. I have become a bit more tone and muscular since the incident. I will never be a victim again. I decide that I need some new clothes for Vegas and ask Rob if he wants to drag me shopping. He happily obliges.

"So what look are you going for?" he asks.

"Well, I would like to look good, not trashy, and don't forget it's like sitting on the sun there right now." I say.

"Are you doing this because you are gonna see Nick?" He asks carefully.

"Not a chance in hell, I just want to know that I look good. This is really the first vacation I've had since we broke up, it's a wedding you know, a celebration and I just want to be on my game." I say, waiting to see how he reacts.

"But you are going to see him." He points out.

"I guess. I really want nothing to do with him. He is there as Tony's best friend. I am Lisa's best friend, apparently. And everyone will act like adults." I take Rob's words into consideration.

We shop and chat and eventually cover what I will need for the trip. I get all the bags into my truck and we head to dinner. Eventually, I make it back home and he helps me pack for the trip to the airport in the morning.

Chapter 3

Ty drives me to the airport in the morning. He is staying at my house and handling a lot at the bar in my absence. He knows Rob will be there to check in on him. It's only a week. I realize I have not been on a plane since my awful ride home by myself. Broken ribs, concussed. Generally looking and feeling like shit. My life changing in an instance. And here I am 13 months later, heading back to the west coast. Same people, different reasons. What the hell did I get myself into? I board the plane to first class and close the shade and order a glass of wine. I slowly settle into the seat and close my eyes.

I am woken by a stewardess upon landing and gather my stuff. Exiting the plane, I text Doug to let him know I have landed and he lets me know he will be looking for my luggage and waiting for me.

I spot Doug down an aisle waiting at a luggage carousel. "Doug!" I shout as I run up to him. He sees me and embraces me back as I run to hug him. "I have missed you so much!" I say.

"You sure you are good with all this?" He asks as he holds me back and looks at me. I'm in a form fitting white sheath dress and matching flip flops. "You look excellent."

"I'm good, should I not be?" I ask as I pull my suitcase off the carousel.

"Let me take that." Doug replies.

We start walking out of the airport and I ask if we can stop for lunch to catch up before we get to the hotel.

He agrees and we put the stuff into a cab and head to a restaurant on the strip.

"What's up?" he asks as our food arrives.

"Doug, I have questions that before I ask, I need to know they will stay between us. No allegiance to Nick?" I ask, studying his face.

"Rain, of course. Normally, to anyone else the answer would be 'no' but…whatever I can answer for you. What do you want to know?" he replies.

"Did he bring a date?" I sound nervous.

Doug laughs.

"What is so funny, Doug? I just want to prepare myself for whatever I feel when I see him. It's not funny. I don't care either way." I say, a bit embarrassed.

"No, Rain, it's funny cause he asked the same thing." He replies trying to compose himself.

"What the fuck did he ask for? I'm the one wronged here. Who the hell does he think he is?" I am getting mad and not even sure if I have the right to be.

"Calm down, he just didn't want things to be uncomfortable. I told him it was just you and he decided to come alone is all. He is just as weirded out about all this as you." Doug says kindly.

"Well, is there anything you think I should know? To forewarn me about, prepare me for anything shocking?" I ask trying to make it friendlier.

"Lisa sister is bat shit crazy!" he laughs. "You are gonna need to keep a drink in Lisa's hand whenever she is present, trust me!" He smiles.

"Huh?" I ask.

"Trust me!" he says as he is checking his phone. "We gotta go, Rain." He continues as he gets up.

Chapter 4

We take a quick cab from the restaurant to the hotel and my luggage is on a bellhop cart. Doug walks me to the desk to check in and Lisa comes running in and hugs me. "Oh, I can't believe you are actually here with me, for my wedding. Oh my god, oh my god!" she shrieks. "I was just heading out to the pool to sit with Tony. Get your shit to your room and come join us...now!" she ordered and headed out the door. I look at Doug and sigh.

"And the whirlwind begins." He says and hands me a keycard to my room. The lady at the desk says my luggage will be in my room in 20 minutes and to head to the bar if I like.

"Doug? Could you go get me a drink and bring it out to the pool? I want to go say 'Hi' to Tony." I say.

"Sure, Jack and coke?"

"No, how about a gin and tonic?" I ask and he nods.

I head out the doors to the pool and spot Lisa and Tony in lounge chairs. I am in a nice white dress and flip flops, I fit right in at the pool. I walk over and Tony notices me and stands up to greet me.

"What a sight you are?" He says as he leans in to kiss my cheek.

"Congrats on the wedding." I reply as I kiss him back. I have my back to the lounge chair next to Tony's and I feel the person beginning to stand up. I turn around and there before me is Nick. Everyone just sort of goes silent as he stands up to greet me. He extends a hand and I am in such shock that he eventually lifts it up to just wave at me. "Hello, Rain, how are you?" he asks.

He cut his hair off. He is clean shaven, he is much more muscular, my god, one might not even recognize him. I realize that I am just staring at him and snap myself back into reality. "Hello, Nick, I'm fine, and you?"

Doug appears at my side with the gin and tonic. I take the glass from him and drink it all in one long chug. I didn't mean to do that, why do I do these things?

"Well, Ive been...good...ok, I guess." he eventually says.

"I think I should get up to my room to unpack." I realize how awful this is going. "Lisa, what's first on the agenda?" I turn to her.

"Oh, 4 at the salon. The bride side of the wedding party." She says.

"I have a copy of the entire itinerary for the week, it should be in your room." Doug chimes in.

"Oh, well, I guess I should go now so I can look it over." I say absently and turn and walk away. I am waiting at a bank of elevators and Nick steps beside me.

"Do you think we could talk?" He asks solemnly.

"About?" I reply back.

"This week? We have a lot to do." He says, studying my reaction.

"What about this week?" I ask. "I haven't looked at the schedule yet." I say as I enter the elevator.

Nick follows me in. "Well, I have and we will be together quite a bit. I don't want you to be uncomfortable."

"Oh, I am uncomfortable all right. But I have decided that Lisa's happiness outweighs that...for this week, I guess." I say.

The doors open back up as we have reached the 15th floor. "All our rooms are together, this way." Nick gestures me out the elevator.

I have a million thoughts going through my head. How did I get myself into this mess? Why am I even talking to him? I have to talk to him. I have to interact with him. Well, keep in cordial and get thru it. "Well, let's look at what we have to do." I say as I open my door with the keycard and let him in. There are flowers and a welcome basket of gifts and a manila envelope on the credenza and I open it. "Sit down and we can go over this." I say to him.

We sit on the couch as I scan the sheet. Today, I have an appointment at the salon. Tomorrow morning is a group brunch with the wedding party. Tomorrow evening is dinner with Nick, myself, Tony, Lisa and their parents. The following day is a fitting for the dresses and then a rehearsal, then dinner followed by a group party. The day after that is a dress rehearsal and then the bachelor/ bachelorette parties. Then Saturday is the big day. Not too bad, not too good, I think. "OK, so what about it?" I say after reading. "Didn't Doug plan most of this out? What's to talk about?" I ask him.

"Well, we have to plan out the Jack and Jill party and the bachelor parties ourselves." He says.

"OK." I reply. "I think I can plan a bachelorette party by myself. Not sure of what you want? Suggestions for the bachelor party? How about cocaine and prostitutes? Isn't that the standard with you guys?" I realize how harsh it was as soon as I spoke. It sounded lighter in my head.

"Rain! Tony is marrying her, that's not going to happen!" He replies back a bit shocked.

"Well, so were we, but…." I trail off, my mind going into overdrive. I am not ready for this.

Nick puts his hand on my arm to touch me and I coil back. "Don't." I say calmly. He pulls his arm back.

"We should really discuss this." He says.

"Discuss what?" I ask.

"Us." He replies.

"Us? What about us? Nick, it's been over a year. There is no 'us'." I say, staring blankly at the wall.

"Please don't be like this." He pleads.

"Be like what?"

"Like this, distant." He says.

"How should I be, what is the appropriate behavior here? Huh? I really want to know what you expect from me to make this easier for YOU." I say, feeling my temper rising.

"Rain, it's not like that, it's more the opposite. What do you want from me this week? What can I do to make you happy this week?" he asks. Are you kidding me, I think to myself?

A long pause while I carefully formulate a reply. "I am happy, I am happy for Lisa, I am happy for Tony. I am here for them, the rest? Well I will just deal with. Can we just get thru this cordially and move on? Do what we have to do for them and let it all be?" I ask.

"I can do that. I will do whatever you want me to." He says, a bit too seriously.

"OK." I say quietly. I'm good with this. Just 4 days and I can go back home. I can be civil and play happy for Lisa. I just have to not take this too seriously and move along. "I guess we have to host a jack and jill, any ideas?" I say trying to lighten the mood.

"I was thinking dinner and a club. Keep it simple, we still have the individual parties." He says.

"Yeah. I have never thrown a party like this, and it's Lisa so the bar is set pretty high for me!" I smile. "Hey, have you ever met her sister? Doug had a sort of cryptic warning, what's that about?" I ask.

"Tony has told me about her, I think she is married with kids and jealous of her little sister. Just kinda miserable?

Not real sure." He replies. This conversation is lightening up a bit. "She is here, but I did not meet her yet. Want to change and head back to the pool?"

Do I? Are we just going to let go of everything and act like nothing ever happened? I think that for the next few days it's going to be what's best. Then back to my life and back to normal. "Sure, I have to unpack and change, I will meet you down there." I say and he smiles.

"I will have a drink and a chair waiting." He says and leaves.

I unpack my things and find a bikini that looks amazing. I put it on and throw a sundress over it and keep my flip flops on and head down to the pool.

Chapter 5

I reach the pool and there are the other members of the band and respective flavors of the week. Tony and Lisa are next to each other on lounge chairs. Nick is next to Lisa and gets up.

"Here, sit here. Next to Lisa." He stands so I can sit down. Lisa rises to hug me again.

"You have no idea how happy this makes me that you are here with me!" she says, smelling of a bit of rum.

"Lisa, anything for you." I reply as Nick sits himself in the lounge chair on the other side of me. Seriously?

"We have about an hour till we head to the salon, manis, pedis, and trying out hair and make-up styles, Oh, my god! You haven't seen the dresses I picked out yet!" she exclaims. "You need to come to my room before the salon and see them!"

"Sounds like a plan." I reply as I reach for my drink. A pina colada, Nick ordered it.

I sit back and enjoy the sun. Not really warm back east yet and this is welcoming after a nasty winter. I reach for my drink and just enjoy the atmosphere.

"Is the drink ok?" Nick asks.

"Sure, its fine." I reply not taking my gaze off the pool.

"I can get you something else, if you want." He replies.

I'm not up for this chit chat shit and decide to get into the pool. I stand up and slip my sundress off over my head and stand there in my bikini. I am all 5'2" of pure muscular toned body. The bikini fits me like it was painted on. A golden string bikini. Abs that are formed and defined enough, but still enough body to not make me look like I'm trying. I can feel a lot more eyes on me than just our group. Tony even takes notice.

"Damn, woman. What have you been up to?" he looks over. Lisa takes notice as well.

"Jesus, you look good. I, I mean you've always looked good, but what the hell? It's my day, not yours." She laughs and says in a way that I take no offense to.

"I'm getting in the pool, anyone want to join me?" I say as I step forward to dive in. I swim around for a bit and realize that there is no graceful way to climb back out of the pool and swim over to the steps to exit the pool in a graceful manner.

"Hey there, you alone?" a man comes up to me with a towel.

"Not entirely, I'm here with friends for a wedding." I say as I take the towel and begin to dry off.

"Ohh, Can I get you a drink?" He asks as I dry off.

"Umm, my friends are over there, I think I have one." I say as I hand him the towel and walk around the pool, him following in tow.

I reach my group and Nick stands up. "Did you cool off?" He says, eyeing the gentleman standing next to me.

"Yeah, felt great!" I say.

The gentleman takes a look at Nick and extends a hand. "Mike." He introduces himself. "I was just asking if the lady was here alone." He says.

"Again, I'm here with….friends." I interject into the conversation. "Rain." I say as I extend my hand to Mike.

"Rain? Not today." He says, shaking my hand.

"No, silly, that's my name. Rain."

"Ohh, that's different. So here for a wedding, you say? You busy later?" He asks

"Don't you have an appointment at 4?" Nick replies. Well, he seems to have my schedule memorized.

"Actually, I do, but not sure what is going on after that." I say, curious to see where this 3-way conversation is going to go. "Lisa? What are we doing after the salon appointment?" I ask, since she appears to be watching this conversation.

"Uhhh, not sure, you could join me for dinner or whatever, nothing set in stone." She replies to see how it will play out.

"Uhhh, I really have no plans, but not sure what's going on so I think I will just pass." I reply.

"Uhh. That's fine, see you around?" The guy says and walks away.

"Well, aren't you turning heads." Lisa pipes up once he is far enough away to not hear.

I take position on the lounge chair and take my drink. I lean toward Lisa with my drink in hand. "To Vegas, baby!" I clink glasses with her and close my eyes while taking a drink.

"I think we have about 30 minutes till our appointment, are you going to need to change?" Lisa asks.

"Uhh, yeah. I don't think this is gonna work. Haha." I say as I get up and slip the sundress back over my head.

Chapter 6

We all head back up to our respective rooms, I think we have the whole hallway. Lisa asks me to hurry and head to her room after I am ready. I enter my room and change as quickly as I can and brush out my wet hair from the pool and head to knock at her door.

"Come on in." She answers in a towel. "We haven't had any time to catch up. What's the deal with Nick? Have you talked to him alone? Are you ok?" she asks as she is changing.

"Yeah, he followed me to my room when I got here. We chatted for a few. I'm good. This is about you and Tony." I say.

"When did he change so much?" I ask her. All the times that Lisa and I have hung out since that fateful night, we have never discussed him. I know that she is with Tony, Nicks bandmate and childhood best friend so I know she knows everything.

"Ehh, you know he went to rehab immediately after well...and then he came out a changed person. Cut his hair, started running. You never asked, I didn't want to give you updates you didn't want to know." She said as she put her arm around me.

"No, I really don't care. I was just a bit shocked is all. It's just I pictured the last time I saw him and that's what was in my head." I say. "I'm good, we both can act like adults for the rest of the week." I smile at her. "Any ideas what you want for your bachelorette party?" I ask, changing the subject.

"You know the male stripper show is here this month, right? Hint, hint!" She says elbowing me.

"Are you serious?" I ask. She looks at me and I can't read her response from her laugh. Is she laughing at my innocence or is she laughing at the absurdity of it? "I will make it happen, lady. I promise." I say and wait.

"I love you, Rain." She says as she finishes her outfit. "We need to go." She gestures to the door.

We head to the salon for our spa time. I meet the other 2 bridesmaids: Heather, her friend from high school that she has kept in touch with over the years and Cindy her sister. They both seem cordial. Cindy doesn't seem too bad. Lisa has this image in her head about how we should all look. Cindy and Heather have other ideas about hair and makeup for the wedding. I could care less. Do what you want, its Lisa's day.

We get facials, and nails and makeup all done. We try different things with our hair until Lisa is content. Then at about 7pm, it's over. "What are you doing for dinner, Lisa, plans with Tony?" I ask.

"Yes, at 8, I figure I look good enough." She says with a smile.

"Maybe the rest of us should all go out and get to know each other?" Heather chimes in.

"Sure, want me to call a restaurant and get us a table." I ask, looking to Cindy for an answer.

"I guess that would be ok. I have to call our parents; their flight will come in tomorrow." She says. She doesn't appear to be bad, I think.

Heather, Cindy and I all head to dinner and enjoy ourselves, telling stories about Lisa and generally have a good time. It's after 10 when I realize how tired I am and end the evening and head to bed. I lie down thinking, one down, 3 to go, not so bad.

Chapter 7

I wake up to my phone buzzing. It's Rob checking in how things are. I call him and we talk for a bit. I tell him it's all good. He promises to check in on Ty running the bar and I let him know that I have to get going. Brunch. A group brunch for the wedding party. All 8 of us. I select a pair of form fitting white pants and lace up shirt. Rob didn't want me to get it, he said it looked like a pirate shirt. Whatever. I slip on some white heels and head down to the dining room that we are booked at. Nick is waiting at the entrance.

"You look amazing, Rain. How was last night?" he asks.

"Good, Lisa is going to look like a princess on Saturday." I say. Princess. Huh, that's what I used to be. I think to myself.

"I'm sure you will, too." He says without hesitation as we walk to the table. It appears we are the last to arrive.

"Am I late?" I ask looking around and checking my phone.

"Nope, I think we were all early." Tony chimes in pulling out a chair. We are seated at a large round table. Tony has another high school friend, Richard, and Nick and the drummer Todd as his best men on half the table, Lisa has myself, Heather and Cindy. Everyone seems to know each other but me.

Cindy is contently staring at me and finally speaks "So this must be great for you to be paired up with Nick. What an honor!" she speaks to me but seeming loud enough for everyone to hear.

I am confused. "What do you mean? I am here for Lisa?" I reply, genuinely confused and quickly becoming uncomfortable.

Lisa shoots her a dirty look. "That's enough, Cindy. Rain knows Nick. Nothing special, nothing to see." She says as the waiter reaches our table.

We all order and it takes the conversation in another direction and off topic. The waiter slowly makes his way round the table and leaves. Nick, Tony and Todd and Richard are making their own conversation and Heather is asking Lisa about the dress. I am fiddling with my phone, which I normally don't do at a dinner table, but it keeps my mind off things.

"NOW I know who you are, you are the girl from the stage!" Cindy bursts out. "Nick broke up with you."

"Oh, my god, shut up Cindy." Lisa yells back throwing her napkin on the empty plate.

"She dumped Nick. Leave her alone." Todd throws in.

"You left him? Why? Who are you with now?" Cindy asks, completely shocked.

"I…I…I've got to use the restroom." I say as I jump to my feet. I feel Lisa getting up right behind me.

"I'll come join you." She says as she is stumbling to get up.

"No, I'm all set, I will be back. Just give me a minute, please." I say. I really don't want anyone following me. I head to the bathroom and enter and go directly to the sink to splash water on my face. I can't do this. I think to myself. I got myself in over my head. Settle down, Rain. You aren't going to leave now. Compose yourself and head back in there. I splash more water on my face and dry it carefully. I head back out of the bathroom. Nick is outside the door.

"What do you want?" I look at him.

"I am so sorry about that." He says.

"What, you didn't do anything." I reply. "I'm sure lots of people have questions. I was this mystery woman that no one knew, thrown against my will into the spotlight then I just disappeared just as quickly as I entered it. People are gonna think what they want, draw their own conclusions since they don't have a clue about the truth." I say with a bit of harshness in my voice. "I'm going back to the table." I say as I walk right past him back to the table to take my seat.

"Cindy, Lisa and I are friends, Nick and I dated, but haven't even seen each other in over a year. This wedding has nothing to do with my previous relationships. It's about Lisa and Tony and who they want here, nothing more, nothing less." I say as I sit down. I begin to place the cloth napkin back in my lap and realize that her mouth is still hanging open.

"I'm sorry." She replies, not knowing if she should speak any further.

"Besides, once it gets out that Nick Stone is in the building, I'm not sure that's a line I want to be stuck waiting in." I laugh, trying to make a joke. Todd and Tony immediately start chuckling but Lisa gives me a sideways look and I return the sideways look letting her know I'm good.

Nick returns to the table shortly before our food. The rest of breakfast is just stuff about the wedding and more stories of Lisa and Tony. The rest of breakfast is good.

After breakfast, I decide to do a little solo shopping and head over to the clubs to see about some male strippers. I buy a 'best friends' charm bracelet for Lisa and myself. I book everything for the bachelorette show to be in the front row and have her dragged on stage. She will love it. My phone is buzzing and its Doug.

Chapter 8

I answer and he asks me to head up to his room, there is some changes in the works. I head up and Lisa, Tony and Nick are in there already. "What's up?" I ask, confused about the group in here.

"My parents missed their flight." Tony says. "Nick's parents did not."

Lisa chimes in "My parents are here, but Cindy seems to think it's more appropriate for her to join us for dinner." She sounds disappointed. "She already told them."

"Ok, it's not upsetting to me to miss dinner." I say still confused a bit.

"My parents know you are here and want to have dinner with you." Nick says. "Tony told them."

"Ummm, really?" I ask.

"I will just tell them 'No'." Nick says.

I stay silent while he is waiting for a reply.

"Why don't your parents just join in place of Tony's parents?" I ask.

"My mother wants to see you." He says.

"Uhh. She knows we aren't together, right?" I am becoming more uncomfortable.

"Well, yeah, of course she does." He replies nervously.

"Lisa, Tony." I look to them. "This is up to you two, I'm here for you guys. I'm yours. Whatever you want." I think this is kind of an easy way to make difficult decisions 'The Lisa and Tony magic 8 ball'.

"Rain, it's really your decision" Lisa says.

"If your family wasn't such a pain, this would not even be an issue." Tony says under his breath to Lisa and I see her sigh from stress.

"Whatever, I will go to dinner. If it will keep things running smoothly, I will join them for dinner." I sigh.

Doug looks like he had weight lifted off him when I reply. Still not sure about all this. But I'm here for Lisa. Whatever I can do to help, I guess.

"Doug, can you make the call for a table? I've got to go see my parents." Nick replies.

"Sure thing, I will text you both with the info." He replies back engaged to his phone.

"Am I all set here?" I ask.

"Yeah, this really helps, Rain." Tony replies.

I head out of Doug's room and I feel Nick following me. "Rain, wait." He says catching up to me as I get to my door.

"Oh, we need to talk." I say opening the door and heading in. "What do your parents know, what do they think?" I ask pointedly.

He sits down on the couch gesturing me to sit. "Rain, all they know is I entered rehab and you broke it off. I stayed with them for a few weeks after getting out. My mother seemed to think that you should have been back with me once I was 'cured'. I don't know what she thinks." He says trying to take my hand. I don't let him.

"So, I'm going to dinner as the villain in all this? Seriously?" I ask

"I think my dad gets it a bit more, he knows some bad shit happened, I don't think he blames you." He says.

"Well, that's fucking spectacular. As long as someone doesn't blame me. Jesus, what am I getting myself into?" I say more to myself at the end.

"It will be fine, we will keep it light." He promises.

"How should I dress?" I ask absentmindedly.

"I think it will be dressy. I will come get you when it's time to go, about an hour? I'll leave you alone now." He says and lets himself out.

I take a long hot shower and begin to pick out an outfit. I settle for a powder blue sheath dress, not real tight, but flattering. I slip on some matching heels and realize that I am ready about 20 minutes early. I check in with Ty and Rob and Tony to see that there is nothing pressing. I check in with my mother and just let her know I'm good and then have a seat on the couch. There is a knock at the door a few minutes later. "Come on in." I say.

Nick opens the door and has his parents in tow as I get up to leave. "What lovely flowers." Liz, Nick's mother, comments.

"Oh, they are. Everything about this is great!" I say as I close and lock the door behind us. We head to the elevator and down to dinner. Sitting at the table, I order an ice water for myself and Nick and his dad order beers. His mother orders a glass of wine. After the waiter returns with the drinks there is just an awkward silence.

"So how have you been, Rain?" Terry, Nick's dad breaks up the silence.

"Good, busy with work all the time." I reply, honestly.
"Hope you didn't take too big of a hit with that dip the market took." He says.
"Oh, that didn't hurt me at all." I say.
"How's that? I lost 8%?" He asks, a bit intrigued.

"Ehh, I am very, very conservative. I don't like risks at all. Everything has to be calculated out. No unknowns here." I reply.

"It's good to take risks in life sometimes." Liz joins in. "Look at Nick and what he's accomplished." Hearing pride in her voice.

"Yeah, well sometimes big risks can end up destroying someone." I say. "I'm really not an 'excitement' type of person." I reply. "I'm content what what's around me." Finishing quietly while I feel everyone staring at me. "So, the wedding is in a few days!" I say trying to change the subject. "I am so happy for them!"

"Yes, they have been together for so long, not as long as Nick and Tony have been friends, but she met them as soon as they got to L.A." Liz replies. "Tony grew up right down the street from us, Nick and him have been friends since they were little." She says. "We are actually good friends with his parents. I can't believe they were late to the airport this morning. I told them they should have rode with us." She says shaking her head at Terry.

"Well, they are on the next flight. Just 6 hours late. Better late than never, dear." Terry replies looking like he has heard this 100 times already.

"I really thought that we were going to see Nick get married first after he met you." She says. Oh, dear lord, did she actually just say that?

"Mom!" Nick blurts out the same time that Terry blurts out "Liz!".

"What?! There is nothing unforgiveable when you love someone." She says looking at me. "I can't imagine what else he has to do to change."

"I need to get a drink." I get up and quickly exit to the bar.

I feel Nick right behind me. "I'm so sorry for that." He says.

"Nick, leave me be. Go sit down." I say calmly.

"Rain, no, let me talk."

"If you leave now, I'm not going to get madder than I already am. Go sit down." I say a bit more forcefully and he turns.

I ask for a shot of Jack and the bartender obliges. Terry sits down next to me. "Well, that probably could not have been worse." He says as he motions for the bartender to bring him one as well.

"Ehh, its fine." I say.

"No, it's not fine. It was completely out of line. I loved when he brought you home. You were good for him, and he really messed up something. I don't know what he did, and I probably don't want to know, but whatever caused you to leave him made him straighten his shit out and I will always be thankful for that." He said. What do I say to that? How do I reply? Glad to be of service?

"Yeah, something like that." Is all I can say in return. I pick up my glass and finish it.

"I understand if you don't, but will you come finish dinner with us?" He asks, putting his hand on my shoulder.

"Sure, we can only go up from here." I say as I slide off the barstool and we head back into the dining room. Spotting the table, I see Nick and his mother in a heated conversation and he takes notice of me heading his way. They both stop and compose themselves.

"Rain has opted to return to the table and I'm sure we can find plenty of appropriate conversation to fill the rest of this dinner." Terry says, eyeing Liz.
"I was out of line, Rain, I apologize. I just know that Nick loves you and always want to see him happy. I..I" Liz says.
"Enough, Ma!" Nick says as he pulls out my chair for me. "I

ordered you a salad with chicken and got you the chicken parm." He looks to his father.

"Thank you, Nick. That's fine." I say as I wish my glass of water was a drink. The remainder of dinner is mundane conversation. God, I wish I was not here. After we finished eating, Terry informed us that Tony's parents had arrived and he thinks they should go check in with them. They seemed to not be able to get out of the restaurant fast enough. Proper good-bye's and not rude, but high tailing it out nonetheless.

"Well, that was fun." I say as I toss my napkin on my plate and lean back in the chair.

"Rain, I am so sorry, it was a bad idea." Nick says. "I had no idea my mother was going to say all that." He continues.

The waiter returns to the table and begins to clear the plates. "Could I get a beer?" Nick asks.

"Two." I interject.

"Rain." Nick says.

"Don't. I want the bill for the bar that you bought me." I say looking at him dead in the eye.

"I bought that for you." He says back.

"No, I want nothing from you. I want to know that I am me, without anything from you, and I want to move on with my life." I say.

"That was a gift for your, for our wedding." He says pleading.

"Well, we never got married so…" I snap back. The waiter arrives with our beers. I begin to drink mine.

"I thought you said we could just get thru this wedding." He says back to me.

"I didn't think it would be like this." I reply.

"I didn't either." He says in a solemn voice.

I finish back my beer and stand up. "I think that it's time for me to call it on today. I'm going to my room." I say, thinking how it began with Cindy and ended with his mother.
"Let me walk you back." He stands up.

"Ahh, fine." I say as I check my phone. No missed calls or texts. "And what are your plans for the rest of the night?" I ask. Not even sure why it came out of my mouth.

"Ehh, there is some band playing Tony said we should go check out. Figured we would head over together. Want to join us?" He asks.

"Not a snowballs chance in hell." I reply a bit too quickly.
"Suit yourself." He says. I'm not sure what to make of his tone.

We walk in silence until we reach my room. "Well, I'd like to say today has been fun, but….let's just be thankful it's over." I say. "After all, tomorrow is another day!" I say with a smile.

"Huh? Why are you smiling like that?" He asks, not sure if he should smile back or be afraid.

"Just something from a movie." I say as I close the door. Yes, tomorrow is another day. God help us all. I take a quick hot shower and get into a robe. I get out my laptop and go thru some items. Tomorrow, I have dress fitting, a rehearsal then dinner then close it out with all of us going out to party. Uggh. I work on my laptop researching some upstarts that might go public and eventually fall asleep.

Chapter 9

My room phone ringing wakes me up. I answer it, not exactly sure how long it's been ringing for. "Hello?" I need to clear my throat.

"I am so sorry about dinner last night." Its Lisa.

"Not your fault. Don't worry about it. How do you even know, as a matter of fact?" I ask.

"Well, Tony went out with Nick and well, hey, why don't you order some coffee and I will be in your room in 5?" She asks.

"Sure, 5 minutes. I will be ready." I hop out of bed. Standing there with just my robe on I order and then throw some clothes on. There is a knock at the door.

"Lisa? Be there in a minute." I say as I rush over.

I open the door and she hugs me "Really Rain, I am so sorry." She says as we sit on the couch.

"Why, nothings your fault, I'm fine. Just learning what I'm made of, haha." I say.

"No, first Cindy then his parents. This is so wrong. You don't deserve this." She says as I interrupt her.
"No. You don't, this is not your worry. What did Tony say anyways?" I am curious how Nick re-created last night.

"Tony said that Liz, that's her name right? Yeah, Liz was super inappropriate telling you that you should take Nick back. She didn't, did she?"

"Well, pretty much. But, again, it's not about that, this is all about you. This week is not Nick drama." I say.

"Tony also said you talked afterward, just the two of you." She was studying my face for my reaction. Huh? What? Were we at the same table?

"Uhh, yeah. I asked for an invoice for the bar, to pay him off and sever all ties." I reply a bit shocked.

"Really? I didn't get that vibe about it?" She is confused.

"Nick is delusional. I gave no hope, trust me. I even told him earlier that we would act like adults for the two of you. Nothing more nothing less." I say.

"Are you sure that's how you feel?" She asks as she takes my hand.

"What do you mean 'Am I sure'? Lisa, you know me." I say, a bit annoyed.

"Just checking is all." She is twiddling with cushion on the couch.

"You didn't ask me to be the maid of honor because of Nick?" I say the words as thoughts start running through my head.
"Oh, Rain, no, no NO! I asked you because you are important to me, because I wanted you to be in it. It had nothing to do with Nick. Why would you even think that?" She asks, taken back from my question.

"You just asked me if I'm sure." I say more accusatory that I wanted to sound.

"Rain, I don't know. I'm so happy this week, Tony would probably not even be marrying me if you and Nick weren't together. Everything that happened set this in motion. And you guys were really good together." She trails off tearing up.

"Yeah, we were good, till we weren't. And that kind of bad will never outweigh the good." I say. Jesus fucking Christ. Again. Glad to be of service. Too many memories begin to flood back to me and I can't watch her cry. I will end up joining her. There is a knock at the door. Room service. I tip the busboy and wheel the cart in. "Coffee, Lisa? How do you take it?" I ask her.

"Oh, just black." She replies as she is blotting her eyes with a tissue. I never wanted to make her upset. I remember the boxes from the jewelry store I got. Her shower gift! I run to my bedroom and get the two small wrapped boxes and bring them back. I sit next to her and hand her one.

"For you! Open it!" I say as she takes it and smiles.

"What's this?" she asks as she unwraps the box.

"Oh, just a little something to commemorate the weekend." I reply as she takes the gold bracelet out of the box and fondles the half heart charm that says 'best friends'.

"It's beautiful." She says as she leans to hug me. "I should get you one!"

She releases me and I pick up the other box and wave it at her. "I got two! One for each of us." I laugh.

"Ohh, I love it. Thank you so much, Rain." She replied while fumbling with the clasp.

I take it from her and put it on her. "What time is the dress fitting?" I ask as she takes mine and starts to clasp it to my wrist.

"It's in a few hours, let's do something!" she says. "Want to go hit the tables?"

"Sure."

We go down to the casino and find some poker tables to sit at and take our seats. It always fascinates me how this place is so busy 24 hours a day. We are playing right along, win some, lose some. Lisa is checking her phone. "Mind if Tony joins us?" she asks.

"Sure, the more the merrier." I reply and within a few minutes he arrives. Lisa slides over a seat and he sits between us.

"How we doing, ladies?" He asks.

"Ehh, up a little, roulette is more suited for me." I say, playing with my chips.

"Hey, aren't you Tony? From that band?" some random guy at the table says.

"Uhh, Yeah." Tony says as he blushes a bit.

"Here with two women, eh?" The guy replies.

"He is marrying me on Saturday!" Lisa interjects while wrapping her arms around him.

"And her?" the guy gestures at me.

"My friend." Lisa responds.

"She here alone?" He moves to the empty chair next to me.

"Not alone, here with the whole wedding party." I say as he moves closer and I realize he has had way too much to drink.

"You got your own room or are you with them?" He asks with a sly smile.

"While I have my own room, I think I will just remain alone in it. Thanks anyways." I realize this is making me really uncomfortable.

"Are you sure, you don't want them to be the only ones having fun." He reaches to put his hand on mine.
"I'm good." I say affirmatively.

"Nah, you look like a pretty good time." He says, moving closer.

"Please back off, buddy." I say a bit louder, the dealer taking notice.

"I think I could show you a good time." He slurs attempting to move closer as I stand up.

"The lady said she's not interested. Got it?" I hear Nick from behind me. The random guy stands up toward Nick. Nick instinctively moves a bit in front of me toe to toe with this stranger. He stares at Nick intently.

"I know who you are! Nick Stone! You're the singer! Damn!" He looks at me to Nick and back again. "I knew she looked like a good time, sorry to have stepped on your toes man! I don't want to take your toy for the weekend." he says as he stumbles back to his seat. Oh, you've got to be kidding me.

"What an asshole." Lisa says.

"Seriously." Tony adds in.

"You ok?" Nick asks me.

"Yeah, I think it time to head back to my room anyways." I say absently as I get my purse and phone.

"I should go with Rain, walk her back. We have to be at the dress fitting shortly anyways." She says as she takes my arm and head out to the elevators. "Well, that was nice of Nick!" she says.

"Yeah, I guess, what an asshole that guy was." I reply.

We head back to our rooms and I get ready for the dress fitting. Lisa picks me back up with her mother, Tony's mother, Cindy and Heather. We head to the dress store. There is a private area in the back. Lisa has already picked out our dresses. We definitely have different ideas. It is a long sliver dress with a lot of sequins on it. A slit from my hip to the ground on one side, floor length. The dress is backless, Im not even sure how much there is in the front. Haha. It seems to clip around the neck holding it all up. It's a beautiful dress. The store seems to have our dresses in the correct size and they have us try them on and make minor pinnings here and there. We wrap up with the bridesmaid's dresses within an hour and move onto the bride dress.

Lisa looks gorgeous. It's reminiscent of a modern English gown. She looks so different. I think I was expecting some sort of showgirl costume. Her mother and Tony's mother dote all over her, assisting getting it laced up the back and helping pin her hair and tuck the vail and all the other things a bride should have done. Her mother hands her a small box. "Something borrowed, old and blue." She says.

Lisa opens the box and is shocked. "Oh, mom, Grandmas sapphire earrings!" she exclaims.

"Now all you need is something new!" he mother says.

"Ohhh, I have that, too." She says, holding up her arm with the bracelet dangling from her wrist.

"Lisa, you don't have to wear that on your wedding day." I say, thinking about how silly a bff bracelet looks.

"No, Rain, I want to, it really means a lot to me!" She says back at me. I sigh and just smile at her. Whatever Lisa wants.

The rest of the fitting goes smoothly. We wrap up and get our tickets to pick up our dresses the following day after alterations are complete and are on our way. Off to the rehearsal.

Chapter 10

We all assemble in the banquet hall. Everyone fidgeting around and chatting. Doug is here with a clip board and I actually feel a sigh of relief. Someone will keep this train on its tracks. Doug and the wedding planner standing next to each other. Could not be farther apart. Doug, looking like some sort of biker gang member and this older woman with every dyed blond hair in place. Doug with his cell phone and her with her headset. It all just makes me giggle a bit.

They pair up Cindy and Todd, Heather and Richard and myself and Nick outside the room. Now Cindy and Todd will head down first and then Heather and Richard. Then Nick and I. Tony's mother has made little papier mâché bouquets for us to practice with. Nick intents on looping his arm thru mine. Nope. Not today.

"We are supposed to be practicing." He says, whining like a toddler.

"Practice walking next to me without touching me." I say, whispering, completely flustered. I am not sure why I cannot walk in a straight line down a damn walkway.

"Just let me take your arm. Everyone else is." He whispers back.

I stop dead in my tracks. Everyone has taken notice. Pushy lady asks "Is there a problem?"

"He keeps touching me." I say, realizing just how dumb it sounds as soon as it leaves my mouth. Tony bursts into laughter. Nick looks mortified. Everyone else looks confused.

"What? Now I can't even touch you?!" Nick asks.
"Why do you want to?" I ask back.

"Oh my god, Rain!" he says back with disgust. Tony's laughter has subsided and everyone is staring at me.

Doug walks up and puts his hand on Nicks arm. "Come on, Nick, you can touch me!" And everyone starts laughing again. We finish the rehearsal and head to dinner.

"What the hell was that all about?" Nick pulls me aside.

"I'm kinda over this entire process is all, I'm tired, Nick. This is more than I was prepared for is all." I say emotionless.

"Jesus, does the thought of my arm touching yours disgusts you that much?" He asks, clearly annoyed.

"Look, Nick, I don't want to talk about this. I'm tired. I just want to be left alone, you, your mother, Cindy, random strangers seeing me near you. It's too much for me. I have had about a year of peace and a clear head. This is just bringing it all back....and I, I don't like it is all, is that ok with you?" I ask.

"Rain, I'm sorry. I don't want you to feel that way." He says, realizing that I am really upset.

"No, I'm sorry. I promised I would do this for Lisa, and right now, I'm not. I need to find my big girl panties and just suck it up. 2 days. That's all. Shit, I've been through worse and made it to the other side. And this is supposed to be fun."

"Are you that miserable here?" He asks.

"Not for Lisa, I am nothing but happy for her and want to see her happy, I don't want to not do it, I just don't need the other attention. I don't know, it's hard to explain." I say. "I just don't want any attention, at all, from anyone, I guess."

"Rain." Nick says solemnly. "Come on, let's just head in and have dinner. Sit next to me." I follow him to the table.

I sit down at the table and realize that I have made this about me, which is the opposite of what I wanted. I pull out my phone while everyone is chatting and Doug has texted me. 'Do you want to go home? Lisa asked me to check.'

'No.' I reply back. 'I'm good now' mental note to have the same awkward conversation I just had with Nick with Doug.

'Just checking let me know if you need anything.'

I have some texts from Ty and Rob. Ty wants to know why I left Rob to babysit him. Rob wants to know if Ty was adopted. Haha. I owe Rob something special when I return.

"Rain, ya there?" I hear Lisa calling out my name. "Nick ordered for you, everything ok over there?" she asks.

"Yeah, just checking on business back east. Sorry." I say.

"It's rude to be on your phone at the dinner table." Cindy snaps at me. Oh, for the love of Saint Pete. Make this shit stop.

"Cindy, she owns a bar back east "Nor'Easter" and she is just checking on business. It's ok." Lisa says.

"No, it was rude of me. I'm at full attention." I say as I make a point to put my phone away for everyone to see. Holy shit. Why am I here?

"So what is the plan for after dinner?" I ask, trying to prove I'm all in.

"We are all going to a club. There is a band performing that Tony wants to check out." Lisa says, smiling.

"Sounds great!" I say.

"Sounds like every other night in their lives." Cindy pipes in. What a peach this one is.

"Well, that's what makes them happy, and they are clearly happy, unlike other people." I say directly at her waiting for her to say something back. She turns away from me.

"So you and Lisa do the same thing for work?" Richard asks toward me taking an opportunity to keep Cindy quiet.

"Yeah, kinda." I say.

"She owns her bar though, I just manage 'The Storm'." Lisa says.

"You own a bar?" He asks, kinda surprised.

"Yeah, a series of odd events, and here I am." I say. "My brother wanted to buy it and things just sort of happened the way that they did." I say, thinking. "But, close enough for him, haha."

"Yeah, that's pretty odd." He replies.

"So you must love the club scene as much as Lisa." Heather joins in the conversation.

"Actually, not really." I say, wishing I had just agreed. "I love the business aspect of it more, not really a fan of dealing with the 'talent', haha." I recover.

"Yeah, some of these band guys think they can do whatever they want and just get away with it cause of who they are." Cindy comments. Lisa's eyebrows go up while waiting to see my reply. Why is she still talking?

"Ehh, they really make so many people happy, what's the big deal if someone is inconvenienced in the process?" I reply.

"I think I'm going to head to the bar." Nick says with a huff and walks off.

"You really never know when to shut up, do you Cindy?" Lisa strains at her.

"You're the one that decided to bring Nick's ex to participate in your wedding." She says to Lisa.

"I brought my best friend to participate in my wedding." Lisa spits back. "They don't have a problem with it, in fact, you seem to be the only one who does. Get your shit in check or you won't be participating in the wedding, got it!"

"Whatever!" Is Cindy's only response.
"She's not kidding!" Tony joins in, putting his arm around Lisa.

"You know what? Enjoy your club tonight, I'm staying in my room. I will see you in the morning." She says and walks out.

"Thank fucking god!" Richard says quietly but loud enough we all hear. He was such a polite, quiet guy. Ha!

"Well, we should all go get ready." Tony stands up and everyone but Lisa and I follow him out of the restaurant.

"Rain, sit." Lisa looks at me.

"What's up?" I ask

"I'm really thinking this wedding thing isn't a good idea." She says nervously with her hands in her lap.

"What?! What do you mean?" I am shocked.

"This all was set in motion when you and Nick were together and now, I'm watching you two and don't want to end up, well...." She trails off.

"Oh, for fucks sake. You and Tony are not me and Nick. You two have been together for ever, you two enjoy the same things. You two are meant to be together. You guys just....are!" I smile at her.

She calls the waiter over and orders another drink while not making eye contact with me.

"Look, everyone gets nervous right before the wedding." I plead. "It's normal." I say, feeling panicked. Why do I feel like this is my fault? I start looking around and notice Nick at the bar. "I have to use the little girls room, stay here, don't move, I will be right back." I quickly get up and head to Nick.

"Hey." I say as I walk up behind him.
"What's up?" He asks, not turning around. Ohh, I am not playing mood games with him. I have to deal with Lisa first.

"Look, we need to get our shit straight here, Lisa is at the table contemplating not getting married because of our behavior." I poke him in the side.

"Huh?" he turns to face me.

"She is at the table over there talking all sorts of nonsense about not wanting to do it." I look at him. "Everyone gets nervous before the wedding and we are probably just the catalyst that set it in motion, but I can't say this has been exactly drama free. Come talk to her with me?" I ask.

"You want us to go talk to her together? Us, the perfect...... anti-couple?"

"Anti-couple?" I ask.

"You know what I mean."
"Yeah, there probably isn't a real word to describe this." I

laugh. I put my hand on his back. "Do this for me? I feel like it's my fault." I look directly at him.

"Your fault?" He asks.

"Yeah, just by being here, not being able to handle my shit. I kind of expected to be able to contain myself a bit better." I say staring at him.

"This isn't your fault, none of this is your fault." He says and takes my hand. I let him and pause for a moment just staring at him.

"Nick! We need to go talk to Lisa. This isn't about us, it's about her." I say as I pull him toward me to get him off the chair.

We return to the table with Lisa. "We need to talk to you." I say realizing I have no idea what to say.

"Rain, you don't have to do this." She says as she takes a drink.

"Yes, Lisa, we do." Nick replies. "Tony loves you, you two belong together. You can't not get married."

"You told him?" Lisa accuses me. Oh, god, I feel awful.

"Lisa, I just want you to understand that you and Tony are not Nick and I." I say. "We were never meant to be together." It hits me when the words come out of my mouth.

"Nick probably loved you more than Tony loves me." She says as I feel my temperature rise. "You know Tony better than I do." She looks to Nick. "You know I'm right, right?" She asks him.

"Lisa, don't say that. He loves you. I know it." He says back to her. "He has always loved you. And will always love you."

"He loves you enough to marry you, he is not taking this lightly. He wants to be with you forever." Nick says taking her chin in his hand.

"What are you so freaked out for at this point?" I ask. "You guys have been together for like a decade!"

"I don't know, I don't know." She said putting her head in her hands. "I think seeing you two here, not together, is messing with my head." Holy shit! Her head?

"Lisa, do you want me to leave?" I ask, kind of afraid of her answer.

"No, I just want...I want...I want you two to be happy." She says, sounding drained.

"I am happy, Lisa." I say, not ready to go any further with this. I look at Nick.

"Lisa, I'm fine with all this." Nick says. "Don't let us bother you."

"Look, this will all be fine. It's just your nerves. Let's go get ready for the party tonight. Come on." I pry at her as Tony walks up to the table.
"Everything ok here?" He asks, staring at her.

"Everything is fine. Just having a little 3-way heart to heart. Why don't you go help her get ready? Meet back at the bar in 30 minutes?" I ask.

"Uhh, as long as you say so." Tony replies as Lisa composes herself and they leave.

"Rain…" Nick says when we are at the table alone.
"Holy Shit, Nick! I can't have this hanging over my head. Look, just be nice to me and I will be nice to you. 48 hours to go?" I say, exasperated.

"I thought I was being nice." He is staring at me.

"You know what I mean. I mean you haven't been not nice, but, Jesus, you were sitting at the table with me." I say. "I've really got to go change for the show." I say, standing up.

"I'll walk up with you." He says.

"Ok, let's go." I say as we head to the elevators.

Chapter 11

We reach my door and it appears that he is just waiting for me. "Are you changing?" I ask.

"Do I need to?" He replies with a small laugh.

"I don't know, but I do. Are you waiting in here for me?" I say as I enter the room.

"I can." He says as he follows me and sits on the couch.

I head into the bedroom and begin to change. "Thank you for talking with Lisa." I say as I slip off my dress. "I know it was really uncomfortable for you." I say.
"Why do you say that?" He asks from the other room.
"Uhh, cause it was for me." I say.

"Oh. Want a drink?" He asks.
"Sure, hey what should I be wearing for tonight?" I ask as he walks into my bedroom and I'm standing there wearing nothing but underwear. "Nick! What the fuck?" I yell.

"Sorry. I. I." and he exits the bedroom. "Wear whatever you want, you will look good regardless." He says and I can hear he is back on the couch.

"Dress or pants?" I ask.

"My vote is a dress."

"Fine, be out in 2 minutes." I reply. I slip on a spandex sheath dress that laces up around the cleavage portion. I lace it up nicely and exit the room.

"Drink now?" He says as I walk around the corner. "Damn you look good, Rain." He says walking up to me.

"Thanks." I say as I take the drink. "Can we just enjoy this evening?" I ask.

"What do you mean?" He says.

"No memories, no bad times. Just, I don't know, a night off from the drama?" I ask.

"Like a date?" he is genuine.

"Umm, I believe those were always drama filled, Nick." I say. "I don't know, I just want a carefree evening. I want to get drunk. I don't want to be worried. I want to have fun."

"Want me to have Doug shadow you?" he asks.

"I don't think 'we' should be drinking at the same time." I say flatly.

"Sooo, you want me to shadow you?" He asks with a smile.

"That might be nice, Lisa sure would appreciate it." I say.

"I can do that for you. Nick's not drinking tonight. I will get you home safely, no matter what you do." He says coming closer to me.

I walk away from him and slip my black matching heels on. "Let's go!"

We head back to the bar and no one is there yet. Nick orders a drink for me and hands it to me. As I'm drinking it,

Todd, Richard and Heather walk up. We chat for a few minutes how this should be a bit better with the absence of Cindy and I see Lisa and Tony walking in. Lisa looks in better spirits. "Hey, over here!" I wave and they spot us.

Tony and Lisa walk up and Nick puts his hands on my shoulders from behind. "How are you Lisa?" He asks.

She gives us a strange glance and says she is fine and we head to the club. Hot damn its loud in here. Lazers everywhere, smoke machines. We find tables right up front. Lisa, Tony, Nick and myself at one and the other 3 at the other table. Tony orders a round for everyone and Nick does not pick up his glass. "You ok, Nick?" Tony asks.

"I am on my best behavior tonight!" he yells back.

"What?! Come on." Tony sounds disappointed and Nick looks from Tony to me. Tony shakes his head. "Got it! Two for you, Rain?" He says.

"Sure." I pick up both shot glasses. "To Lisa." I drink one. "To Tony." I drink the other.

The lights go dim and a band takes the stage. Not too bad. Lisa is rocking out with Tony. They play a few songs and then break. The singer comes out and announces that Tony and Nick are center stage and the place begins to get loud. Lisa is loving it. I have had way too much to drink and start prodding them as well. Nick is shocked. "Really? You want me to go up there?" He says laughing. "Should we, Tony?"

"Whatever, man. Let's do it." Tony is drunk but you can never really tell how drunk. They scoop up Todd on their way and hop on stage. "What the fuck do we do now?" I see Tony ask Nick.

"Play something? He replies. It's funny that they did this with literally no plan. "Rain, what do you want us to play?" He shouts at me.

"Me? Nah, its Lisa's night." I scream back. Lisa has her arm around me. "What's it gonna be, Lisa?" I ask her.

"Oh, shit, I don't know. You pick something? What's appropriate?" She asks as she tips into me. Neither of us can stand on our own. I cannot process anything in my brain. I could not name 3 Heavensent songs right now if my life depended on it. I realize that we are taking way too long. The room is not waiting for us.

"Simple Man." I yell out. Nick, Tony and Todd have a short meeting of the minds and pick their spots and begin. The entire place erupts into cheering when they begin to recognize the song. Some sketchy spots at the beginning, but the original band comes out and joins them as well. This is amazing. Lisa and I are swaying to the song at the front of the stage. Tony has his eyes locked on Lisa from the stage. I look to Nick and suddenly wish I was sitting up there with him. I have had too much to drink. What the hell am I thinking? Water. Now.

The waiter comes over and I order water. It finally arrives by the time the song is over and everyone has returned off the stage. The band makes a big deal thanking the guys and begin to return to playing.

"Excellent song choice, ladies." Tony says to us and Lisa basically climbs on top of him. I think the honeymoon started early. Nick and I are at the table. He is a bit sweaty.

"That was fun." He says to me. "Did you enjoy that?"

"Nick, it was amazing, as always." I say sounding as vulnerable as I feel. "I'm drunk." I announce.

"I see that." He laughs.

"No, I'm really, really drunk. I think I should go." I say.

"Where do you want to go?" He asks, still smiling.
"To go lay down. Hopefully not in my own puke." I say.
That snapped him back.
"Oh! Do you feel ok now? Want some water?" He hands me the glass and I drink most of it at once.

"Let's just go." I say as I stand up and sit right back down. Heels are not going to work. I lean right down, almost tipping out of the seat and take them off. Bare feet. Solid ground. That feels good.

"Hey, guys, I'm gonna get Rain to her room." Nick is trying to interrupt Tony and Lisa making out. They kind of broke apart at the mouth to acknowledge Nick.

"Yeah, we probably should too." They sort of reply as I put my shoes on the table.
"Let me get those." Nick picks up my heels. "Do you have

the rest of your things?" he asks and I hold up my arm with my wristlet hanging off.

"Do you need help?" He asks as I stand up and realize how crowded the room is. He takes my arm and begins to guide me. I am stumbling a bit, but maintain a bit of composure.

"Lead the way." I slur. We begin to exit and he has people trying to get to him and he just sort of pushes forward, ignoring them. My foot gets stepped on by some guy in boots. "Oww!" I exclaim and kind of tumble. Nick reacts and stops and just stares at me, laughing. "My foot hurts!" I say and he leans down and helps me up. I take 2 steps and limp. He scoops me up and carries me out to the elevator.

"Can you stand?" he asks when we reach the inside of the elevator.

"I think so." I attempt to and brace myself against him as he instinctively puts his arm around me. "Thank you." I say

"I wouldn't leave you on the floor. You wouldn't have been rushed if people didn't know who I was, it's my fault." He says.

"No, thank you for tonight." I say. "I really had a good time." I say quietly.

"I'm glad you did." He says rubbing by back.
"Sorry you didn't drink." I really feel emotional.

"What? I had a great time, I didn't need to drink." He says.

"I'm sorry for all this." Why am I tearing up? Get it in check girl. The elevator doors open and I head out toward my room. He is following right with me. I am stumbling with my purse to get my keycard and he takes it from me and opens the door. I rush in and lay down on the couch beginning to cry.

"What's 'all of this'? Why are you sorry?" He asks.

"Just for everything, causing this drama, facing you, coming here, just everything." I say. How did I get this upset?

"Baby, come here." He says as he gets me to sit up on the couch and sits next to me.

"No, Nick, please don't. I should have just stayed away. I shouldn't feel this way." I say as he pulls me to lean on him. I don't even have the strength to stop him.

"Feel what way?!" he asks. I am slipping into sleep. "Princess, talk to me."

Chapter 12

I wake up groggy, laying on the couch in the same clothes I had on last night. I have a headache. I begin to open my eyes and see Nick sitting across from me, wide awake, staring at me. Oh fuck no. What did I say, what did I do? I should not drink.

"Want some coffee?" He asks.
"That would be good." I reply slowly sitting up. "Have you been here all night?"

"Yeah." He says getting me a cup.

"Why." I ask. Did I invite him? What the hell happened? I remember shots, I remember singing 'Simple Man' with Lisa. Why does my foot hurt? "Why does my foot hurt?" I ask, rubbing it.

"You don't remember getting stepped on?" He asks.

"No."

"What do you remember?" he asks.
"What should I be remembering, why are you staring at me like this?" I ask, getting nervous.
"I think I liked you better drunk." He mumbles as he gets himself a cup of coffee.

"What is that supposed to mean? What happened?" I feel sick.

"You were nicer to me is all, more open." He says.

"Nicer? Nicer how?" I am so confused.

"I don't know, happier? I guess, you were happy just to be with me." I can tell he is searching for the right words.

"Oh, nothing happened though." I say, relaxing a bit.
"Jesus, Rain, I wouldn't take advantage of you, you couldn't even walk." He says, clearly irritated with my thoughts.
"Well? How was I nicer then? What did I say, do?" I am morbidly curious, but not sure I even want the answer.

"You didn't freak out when I touched you. I don't know. I guess, you didn't have the guard up like you do now. You weren't trying to calculate everything like you are now." That hurt. "You were just happy to be with me and I was happy to be with you, is all." That hurt more.

"And you're not happy here with me now?" I ask.

"Jesus, this is what I'm talking about Rain." He says becoming frustrated.

"I don't know what I'm supposed to feel thru all this." I say, sulking a bit.
"You are supposed to feel whatever you feel, not try to feel a certain way on purpose. What do you feel right now? Are you happy, are you mad?" He is getting more flustered.

"You want the truth?" I ask solemnly.
"NO! Fucking lie to me!" he replies back and I shrink into the couch. "Rain, I'm sorry, you are so frustrating." He says quietly moving to sit on the coffee table in front of me.

"Truth." I stare directly at him. "I am kinda enjoying being around you in bits and pieces. I hate you! I hate you for what happened! I hate myself for even speaking to you. I hate myself for feeling happy to be near you." I look down into my lap. "How do you feel right now?"

"Rain. Oh my god, I don't even know what to say." He says taking my hand.

"OH? You feel what you feel. Well, what do you feel? Huh?" I ask.

"What has Lisa said about this? Or even Doug or Tony?" He asks.

"What are you talking about? They have never said anything to me." I am confused now.

"What? I've always told them not to push you, but to be 100% honest about anything you ask." He says.

"I've never brought it up." I say matter of factly.

"OK, well who did you talk this out with? Rob? Ty?" He asks.
"Oh my god, are you insane? No, I've never discussed it with anyone, ever." What the hell is he thinking?

"You mean everything you went through....no one? Ever? You just let that shit rattle around in your head all this time?" He is shocked.

"Well who was I supposed to talk to? My mom? My Brothers? No, it's bad enough I lived it, I was not sharing that humiliation with anyone." My headache is easing up the madder I get.

"Maybe go to a shrink? I don't know." He blurts out.

"Have you? Who did you sit down and talk to?" I ask, almost accusatory.

"A shrink, a therapist, actually lots of each." He says. I realize that he discussed this with other people. Oh, this is so much worse. I begin to shake a bit.

"Really? You have a team of doctors waiting to hear your version? How does your version go?"

"Rain, what the hell do you think I did in rehab? I talked to a lot of doctors about a lot of things. Especially the trigger that made me go."

"I'm a trigger?" It sounded funny to say out loud.

"No, this is the trigger." He says as he pulls a chain out from under his shirt. The chain has 2 rings on it. The two rings that I handed back to him from the car that day. "I've never taken it off. Any time I feel like doing something I shouldn't, there is a constant reminder of what I lost." He says sounding sad. "Half the people I talked to wanted you to come in, I wouldn't allow it. I did not want any one of them contacting you. The professionals insisted that you would contact me and I insisted that you wouldn't. 'For closure' they kept saying. I just gave you your space."

"I don't know what to say. I don't know what you want me to say." I look at him.

"Say what you feel, whatever you feel right now. Please."
He says.

"I feel....empty. Like, everything you just said makes me feel sad for you. But in reality, how fucked up is it that I feel bad for you?" I say.
"Rain, never feel bad for me. For this. Ever." Nick says as he stands up and pulls me to my feet to hug me. I begin to cry and he hugs me tighter. "Rain, I will always love you. I will, whether you love me back, hate me, go to the press and destroy me. Doesn't matter, I will always love you and I deserve whatever you decide happens." I actually hug him back. I don't know if I feel better or worse.

"You should go, we have dress rehearsal soon." I say flatly as he releases his grip. He looks me directly in the eyes. Keeps the stare for a few seconds and leaves.

Chapter 13

I head over to Lisa's room and find Lisa, Heather and Cindy. "How are you feeling this morning?" I smile at her.

"Refreshed!" she says with a sly smile. "What about you? Looking like you had a fun time."

"I did, Lisa, I really did." I smile back at her.

"Did you make it back to your room ok? You were looking a little sloppy there at the end." She says.

"I'm surprised you noticed!" I laugh.
"I saw Nick carrying her into her hotel room." Heather laughs. Lisa's look changes in an instant.
"Why yes, yes he did. And he was a complete gentleman about the whole thing." I look at Lisa to reassure her. "We are quite the anti-couple, aren't we?" I laugh and Lisa joins in.

We head to the dress store to try on our dresses. Lisa tries hers on and takes it back off. "I spent way too much time picking it out to let him see it early." She smirks. We all complete getting dressed and head out to the ballroom. The guys are already there in tuxedos. They all look good. Nick looks so clean and amazing. Short hair, actually combed, clean shaven. Tall. I could go on forever. Completely opposite from the hot mess that signed a Christmas card many moons ago.

Doug joins us in a suit as well as the snotty woman with the headset. "Are there any ground rules before we begin? Is anyone not allowed to touch anyone else? Did someone show up with cooties that everyone else might not be aware of?" He laughs.

We all start outside in the hallway and practice over and over coming in. walking down the aisle. Taking our places, blah, blah. Over and over until we do it twice in a row with no mistakes. Finally, we are done.

"Is it what you want, Lisa?" I ask her. "Anything else we need to do? Speak now or forever hold your peace." I say.

"I think it's exactly what I wanted." She says, beaming. The lady with the headset says we can go.

"So, dinner is in an hour?" I ask Lisa.

"Yeah. See you then." She replies and takes off with Cindy.

I head to the elevators and feel Nick beside me. "You look amazing." He says.

"Thanks, Lisa dressed me." I make a joke. "You clean up pretty nice yourself." I wink at him.

"Thanks, I think Lisa dressed me, too." He smiles.

We step off the elevator and head to our rooms. Inside mine, I realize I am alone and can't get the dress off. Shit! I walk back to Nick's room and knock. "Coming back for a second look, can't resist me, can you?" He smiles.

"Come to my room and undress me!" I say. The look on his face.
"Rain, stop it!" He says.

"Actually, I'm serious. I can't get out of the dress and I can't have anything happen to it before tomorrow." I look at him.

"Well, turn around and let me see." He says.

"Not here, you idiot. I'm not gonna walk back to my room naked carrying the dress."

"Ahh, alright. Can I change first?" He asks.

"Fine, hurry up." I say. "So, what are you doing for Tony tonight?" I ask

"Cocaine and prostitutes." He replies.

"Shut up."

"Nah, we are going to keep it calm. Some gambling, drinking and just go back and see that act we saw last night again. Tony wants to possibly see about the bass player. And you girls?" He asks.
"Strippers, obviously. And way too much to drink." I say.
"That is sooo you. But what are you really doing?" He smiles.

"I'm not kidding. I got us a table for the male stripper show. Right up front." I say and smile.

"Get the hell out of here, you didn't plan that yourself." He says as he comes out of his room in jeans and t-shirt.

"Yes, I did. I thought to myself, what is the exact opposite of what I would do, and I did it. I wanted to get tickets to the cirque de solil show."

"That sounds like you." He laughs.

"Exactly!" I say as we head to my room.

"First strippers, and now you are begging me to undress you, it's a slippery slope, dear." He smiles.

"I'm not begging, I'm sure I could head out in the hallway and a line would form to service my needs." I give him that 'don't push me' look.

"Baby, I'd be first in it." He says as he starts to assess the zipper in the back.

"You better not fuck up the dress, Lisa will actually kill me." I say feeling him tug a little too much.

"Got it!" he says as I feel the dress release off me. I grab the front so it does not fall to the floor and head to my bedroom. I opt to wear pants and flats tonight. No more heels. Tight low-cut tank top and spandex jeans with gladiator sandals. I come back out of the bedroom.

"Want a drink?" I ask him.

"Sure, a beer is fine. Are you having one with me?" He asks as I take two out of the mini fridge.

"Is that ok?" I ask.

"Take it easy tonight? You are so vulnerable when you are drunk and it's just you girls out there." He says completely serious.

"Oh, are you protective of me now?" I ask.

"I've always been protective of you." he says.

"I…" I actually stop myself for once.

"What?" he asks.

"Nothing, I have to keep up with Lisa tonight." I say.
"If you try to keep up with Lisa your liver will shut down."
He says.

"No, I mean, take care of her. Not attempt to keep up with her drinking. I don't have a death wish." I laugh."

We drink our beers and get ready to go.

"You better have Tony take it easy too. It's his big day tomorrow." I say as I get my wristlet and check the contents inside. I take my phone out and check for messages. Nothing. Jeeze, I wish they would check in with me a bit more.

"Ready?" He asks.

"Always!" I reply and we head back to the bar.

Chapter 14

There seem to be two tables congregated. Doug is joining
the bachelor party and we are still the 4 girls. We take off
in separate directions. We reach the club and I go the box
office to get our tickets.
"What is this show?" Cindy asks.
"Strippers!" I laugh.

"Awesome!" She smiles. Finally, something she approves
of.
We take our seat and a man in leather hot pants comes to
take our drink orders. "2 rounds of tequila and keep them
coming." Cindy pulls out 2 hundred-dollar bills. Dear Lord, I
wish this Cindy showed up earlier.

I toast one shot to Lisa and then ask for a water. Lisa is
drinking like a fish. Along with Cindy.

"This is what they have in common?" Heather laughs and
asks me.

"Maybe it's in the dna? I ask and she giggles. "I'm not even
gonna try to keep up." I flag down the waiter. "May I get a
very weak pina colada?"

"Sure thing." He says.

"Make that two?" Heather asks.

I hand him my credit card. "Can we just open a tab? 25%
added for you?" I ask.

"Sure thing, I will be right back."

"You didn't need to do that." Heather replies.

"It's no big deal and I kinda want the evidence." I laugh.

We continue to drink at about the quarter of the pace that Cindy and Lisa are. They are getting plastered, but getting along so all is good. The show is getting better. Women screaming, men dancing around. Money flying all over the place. Everyone having a good time.
"Do we have any brides to be in the audience?" I hear from the stage. Cindy starts flailing her arms. "Well, come on up then." What the?!?

"Hey, bitch, I'm the bride." Lisa slurs as Cindy starts racing her to the stage. They push and shove each other to make it to the stairs and both sort of land at the same time.

"Why don't we just celebrate you both?" the MC says to them.

"Shit, I would have said I was a bride to be, too." Heather leans over to me.

"For real, though. Ehh, just as long as they both remain tame, is all I care. They look like they could go at it." I laugh. On stage, they have both taken seats in folding chairs set up side by side. The dancers are making their way around them. A fireman and a cop. I wonder if the rest of the village people will join them on stage and laugh to myself.

"Why do you have to ruin everything?" Lisa shouts from the stage and lunges at Cindy.

Heather taps me on the shoulder to gain my attention from a gentleman that seems to think I'm very interested in supporting him. "Uhh, should we go help?" she asks

"Is this actually happening?" I say, mostly to myself.

The cop in his underwear is clearly overpowered trying to separate them. The fireman is sort of useless as well. I head for the stage, thinking I should have just drank myself into a coma tonight. Some other dancers attempt to stop me. "She's with me." I say. I guess I looked sober enough to let me up there and I go up and attempt to drag Cindy away from Lisa. She has grasp of Lisa's hair. "Let her go!" I wrestle with her. The cop manages to get Lisa. This is particularly hilarious to me. We gain control of the two of them and drag them to the side of the stage. I am apologizing profusely and they seem to be gaining some composure. They are still bitching at each other. Something about a cat when Cindy was 10 and a book cover that was ruined. They promise to settle down and we release them from our grips.
"Fuck you, Lisa, you always get everything you want." Cindy spits out as she takes a swing at Lisa.

"I hate you, Cindy." Lisa begins to swing as well. I rush to grab Cindy's arm and stop her as the cop steps between them as well. I stop Cindy and Lisa connects with the cop's face.

"Holy Shit!" He is screaming like a small child. The fireman rushes over and Lisa empties the contents of her stomach down the front of him. I think I may be sick. The blood on the 'cop' and the puke on the 'fireman' seems to have brought Cindy back to reality for a moment.

"I think it's time to go." She slurs.

"Ya sure? Now it's time to go? Get the fuck out of here." I say as Heather steps over glancing at me for direction. "Can you take her and do something with her?" I ask Heather.

"Where do you want me to bring her? She asks as she is guiding her to the exit.

"I don't care, the dumpster? Ha, ha." I laugh nervously. "Her room would probably be best. I will catch up with you later?" I say and Heather leaves with her.

I look back down and Lisa is passed out on the floor. Dear lord. I look at the cop and the fireman. "So, Im sure this has happened before. How does this work?" I ask them.

The fireman has his arm around the cop consoling him, "This does not happen, I don't fucking know what to do. Who's going to pay for this?" He asks, clearly upset.

"I will, I will take care of everything. I should probably get her out of here first. Can you help me with her?" I ask him.

"Fuck you, deal with 'that' yourself." He says. His cop friend whispers something to him. "Sorry, I'm just worried about Mark here. I can help, but I don't know what to do. It'd be like moving a 150-pound suitcase. Even the luggage has wheels." He says a bit calmer.

"Uhhh, could we find one of those bellhop carts?" The idea pops into my head at the mention of her being luggage. "Then if I can just get her onto it, I can just wheel her into her room." I am pretty proud of my idea. The fireman leaves and speaks to someone who quickly returns with a bellhop cart. We work to carefully get her on the cart and I tell them to give me 20 minutes and I will be right back. I start wheeling her out of the back entrance and to the bank of elevators.

In the elevator, I pull out my cell phone and see a text from Nick asking how the night is going. How ironic. Ehh, he is with Tony and I will just ignore it. I push the cart into her room and realize that I probably shouldn't just leave her on it. I do for a moment and go to Cindy's room next door and knock. Heather answers. "Where is Lisa?" She asks me.

"Come with me, I will show you." I say and we head back to Lisa's room.

Heather bursts out laughing. "Oh, my god!"

"Well, I had to get her up here, she is out!" I say, pretty proud of my moving job, with my hands on my hips. "But I need a favor, I need to get her into bed and have you watch her. I have to go back to see their new stripper friends and work this mess out." I say.
"I will babysit these two, go." She says and I head back out.

I reach the club and am blocked by security when I try to get back in the way that I came. I spot the cop with a towel over his face. I wave to him until someone notices and lets me thru. "You have no idea how sorry I am about all this. What do you want me to do?" I ask.

He removes the towel and the bleeding has stopped. "What can you do? Look at me, my nose is broken. I'm not going to be able to work for days." He says.
"Can I take you to the doctor, money? Whatever you want." I say.

"Your friend is crazy, ya know that?" He looks at me. "And really? They are both getting married?" He says, lightening up a bit.

"Ehh, the one that hit you actually is, the other is the jealous sister." I say. "You ever heard of Heavensent?" I ask him, curious to his answer.

"Yeah, who hasn't?" He says.
"She is marrying the guitarist, tomorrow, here!" I say.

"No shit?!" He is really surprised. It's not like me to name drop, but I'm really just trying to undo this mess. "So, are you like her assistant or something?" He asks, engaged a bit more in the conversation.

"Nahh, just the maid of honor, and apparently I am now the actual 'maid'." I laugh.

"But with honor!" He laughs too.

"Can you change into some clothes?" I ask.

"Huh? What?" he replies.

"Sorry, that sounded a little harsh. Change, clean up, I will take you to go get something to eat and we can discuss how I can fix this all for you." I say as nice as I can.

"Uhh, sure? Give me 10 minutes, I will be right back." He says and heads into another area.

The 'fireman' comes over to me and asks what's going on. I explain the last few minutes to him. "She is really marrying the guitarist from 'Heavensent'?" He asks.

"Yeah, crazy, huh!" I say.

"And what's your relationship to them?" He asks.

"Relationship? Umm. I'm friends with them, not attached to anyone, if that's what you mean." I say.

"Oh, bands like that usually turn into little families, that's all." He says.

"Like you and the cop?" I ask, smiling. Did I just say that?

"The cop? Oh, you mean Mark. Ahh, haha, I'm Tim. Is it that obvious?" He asks, a bit nervous.

"Well, when he was bleeding all over the place, you were protective....in a good way, is all." I say, kindly. "I told him to change and I'm taking him to get some food and discuss how I can get this all fixed. You are welcome to join us." I say.

"Uhh, let me check with him, I will be right back." He says and he leaves.

Tim and Mark both return wearing jeans and t-shirts. It looks like they just stepped off the Jersey shore. Mark looks a lot better, swelling and redness, but he is not going to look good in the morning. "Where do you want to eat?" Tim asks me.

"I think you know the place better than I do, lead the way." I say as we head into the main area of the hotel. We settle on a steakhouse and we order. We chat about the two of them, what I do and so on. I explain that I have a club on the east coast. We discuss how cool it would be for their show to make a stop at it for a few dates. Wow, I can't wait to tell Rob about this one. Dinner is good. Shortly after eating, Tim gets a text and has to go. Mark and I are left at the table.

"Do you want to see a doctor tomorrow?" I ask.
"Nah, nothing they can really do for a broken nose, it just sucks I will miss a few nights of work if I am all black and blue." He says, playing with his drink.

"What do you usually make in a night?" I ask.

"Depends, 800 on a weeknight, maybe 1500 on a Saturday? We don't go on every night, though." He says.

"What's a number that will work for you?" I ask, pointedly. No response. "Five thousand?" I throw out there.

"Ohh, are you kidding? That's too much." He says.

"No, there is still your aggravation."
"Are you sure?" He asks.

"It's fine. I feel so bad about the two of them and their behavior. I'm embarrassed." I say, honestly.

"If you are ok with it, so am I. And I really want to talk to the manager about heading to the east coast, too." He says, smiling.

"Let me get you my number, you guys can call and we can try to work something out." I reach into my purse and have no pen or paper.

"I can go to the bar and get something." He gets up.

Sitting at the table, I rub my temples. One day left. How fucked has this whole trip been, I think. At least I didn't cause the drama tonight. Not that I'm happy she caused it, but it's easier on my brain that I did not for once.

I hear a loud familiar group coming into the restaurant. Tony and his bachelor party are coming in with the band they went to see. He notices me from across the room. "Hey, where's the girls?" He asks, laughing jovially.

"Their rooms, all tucked in for tomorrow." I smile.

"Tame evening? Already in bed?" Doug asks.

"Ehh, I guess." I say.

"You aren't even drunk." Todd stumbles over.

"Nope, not tonight." I say as Nick sits down at the table and notices 2 drink glasses at it.

"Who ya here with?" He picks up the glass and looks at it.

"No one in particular, just having a drink." I say.

"Did you girls have a good time tonight?" he asks.

"Yeah, some more than others, I think." I say as Mark walks back up to the table.

"Holy shit! Look at you guys." He exclaims. "The whole band is here, Nick! It's an honor, can I get your autograph?" He is beaming.

Doug steps in, acting security mode. "Sir, this is a private party, you will have to be on your way." He sounds so authoritative. I laugh out loud.

"Ohh, sorry, I was just coming back to the table for Rain to give me her number." He says innocently standing there in awe of all of the guys.

I have to physically take the paper and pen out of his hand and write down my info. "Here, Mark." I say as I hand it back to him. The other guys in the party are quite confused. I lean over to Mark and whisper in his ear to call me in the morning and I will get him the cash. He leaves.

Nick stands up in a huff. "Well, I guess some of you did have more fun than others. Come on guys, our party will continue." He gets up and everyone follows.

Back at the table alone, I finish my drink and settle the bill. I sit there for a few minutes in silence and notice the crew at the bar getting all the attention from the ladies. Tony is having a blast. Everyone is. Why couldn't my night go like that? Ehh, so is life. Time to head up and check on my sleeping beauty boxers.

I reach Lisa's room and knock quietly. Heather answers the door. "You were gone for a while."

"I had dinner, cost me five grand." I say.
"Holy shit! How did dinner cost so much?" she asks.

"Haha, not dinner, that's to cover him missing work from the broken nose."

"Oh, yeah. Sorry, I'm just really tired, my mind is not functioning at 100% right now." She says, yawning. "But... I got her undressed and into bed, and I got her to drink some water." She says with sarcastic pride.

"And the other one?" I ask.

"She's on the floor, I left her there." She giggles.

"Good. You can head back to your room if you want?" I notice the clock, its 2:30am. "Big day tomorrow, not sure how, but, whatever."

"Lisa will wake up fine, as always." She says as she is gathering her things.
"Yeah, you're probably right." I say as I close the door on her.

Chapter 15

I stay in Lisa's room for a bit and clean up. I rinse her
clothes off and straighten up a bit. I look at her in the bed.
I carefully take her earrings off and bracelet off. 'best
friends' She is still wearing it. I place the items on her night
stand and head out of the bedroom. I order some coffee
and settle on the couch and flip the tv on. Flipping through
the channels, I settle on some mundane cooking show. The
coffee comes and I drink about 3 cups and glance at the
clock. 3:30 am. Shit! I need to go to bed. I check on Lisa
one last time and head out. I hear the guys before I see
them and stop and wait. Nick comes stumbling down the
hallway with a woman draped around him. My stomach
sinks as he meets eyes with me.

"Looks like we are all having fun tonight." He says. Fuck
you Nick.

I turn and Tony is already heading into his room. "Where is
Doug?" I ask kind of top volume at everyone.

"Not sure, you need him for something?" Todd replies.

"Well, there was a big problem tonight that I'm trying my
best to handle, but I should probably let Doug know." I say
to him. I see Nick moving closer to me to hear.

"Didn't look like any problem earlier." He says at me with
this girl playing with his hair.
"Where is Doug?" I ask.

"What is the problem?" Nick asks while his new friend is
still clinging to him.

"Not doing this like this." I say flatly, pointing to her. "Just go. She clearly needs your...attention." I say. "You know what? I'm going to bed. If someone sees Doug, please have him find me." I say and head into my room, slamming the door. I start undressing and there is a knock at the door. Doug? I scramble to find a robe and wrap it as I answer the door.

"Nick?" why is he here?

"Where is your friend?" I ask, looking down the hallway.

"I sent her home." He says.

"Why, you two looked like you were gonna have a good time." I snark at him.

"Rain, stop."

"Stop what?" I ask.

"Who did you have dinner with? Huh? Looks like you were being awful nice to him?" He says.

"So you see me being nice to some guy and have to one up me and find someone to parade back to your room in front of me, is that what that was?" I ask. I am so over tired.

"Look, I ain't gonna lie, I kinda thought we were here, single....for the wedding. It's not my business who you are with."

"Got that shit right." I interrupt him while he speaks.

"But it got under my skin is all, I reacted." He says.

"Nick, I'm tired. I can't do this right now." I plead.

"I never pictured you just picking up some random guy." He says.

"Picking up some random guy? You want to know what I was doing? I was paying off the guy Lisa punched in the face, if you got there earlier you would have seen his boyfriend there with us. Fuck you Nick. Leave." I shout.
"Wait, what?"

"Oh my fucking god. Lisa and Cindy had way too much to drink, got into a god damn brawl on the stage, Lisa punched a stripper and threw up all over another one. Her and Cindy were rolling around on the stage fighting. That was my night. I spent the rest of the night putting everyone in their respective beds, cleaning puke, paying off people and then I get to finally reach my bed and see you with some bimbo draped all over you. Perfect fucking end to a perfect fucking night."

"Holy Shit!"

"And how was yours?" I snap.

"Well, sounds like it was better than yours." He says as he laughs and puts his arms around me.

"Don't." I say as I take them back off me.
"What?" He tries to look sympathetic.

"You just had your hands all over some other woman. No." I say.

"Rain."

No, you literally went and picked up a woman because you saw me with a guy at a table." I say.

"Rain."

"Stop saying my name. I'm worn out."

"We have breakfast at 9am. Want me to come get you?" he asks.

I glance over at the clock. 4:15. "Oh, I'm gonna be so tired." I sigh. "Look, don't say anything about last night to anyone. Goodnight." I say.

"I will be here at 8:30 to get you up. Lips are sealed." He says.

"Take my keycard, I am not gonna get up to let you in." I say from my bedroom. "I think it's on the table." I feel my eyes closing and I am out.

Chapter 16

"Rain, Rain?" I am being shaken awake.

"NO, let me sleep." I say as I pull the sheets closer around me.

"Rain, you have to get up. I have coffee for you." I hear Nick.

"Go away!" I say and turn over.

"Rain, there is a wedding today. You can't sleep all day." He says, trying to get the sheets out of my grasp.

"After last night, I can do whatever the hell I want." I say beginning to wake up. My robe is still on so I let him pull the sheets.

"Come on, clothes. Where are they, I will get them for you."

"How the hell aren't you tired?" I ask as I sit up.

"Just the lifestyle, I guess. Years of conditioning." He shrugs his shoulders. "Coffee, here." He hands me a cup.

I start drinking the coffee and see him rummaging thru my luggage. "What are you doing?" I ask.

"Getting you something to wear. Did you have something specific you want to wear?" He asks.

"Don't care, its breakfast." I reply. He pulls out a dress and some underwear and a bra, tosses them to me and leaves the room.

"Five minutes." He calls out.

"Maybe you should be next door making sure Lisa is up?" I ask as I get dressed and start brushing my hair.

"I told Tony it would be romantic for him to go wake her up. Texted him when I got up." He laughs.

"Bahaha!" Is all that comes out of my mouth as I am brushing my teeth.

I come back to the main room and Nick is sitting on the couch. "You know nothing happened last night." He says. "Ohh, that's where you are wrong. Lots of shit happened last night." I reply, shuddering at the thought of it all. "I mean with that chick. We didn't do anything." He says.

"Why are you telling me this?" I ask while getting my purse.

"I just thought you should know is all." He says as we head out the door.
We continue talking as we head to the elevators.

"We are not together, it does not matter what you do." I say.

"I'm just trying to be respectful of you here, is all." He says as Todd and Doug walk up. The elevator doors open and we begin filing in.

"Nick, you didn't respect the sanctity of monogamy when we were together, why do it now when we are not even together?" I ask.

"Uhh, let's just catch the next one." Doug says loudly and him and Todd step back off the elevator.

"See, there you go again." He says. "You are trying to figure out how you are supposed to feel."

"Huh? What the hell is that supposed to mean?" I ask.

"I know what I saw, last night, you saw me with her and it hurt you. Accept it." He says as if he won something.

"Are you for real?! Am I in the fucking twilight zone? Yes! Yes, Nick, your actions hurt me. Seeing her draped all over you hurt. Is that what you wanted to hear me say?" The elevator doors open and I beeline to the restaurant.

He is following at the same pace. "I didn't want to hear you say it. I'm just saying I don't want to see you hurt. I would do anything to not see you hurt. I am taking your feelings into consideration. Just let me know what they are. Honestly." He says.

We reach the table. "You need to stop right now." I say, thankful we are the first at the table and no one else is here. "Fine, you know you hurt me, you are trying not to. Thank you." I say and sit down. Doug and Todd are reaching the table.

"You two good?" Doug is studying us.
"Yup" I say. "I need coffee. Now." I say, looking for a waiter.

"I will go find you a cup." Nick says and walks away.
"Todd said you were looking for me last night, are you sure you are good?" Doug asks, pulling his chair closer to mine.

"Oh, last night. Yeah, I think it's all set." I say, absently.

"Well, Nick was shocked when he saw, then he picked up that woman at the bar to get back at you. I was so mad I went home." He says.

"Yeah, I met her." I say. Here we go again.

"Ohh, are you sure you're good with it?" he is prying.

"Doug, we talked. He sent her home, what he saw was a complete misunderstanding on his part. Its fine." I say, hoping my tone puts an end to it.

Heather and Richard start walking up and take a seat at the table. "I'm surprised you're even up!" she says as she rubs my shoulders.

"So am I, still haven't seen the twisted sisters yet." I laugh. Nick returns to the table with coffee in a to-go cup and hands it to me and takes a seat next to me.

"Ohh, I meant to give you this last night. The waiter, uhh. The tab. Here is the final receipt. I signed your name in a squiggle. Probably more appropriate than trying to find you." She hands me my credit card and an extremely long receipt.

Doug snatches the paper receipt and starts scanning it. "$1,200 fucking dollars? Jesus, and you guys called it an early night? You didn't even seem tipsy when I saw you?!" He exclaims. "What did you guys do?"

"Let's just wait till the table is full." I say.
Tony and Lisa walk into the room and up to the table. "Can we chat in private?" Lisa asks me.

"Nahh, not right now." I say. "Anyone seen Cindy?"

"I knocked at her door and she said she would be about 15 minutes late." Tony says as Heather rolls her eyes at me.

"Rain, will you join me in the bathroom." Lisa prods again.

"If I must." I stand up and we head out.
"What the hell happened?" She is pulling at my arm.

"What is the last thing you remember?" I ask her.
"I remember having way too much fun and then just sleep. But I had this dream that I beat the hell out of Cindy, I have always daydreamed about finally shutting her up, and the cops broke up the fight. But they were hot cops. I mean really hot." She says, looking at me.

We reach the bathroom. "Do you actually have to go in there for any real reason?" I ask.

"No, I just wanted to talk to you." She says.

I just start laughing, I can't stop. I lean my back against the wall and continue to laugh. I eventually slide down the wall until I am sitting on the floor.
"Rain, what the hell is so funny. What happened?" She is kneeling on the floor, pulling at my arm.

I open my eyes and see Heather running over. "Are you ok? What happened, are you hurt?" she asks.
I have tears streaming down my face and can barely breathe from laughing as Heather walks up to us.

I laugh out "Heather was there, Lisa, tell her about your dream." Beginning to laugh again. It hurts to breathe. This is what mental exhaustion feels like.

Lisa repeats her version of events as Heather has this look of utter shock on her face. "Let's just get Rain off the floor and back to the table. Did you tell Tony about your dream?"

"Yeah, he said I should just clear it up with Rain." Lisa seems almost annoyed.

"Let's go back to the table." Heather helps me up as I wipe tears and try to compose myself.

Cindy is just sitting down at the table. She is stuck in a seat between Richard and Todd. Better to be away from me. "Good morning everyone." She says.

"How did you sleep, Cindy? Heather asks.
"I've had better." She clearly remembers more than Lisa.

The waiter comes and takes our orders. I am starving. I think I ordered one of everything.

I lean over to Nick and whisper for him to follow Tony to the bathroom and ask him about Lisa's dream.
"Huh?" he replies.

"Just do it, trust me, and you don't have to keep my secret from last night!" I smile.

As soon as Tony places his order he excuses himself to use the restroom. I nudge Nick and he follows.

I'm not sure what transpired in the bathroom, but I have a pretty good idea. Tony and Nick return to the table and Tony takes my hand and pulls me to my feet. He kisses me right on the mouth dipping me backward and returns me to my seat. Lisa looks shocked. Nick is standing there smirking. "Thank you for getting her home!" he says and returns to his seat.

Lisa looks like she is ready to pounce on him. "What the hell is going on?" She asks.

"It wasn't a dream, baby!" He starts laughing.

"Huh?! What the hell do you mean? I woke up in bed, I didn't get arrested." She says, clearly confused.
"Nope, the hot cops did not arrest you." He says in full belly laugh.

Heather and I are laughing again.

"What the hell happened last night?" Doug asks. Heather retells most of the story and I interject occasionally, filling in things here and there. The food arrives and I begin to just eat. Like I've never eaten before. Lisa sits there the whole time in amazement, I think I even see Cindy laugh a couple of times.

"How did you get me to my room by yourself?" She asks as if she does not believe this.

"A luggage cart, we rolled you on then rolled you off." I realize the absurdity of everything that occurred.

Nick squeezes my knee from under the table. "I'm so sorry about last night." He says leaning into me.

"Its fine, it's kinda even funny the next morning." I say smiling.

"No, what I did." He says with sadness in his voice.

"Well, he was a pretty hot cop!" I laugh.

Nick just takes my hand and squeezes it, not finding the humor in it.

We wrap up breakfast and have a few hours of quiet, vows are at 6 and we have to start getting ready at 3. I think I will just nap at the pool.

Chapter 17

I get ready to head out to the pool and find Nick coming down the hallway. "Where are you headed?" He asks. "I'm thinking a nap at the pool is in order. I ate a lot at breakfast. I am so overtired, I just want to relax before tonight." I say.

"Can I join you?" He asks. "I can change real quick and grab a towel."

"Sure, but no talking. Quiet time." I say not sure if this is a good idea. I really just want to clear my head.

2 minutes later he is back wearing shorts, flip flops and the chain around his neck. Don't stare at it for too long. Don't. "Let's go." I say.

We reach the pool and I find two lounge chairs next to each other. I put my towel down on it and lay down. Nick follows suit and is quiet. Finally, sleep.

"Rain. Rain, wake up!" He is poking me.
"No talking. That was our agreement." I say and turn my head away.
"You need sunblock or you are going to burn." He pokes me again.
"So put it on me. Quietly." I say as he starts to rub my back. Oh, that feels good. I hear splashing in the pool and it is reminiscent of Malibu. Him rubbing my back and hearing the water. Not the same as waves crashing, but close enough to flood me with memories. Just go to sleep.

"Rain, Rain" He is poking me again. "Time to get up, you've slept long enough." He says.

I actually feel quite rested. I think it was a food coma after all the breakfast I ate.

"Do you want lunch before you have to go get ready?" He asks.
"Nah, I ate too much earlier" I reply.
"We don't have dinner till 7:30. Are you sure?" He asks.

"It sounds like you are hungry. I can go watch you eat, if you like." I say. "Maybe a side salad or something."

"Do you need to change?" he asks me

"Do I have to?"

"I don't know."

"I guess we will find out." I say as we head to a restaurant outdoors near the pool.

We get a table and no one says anything. We sit in silence until the waiter arrives. I order a pina colada and a salad. Nick gets a burger and fries with a beer.

"Why aren't you saying anything? Are you mad at me for something?" I ask.

"No, you told me not to talk to you. I'm being quiet." He says.

Are we 4 years old now? Why is dealing with him so much fucking work? "I meant when I was trying to sleep. I needed rest. Nick, you know I like a boring, drama-free existence. This week is really taking a toll on me. I'm sorry." I say genuinely.

"Well, today is the last day, you must be thankful for that." He says.

"Kinda. Well, I will miss everyone, but you know...this is too much for me." I reply. "I don't really get to see everyone as much as I want. They don't really come out all the time." I say.

"You could always come out to Cali?" he says.

"Ehh, this is actually the first time I've been out since....." I trail off.

"You can come out whenever you want. Lisa would love it." He says.
"I don't know. I like my routine. And I'm really not a fan of flying." I say.

"Are you gonna miss me?" He asks, waiting for my reaction.

"What?" I ask.

"Are you going to miss me, when this is all over." He is direct.

"Huh, I don't know." I say, thinking about it. "Are you going to miss me?" I redirect.

"Of course, I am. I missed you all this time, Rain." He says.

The waiter brings our food. I am still not that hungry and pick at the salad while he eats.

"You stayed away from me just the same that I stayed away from you." I say.

"You didn't want to see me. I didn't want to make it worse." He says. He is right. I would have set him on fire if he showed up.

"Let's not talk about the past. Happy thoughts." I say.

"When will I see you again?" He asks and I do not reply. "Will I see you again?" He asks.

"Nick, I don't know. I have no reason to come out here. You have no reason to come back east. Maybe we will run into each other at some point down the road." I say. "We'll see."

"Do you ever want to see me again or do we just go our separate ways forever?" He asks.

Forever. It sounds like such a long time. Getting off the plane a few days ago, I would be ok with never seeing him again. But now I am just confused. Really confused. Why is he asking me all this?

"Why are you asking me all this? It's too much." I hear my voice breaking as I speak. Don't cry.

He slides his chair closer to mine and puts his arms around me. "Princess, don't cry." And there I go.

"Nick, please, I can't do this right now." I fight a full bawl.

"But you are leaving tomorrow morning." He pleads. "I don't want to miss a chance to make you happy before you go." He says while rubbing my back.

"Talking to me like this does not help." I say as I gain my composure.

"Rain." He says.

"We have all night." I say not sure of what it even means, but whatever makes this conversation right now end will work for me.

Nick is done eating and I never really started. We decide to head up to start getting ready.

Chapter 18

I gather some things from my room and head to Lisa's to see if she is ready.

"How are we today?" I ask as I enter her room. There is no one here but her. "Any fallout from Cindy last night? I throw my purse down and grab a beer.

"Oh, Rain, I can't believe that all happened!" She is smirking at me. "There is blood on my shirt." She points to it.
"You are lucky you didn't end up with real cops arresting you." I point out.
"How did you handle all that? Heather just said you took care of it."

"I paid them off. How do you think handled it?" I ask.

"Oh, how much. Let me pay you back." She is shocked.
"Nahh, we will call it your wedding present." I say.

"What is the deal with your sister, though?" I ask.

"She is older than me by 2 years, always done everything the 'right' way and thrown it in my face. She went to college, I worked at a bar, she got married, I started dating some random guy in a garage band. She played by the rules as she says it and I fucked off. Well, I 'hit the jackpot' according to her and she just can't fucking stand it. She is jealous is all." She says. "She will be here shortly, we had lunch with my parents today and she will behave tonight."

"God, I hope so." Is all I can say. I guess I'm thankful for my brothers, we joke, but we are all genuinely happy for each other. Tony wanted that bar and I ended up with it. He has no idea the sordid details behind it, but never acted pissy about it once. And I let him pretend like he's the boss some nights. Haha. I check my phone. A text from Rob confirming when to pick me up from the airport. A pic text from Ty of the bar with a caption that he did not burn it down. A text from Melissa saying she is really messing up Tony's office and to see her before him when I get back. I reply to them as Tony's mother and Lisa's mother arrive. Lisa's mother is almost in tears. Awww. Heather arrives shortly after followed by Cindy.

"Ready Girls? Let's head to the salon." Lisa leads the way.

We all start getting our hair and make-up done, each to Lisa's standards. I have never had this much make up on in my life. She insists it will help with pictures. I let her command the stylist. My hair is upswept on my head with random little curls falling out of the back. There are about 50 bobby pins in there and they hurt. But it is Lisa's day. The woman wraps it up with about a quarter of a bottle of hairspray. I need to keep a mental note to be careful smoking. I get assistance getting into my dress and platform heels. Jesus. I'm walking around like a baby calf. I slowly get my groove. One by one we are each completed and the stylist leaves to add to Lisa's team working on her. They finish. She looks stunning. She stands before us.

"Well, Did I clean up ok?" she asks, spinning in her gown with her blonde hair perfect and makeup on point.

I laugh.

"What? Is something wrong?" She looks worried.

"You cleaned up great from last night." I laugh again. "You look perfect, amazing." I say as I go in for a hug.

"Oh, wait, one more thing." She says as her mother hands her a bag. Wedding gifts." She says as she hands us each a small wristlet matching our dresses.
"Aww, they are beautiful." Cindy says. Heather and I thank her as well. I begin switching items from my current purse to my new one. And we are on our way. We are taken to a private room where Lisa can wait away from Tony and the lady with the headset has Doug in tow with her. He has a headset as well.

"Trying to be like her?" I ask elbowing him.
"You look amazing!" he says as he kisses my cheek.
"Thank you." I reply. "You should get a glimpse at Lisa, makes me look like a trash bag." I laugh.

"Follow me, ladies." The woman with the headset commands. "All except you, Lisa" She says.

I kiss Lisa one more time before being prodded into the hallway.

I see Nick escorting Tony's father to their seats up front, I notice they are sitting next to his. How sweet. Nick starts walking back. Todd is escorting Lisa's mother in as random piano music is being played. Nick walks up to me.

"Oh, my god, Rain, you look absolutely stunning." He is beaming. I feel a bit taller in the platforms. I lean into him.

"You look pretty stunning yourself." I say as I rub my hand on his cheek. Headset lady begins pairing us up in formation.

Richard and Cindy. Check

Todd and Heather. Check

Nick and myself. Check

Up front is Tony and his Mother to walk him down the aisle.

They begin. Why do I feel so nervous? Nick takes my hand and squeezes it, I squeeze it back.

We slowly begin our descent down the aisle and reach the alter that was made of flowers.

We wait. And wait some more and finally the wedding march begins.

Lisa and her father enter the room and there are so many gasps and flashes going off. She does look beautiful. I begin to cry for her. I look across and see Nick staring directly at me.

The ceremony begins and we get thru the personal vows that they each wrote. Finally, you may kiss the bride. 200 plus people erupt into cheers and hand in hand they exit the room. We file out in reverse order the same parings that we came in and all have to line up in a certain order because headset lady says so. Eventually, our receiving line has received everyone and we head to another area for pictures. Lisa has only about a thousand different combinations that she wants and we all comply without complaint.

"Who is ready to eat?" Tony shouts out and we head to the ballroom. I should have listened to Nick earlier and eaten more salad. Its almost 8 and I'm starving. Headset lady is blocking the door.

"There is an order. Richard and Cindy, you are announced first." We hear them announce it inside and they go in. Next is Todd and Heather. Then I can hear them announce us. I am about to walk thru and Nick picks me up in his arms and twirls us into the room. He kisses me right on the lips as he sets me down.

"Well, that was unexpected." I say.

"Are you mad?" he is looking at me.
"Not at all." I smile as I squeeze his hand and we head to our seats at the head table.

Formalities and announcements. Lots of clapping over and over again. Toasts and drinking. This is all going very smoothly and everyone is enjoying themselves. We are eating and the DJ announces that first dances are to begin. Heather and Todd dance to a song, Cindy and Richard dance to a song. They call for the maid of honor and best man to take the floor and we oblige. From the speakers I hear the first few chords of Simple Man come on. I take Nicks lead and begin to dance with him.

"Did you have anything to do with this? I ask him coyly.

"What?! It's a really good song." He smiles and kisses the top of my head. We dance very slowly and very close together.

"I think this is our first dance." I say.

"It doesn't have to be our last." He replies squeezing me.

I don't want to screw up the moment so I just lay my head on his chest and continue to dance.

The song slowly comes to a close. "Kiss me." Nick says.

I just lean up and kiss him. No hesitation, no forethought. Done. It feels good too.

The tables begin to clap and for a moment I forgot we had so many eyes on us.

The DJ calls the newlyweds up for their first dance. The four of us meet at the side before Tony and Lisa take to the floor. "Jesus, how am I supposed to out do that?" Lisa squeezes my arm and winks at me as they head out on the floor.

Nick is guiding me back to my seat. "I know I should be watching this, but I need a cigarette." I say.

"You can smoke out on the balcony, come on, I will go with you." He says as I walk out with him. He lights me a cigarette and I smoke it while staring off into the Vegas desert. "It's not a beautiful as you." He says wrapping his arms around me from behind.

"I prefer the ocean." I say absently. "I was just thinking about all this week. How Lisa and Tony are actually married right now. It's all crazy, isn't' it?"

"Yeah, kind of." He says.

"We should get back in there before we miss something." I say and we head back in and take our seats. Headset lady does a few more required dances. Lisa dances with her father, Tony dances with his mother and so on and so on. The floor is finally open to the guests and Doug is at my side.

"Dance?" He takes my hand. Doug dances? He leads me onto the dance floor. "We haven't had any time alone since the cab ride from the airport. How ya been? Is it as bad as you thought?" He asks.

"It's had its moments. But I would do it all over again." I say.

"What's up with you and Nick?" he asks.

"Huh? Oh, Nick taking advantage of the moment, I guess." I smile.

"Please just don't lead him on." He says.

"Ahhh, now don't you start talking to me. I've talked enough about this all week." I say warning.

"Ok, ok. You look beautiful, by the way." He kisses me on the cheek as the song ends.

Tony wants to dance with me next, then Nick, then Heather, random people I have met, Nick's Dad, Nick's mother. Then finally Lisa. "My feet are killing me, how about instead of a dance, we go have a cigarette." I suggest to her.

"That is the best thing I have heard in the last hour. Let's go." She drags me with her by the arm. She grabs a bottle of champagne and cigarettes and a lighter off the table and we head to the balcony.

"I'm married!" she exclaims holding out her newly ringed finger. I take her hand and look at it.

"It's beautiful, you're beautiful. This entire night is amazing. I am sooo happy for you!" I beam.

She lights me a cigarette and hands it to me. "Quite a dance you and Nick had there." She says as I reach for the bottle and pry the cork out. I take a long swig from the bottle and put my feet up on the chair across from me. She follows suit and reaches out for the bottle.

"Let's not talk about it." I say taking a drag from my cigarette. "I just want to enjoy the moment." I say exhaling the smoke.

"I hear ya, thank you for everything this week. I love you." Lisa says passing me back the bottle.

"Well, isn't this the epitome of being a lady, look at the two of you!" Tony pulls up a chair.

"Would you like a drink?" I don't sit up, just leaning over with the bottle.

"Got my own." He says pulling out a flask from his tuxedo coat. "Rain." He starts

"She is not talking about anything. Leave her alone." Lisa says reaching over to touch his arm.

"Look at you two, reading each other's minds like you've been married for decades." I laugh.

"So this is where we are all hiding?" Nick pulls up another chair.

"I'm sooo tired." I say out loud laughing.

"I can bring you up to your room." Nick replies.
"Nah, I can sleep later. I want to see the cake and the bouquet and everything." I say.

We sit in silence and finish our cigarettes and begin to head back in. "Wait.' Nick says.
"What?" I reply as he takes me and kisses me again. A long slow kiss. I don't fight it.

"Nick, why? I am leaving in the morning, you remember that, right?" I ask slowly.

"But will you miss me?" He asks.

"Of course, I will miss you. Don't play games." I say, fidgeting. "Let's go back inside."

We head back inside and I see Doug and Jen dancing together. Jen, that sweet little girl. I need to go say 'hi'.

"Do you mind if I cut in?" I ask gaining both their attention. "Oh, Rain, Its Jen, do you remember me? I will go sit down, you can dance with Doug, Doug, I will be over there when you are done." Holy shit she talks so fast.

"Doug? Can you sit down while I dance with Jen?" I ask slowly so there is no confusion.
"Ha, sure." He says and leaves me there standing with Jen.
"You want to dance with me? Oh, I didn't even know that you remembered me." She says, clearly flattered.
We begin to dance and I ask how she has been and she explains she still works at the bar; she and Todd broke up. She has been seeing Doug on the sly, she let it slip and looked scared. I promised it would be my secret. We finished the dance and I pass by Doug back to my seat.
"Your secret is safe with me!" I smile at him and wink. He just smiles and shakes his head. Huh. Maybe they would make a nice couple. Neither of them have a conniving bone in their bodies. She is so innocent, Doug is well...Doug. I can't ever recall seeing him with anyone. Well, at least he keeps it clean. I am happy for them.

Headset lady goes flying by me on a mission. She has a bouquet in her hands and is looking for Lisa.
We get thru the bouquet toss. Some random date of a cousin of Tony's catches it. I now have no interest in the garter toss and I head to the ladies' room. I decide I need another cigarette and go to look for someone that has some. Lisa and Tony are preoccupied with the garter toss. Nick is nowhere to be found. Hey. I put all my stuff in the gift wristlet Lisa gave me. I have my own.

Chapter 19

I find it on the seat of my chair and head out to the balcony. I take my phone out. It is lighting up like the 4th of July. 35 missed calls, more texts than I can scroll thru. TY, Melissa, tony, Rob. Call home, call home. Call home. I scan through the missed calls, home, the bar, ty, tony Melissa, Rob, New Haven CT?

I play a voice mail; its Ty and he sounds scared.

Dad was in a car accident, I don't know, it's serious. Call me.
 OH FUCK.

New Haven number voice mail.
We are all at the Yale Hospital, Dads here, you have to call us.

My stomach sinks. I have to get out of here, what do I do? What do I do? I hit redial on Melissa's number and she answers on the first ring. "Rain, you have to come home, NOW!" she is crying. This is not good.

"OK, OK, what happened" I ask as I begin to tremble.
"He was hit by a car that crossed the line. Head on, it's not good. Just get here as soon as you can."

"OK, Im gonna get on the next flight. I will be there soon."
"Hurry." She said with such seriousness in her voice.

Doug, I have to find Doug. Jen is walking past. "Jen!" I yell out. She turns and rushes over to me. "Find Doug now, it's an emergency." I say. I think she understands the importance of the situation from how I look and she rushes off and returns with Doug.

"What's wrong?" Doug asks.

"I need to go home right now. My dad was in a bad accident. I have to go...Now, Doug." I say.

He pulls out his phone and starts typing things in. "There is a flight that leaves in 30 minutes but..."
What airline? Get me on it, Doug!" I say.

What about your stuff, you have to pack?" He asks.
"Doug, I'm going like this, I don't have time" I plead.
"I will take care of your stuff, Rain." Jen is trying to be helpful.

"Ahhh, get to the airport and I will have the ticket waiting." He says.

"Tell Tony and Lisa I love them and am sorry." I shout as I head to the lobby. Cab next.

"Rain, wait!" Nick is running behind me.

"Nope, gotta go." I say as I carry on.

He runs up and grabs my arm. "Let go, Nick, I don't have time for this." I say and pull away.

"Wait, talk to me for a minute." He pleads.

I glance around and there are a ton of people coming in and out of the hotel. "Holy Shit, is that really you? Nick

Stone from Heavensent! It really is you!" and people start to swarm him and I escape to the portico and hop in a cab.

I tell the driver to get me to the airport and pull out my phone. Texts. Rob. I text him.

On my way to airport. Have 10 minutes call me.

My phone rings a minute later.
"Rain, oh my god."
"What is going on? I talked to Melissa."

Rain, get home. I got the bar under control, just get to the hospital." He says. "I will close later and get there. Call Tony."

"OK, I will text you when I land home." I say and hit end.

I look at my phone and dial my brother Tony.

"Rain, where are you?" He answers on the first ring.
"In a cab, on my way to the airport. What happened?" I say, my voice shaking.

"He was on his way home from work and someone crossed the line, hit him head on." His voice is getting quieter. "Hold on, I'm going out to the hallway..."

"Tony!"

"OK, Mom's in there and she doesn't need to keep hearing it over and over....He was coming home from work and someone crossed the line straight into him. Head on collision. He's bad Rain, real bad." I have never heard Tony sound so worried. "They put him into a coma to try to control it all. Mom's a wreck, Ty is a wreck, you need to get here. Melissa is trying to help, but she's due soon and doesn't need the stress." He says.

"Where is Bella?" I ask.
"Her parents drove out and took her." He said.

"I'm racing to the airport now, I checked my phone and just saw it. I left as soon as I talked to her. I'm sorry Tony, I'm on my way. I think I will be on the next flight out. I will text you when I land." I say.

"OK, just hurry."
I hit end.
I see signs that we are nearing the airport. I text Doug.
What gate?

He replies: 12, it leaves in 15 minutes. You fly to Kentucky with a 15 minute layover then onto Laguardia, you are closer to New Haven.

I hit dial. He answers on half a ring.

"Doug, do not say anything to anyone. Just tell Lisa and Tony there was a family emergency, I don't want to ruin anyone's good time."
"Rain, do you need anything? I am trying to get a car service ready for you as soon as you get off the plane."

"Uhh, just get my stuff out of my room?" I ask. My mind is racing.

"Jen said she will take care of packing and getting it to you. I think she is proud to do it. She loves you." He says.

117

"By the way, I am hurt you never mentioned her to me. We will save that conversation for a later date."

"Rain….we will talk, don't worry." He says.
"Gate 12, please, as close as you can get." I say to the driver.

"Gotta go, Doug." I say.
"Take care." He replies and I hit end.

The taxi stops and I throw him a $100 bill and run out. I get to the counter and get my ticket and head for security. I make my way thru pretty fast. I explain I was participating in a wedding and have to get home as my dad was in a bad car accident. They seem to be sympathetic. Probably helps that I don't even have a carry on.

I immediately board the plane. First class. First class to Kentucky. Haha. It seems funny. I ask for a glass of wine and settle into my seat. God, I hate flying. What a day. The last 24 hours flash before my eyes. Strippers, assault, a cat fight. A wedding. Kissing Nick. This outfit. I feel drained. I ask the stewardess to ensure she wake me up 10 minutes before we land and she assures me she will and brings me a pillow and blanket. I close my eyes and am so tired but can't sleep. My mind is racing.
I wake up to a gentle nudge from the stewardess. "Landing in 10, buckle up please." We land and I don't leave the holding pen, I am not going to go the security check again. I wait for the next flight to be called and board Kentucky to New York.

"Why aren't we taking off." I start to ask the new stewardess.

"About a 10-minute delay, sweetie, can I get you anything?" She asks.

"How long is this flight?" I ask.

"About an hour."

"Could I get a coffee?" I ask.

"Sure thing, sweetie. You look great, where ya going?" she is smiling.

"My dad was in a car accident, I'm trying to get home to him." I say and see a bizarre expression on her. "Oh, I was in a wedding in Vegas when I got the call." Realizing that I am still in the dress.

"I will get you that coffee right now." She pats my arm. She brings me back the coffee and a nip bottle of Irish Cream. "Not sure if you needed a little something in the coffee." She says as she puts it next to the cup.

"You are an angel." I reply dumping it in.

"There now." She braces herself on the seat. "We are taking off."
I drink the coffee and wish I had checked in with Doug about the car. I lay my head back and rest. I try to clear my thoughts. I can't. I wake up again to being nudged. We are landing. Thank god!

I exit the plane and see Nick at the gate. What the hell?

"Rain, over here, I have a car." I rush to him.

"How the hell are you here, I left you in Vegas and just got off the goddamn plane." I say as we head to the exit.

"If you took a minute to breathe, there was a direct flight that left after the one that you got on. Doug felt horrible, but he said you were freaking out and he put you on the first one out. I've only been here for an hour. I got you a coffee." He says handing me a Styrofoam cup.

"I talked to him and he didn't say anything." I say absently as we reach a waiting car.

"I told him not to." He says as we get in.
"Huh? You wanted to surprise me?" I am tired and confused.

"No, you would have been stressing the entire way about the time if you knew." He says.
The driver announces we are about an hour and 50 minutes out as we pull out.
"There is no traffic, $200 tip if you do it in an hour and a half." I say. "What did you say to Lisa and Tony?" I ask him.
"I just said you had a family emergency and you would call them." He replies and begins to rub the back of my neck. All I want to do is sleep. I just want this whole week to go away.

I think I doze off again as we are pulling into the hospital in New Haven. Nick wakes me up and tells me we are here. I rush into the hospital and ask where to go. I am frantic and reach the room I am directed to. The nurse knocks quietly at the door and opens it. I see Tony and Ty and my mother sitting around the bed. I rush in and break into tears.

"Rain, you made it." My mother says hugging me. I look at my father, completely broken and machines hooked up to him. A tube down his throat. Eyes closed. The slow, steady beeping of the machines.

"Oh, my god, how bad is it?" I ask and my mother starts crying.

"Nick, shock to see you here." Ty shakes his hand.

"Nick? Oh, I'm so glad to see you come back with Rain." My mother lifts her head.

"Oh, no problem, I just want her to be ok." He says absently. He puts his hands back on my shoulders.

"We've been here since about 7 last night. We are just waiting now. Specialists will be in in a few hours to give us some news. We should know more when we talk to them." Tony says.

"Where is Mel?" I ask.
"I sent her home with her parents. She needs to rest." He says. I can hear the heaviness in his voice.

"What time is it now?" I ask.
"Almost 5am." Ty says, yawning. "Rob stopped earlier after he shut the bar down. He went home. Oh! He said for you to call him as soon as you got here."

I pull out my phone and send him a text. He is probably tired. The craziness from me bursting in and crying seems to have subsided and we are all just hovering over my dad. "You look nice, by the way." Ty says as he kicks my foot. "Yes, you two make a perfect couple. Nick, you are so handsome." My mother chimes in. "How was the wedding?" she asks. I am tired and just sort of shrug my shoulders to answer her.

"It was everything Lisa wanted." Nick replied. "It was like something out of a movie." He continues.

The nurse comes in to check on my father, pokes some buttons and records some info on her clipboard and turns to leave. "Are you all family?" She asks, eyeing Nick.

"Yes, all the kids are here." My mother replies.

"I swear you look like someone." She is still eyeing him.

"Nick Stone. Right here in the room." I say flatly.

"Oh, I thought you looked familiar." She shrugged her shoulders and left.

"Why did you do that to him?" Tony asks me.

"Second time today." I laugh.

"Its fine, she is really tired and annoyed with me a bit, probably." Nick replies.

"Maybe, just a little." I feign a smile. "Do you think you could find me another cup of coffee? Maybe a Danish or something?" I ask.

"Sure, does anyone else want anything?" Nick replies.

"Coffee would be great, even better if it's not from the vending machine down the hall!" Ty replies and Tony and my mother nod along as my phone buzzes. Its Rob.

"I'm on my way, need anything?" Rob texts.

"Wait, Rob is on his way. I can get him to stop at a coffee shop?" I say.

"Ohh, that would be so much better." Ty replies.

I text back what everyone wants.
"He will be here in about an hour." I say. We sit in silence for a bit longer.
"When is the doctor supposed to come in?" I ask.

"When they get here." Tony replies.

"I'm gonna go lie down on that couch in the waiting room." I say as I stand up. "Come get me when the doctors get here." I say as I exit the room. I reach the couch and look at it. I begin to try to lay down but realize that this dress is not helping.
"Cover up with this." Nick puts his tux jacket over me.

"Why are you here?" I ask him while lying down.

He is seated on the couch across from me staring at me. "I told you, I don't want to see you upset." He says.

"Well, that makes no sense, you'd think you would have stayed in Vegas. I'm upset. See." I say.

"You make no sense." He says. "I'm just trying to be supportive for you."

"I'm sorry, I'm just really tired." I say as I fall asleep.

"Wake up, Rob is here." Nick nudges me.

"Huh?" I sit up not even knowing where I am for a moment. "Oh, coffee. Thanks, Rob."
"I will leave you two alone for a few. Want me to take those?" Nick points at the tray.

"Sure." Rob hands Nick the coffee and bags and he heads back to the hospital room. "How you doing, Rain?" Rob sits on the edge of the couch and rubs my shoulders.

"Could be better." I say sadly.
"How was Vegas? I know you have stories to tell. You and Nick rekindle?" He asks trying to make me smile.

"No, I think I have a new shadow though." I say.

"Aww, don't be like that, you have a crisis. He is being there for you. Do you call me your shadow behind my back?" Rob asks.
"Are you trying to sleep with me?" I ask right back.
"Yes, Rain, I'm taking the slow and steady path. 13 years in, almost ready to make my move." He deadpans as I laugh. "What's the craziest thing that happened in Vegas? I've been dying to hear about the trip?" He asks. That question. Wow. How do I even answer it?

"Ummm, Lisa punched a gay male stripper in the face, dressed as a cop, broke his nose, blood everywhere." I say, smiling, staring at him.

"How did you know he was gay?" He asks.

"His boyfriend let the cat out of the bag." I say.
"Oof. Was he a stipper too?" He is rubbing his hands together.

"Yup, A firefighter, and Lisa puked on him." I say, laughing.
"Holy Shit!"

"Yup, and I have not had more than 6 hours sleep since
that happened ummm, Friday night? Hey, What day is it?"
I ask.
"Sunday. You need to sleep." Rob replies.

"Yeah, yeah. It will happen eventually. The strippers are
interested in doing a show at the bar. I dub thee 'talent
management' you can deal with them when they come in.
Early Christmas present we will call it." I smile at him.
"God, I missed you this week." He hugs me. "We should
probably head down and see what's going on in there." He
says as he helps me to my feet and we head back to the
room.

"Oh, you just missed the doctor." Ty says.
"What the hell, I said to come get me." I reply instantly.

Nick takes my arm "Calm down, he wants to actually set
up a meeting in a little conference room after he finishes
his rounds." Nick says.

I look around the room and notice everyone is a bit more
worried than when I left the room. Rob is sitting with my
mother.

"Hey, Rain, I think I'm gonna take off. There is no reason
for me to be here. I am heading home. I'm sure my mother
is cooking up some lasagna. I will bring it back if you
want?" He looks around the room.
"That might be nice dear. Say hello to Corinne." My
mother says. "Rain will let you know." And Rob heads out.

I follow him out to the hallway.
"You can stay for the meeting." I say.

"Nah, I don't want to be here for that." He says. "Let me know if you need anything." We hug and he leaves.

I head back into the room. I see Tony is on his phone. Probably talking to Melissa. I go over and put my arm around Ty. "What the hell is all this?" I ask him.
"Surreal, I know." He says, staring at the floor.

Nick walks over "You want me in this meeting?" He asks and puts his hands back to rubbing my shoulders.
"Come with me for a minute?" Tony asks Nick and they head out into the hallway.
2 minutes later they are back in the room. "What was that all about?" I ask Nick.
"Uhhh, Tony asked me to stay." He says, looking to Tony, nervous.

A nurse knocks at the door and comes in. "The doctor would like the family to come with me." We all slowly start following her to a room. There are 2 doctors sitting at the table.
"Have a seat. Barb, is this all the kids?" He asks my mother.

"Yeah, Well, Melissa isn't here, Tony's wife. But she's pregnant and needs her rest." My mother is looking at the table.
"And you must be Rain." He leans over to shake my hand. "Dr, Roberts."

"Nice to meet you." I say flatly.

"And you are?" He extends a hand to Nick.

"Oh, Nick, I'm here with Rain." He says.

"Matched set, I can tell." He comments looking up and down our outfits.

"Well, I have brought in a colleague to go over the test results. We have gone over them again and again. There is nothing that makes us think there will be any forward progress." He says solemnly.

"Forward Progress? What the hell does that mean? Are we at fucking attempting first down?" I spit out.

"Rain, Sit." Nick tugs at me. My mother is visibly upset. Ty is holding his head in his hands on the table.
"What my eloquent sister is asking is for you to put it in simpler terms? What exactly are you saying?" Tony asks, standing up and resting his hands on my mother's shoulders.

"It means that he will not improve. He cannot survive off the machines. The coma is non-recoverable."

"Oh my god." I scream. "NO, NO this is not happening." I begin to sob and Nick takes my hand.
"Now, ultimately, it's your decision if you want us to keep him on the machines. Does your husband have any medical directive Mrs. Brady?"
"I believe he does, it's at home in the safe with the papers." She says blankly.

"Do you know what he would want you to do?" Dr. Roberts asks.

"He wouldn't want this." She slowly begins to sob.

"Well, you don't have to decide now. You can go home and get your papers. You can discuss this with your family. We are here all day and always available on call." The two doctors get up and shake hands and exit.
"This is not reality. This is a nightmare, I have to wake up." I speak first.
"Rain." Nick says.
"Stop saying my fucking name. It's not helping." I say out loud.

"Ma, are you sure this is what he wants?" Ty asks.
"Sounds like him." Tony says.
We all look at my mother. "He has always said people that stay on machines are living a 'fake' life, as he put it. I think I should go home and get the paperwork." She doesn't seem like herself.

"I'll drive you." Ty said.

"I should go home and check on Mel." Tony says. "You should go home and change, Rain. You look like someone snapped you off a trophy or something." He shakes his head at me.

"And your makeup is starting to droop." Ty chimes in smiling. "You look like some haggard prom date the morning after." He laughs.

I start yo giggle a bit. Ehh, everyone can loosen up at my expense. I start to laugh and then just begin to cry again. "Oh, Rain." Tony hugs me and Ty is hugging mom.

"How do I get home?" I ask looking at my brothers and my mother.
"Shit, how do I get home? Mel and I drove together and she went home." He says, clearly annoyed.

"Well, my car is here and Ty drove here too." My mother pipes in.

"Ty will take me home in mine and Tony and Rain will take Ty's. Drop them off at her house on the way." She says simply.
"Great, we get the bucket." Tony elbows me trying to make a joke.
"Well, I'm certainly not riding in that thing." My mother says sounding so proper.
Tony and I burst out laughing.
"And you shouldn't have to." Tony says to her as he kisses her cheek.

We all slowly head out of the room and exit the hospital. Ty gives Tony the keys. "Be careful, man, she is my pride and joy." He dangles the keys out for Tony to grab them.

"I'm not riding in the back" I say standing there in front of Ty's tiny Cobalt.
"Yes, you are." Replies Tony.
"Scuse me?" I

"Nick wouldn't even fit in the backseat, get in. And try not to touch anything, it's a bio-hazard back there." He replies.

"I can just ride in the...."Nick starts as he looks into the back seat. "Nevermind." He finishes, shaking his head. "Really?"

"Yup, this is why I won't give him an office." Tony chuckles as I climb into the back seat, shifting trash and clothes over to get into the seat. Tony and Nick get in the car afterwards and we head home. It's a very quiet ride.

We reach my home and locate the hidden key in the flowerbed and we head in.
"I really shouldn't stay, I need to go get Melissa." Tony says.

"Ehh, I have to just shower and put on something a little less fancy and then I will head back." I say, quietly. I really don't want to go back understanding that it's just goodbye.

"Well, I'm probably gonna be about two to two and half hours so take your time." He replies.

"See you there." I say as he gives me a side hug and leaves.

I take a seat on the couch and just sigh. How did I end up here? I can't lose my father. Who is going to walk me down the aisle some day? Who is going to keep me grounded? Who is going to take care of my mom? Jesus, a week ago, I was waking up late from closing the bar and heading to the house for Sunday dinner. I feel tears forming in the corner of my eyes and put my face in my hands and just breathe.
"It's gonna be ok." Nick says. I almost jump. Holy shit, here he is in my house. Again. After all this time.

"I need to go shower." I stand up and head upstairs to my room. I sit down at the mirror and look at it. My hair has been going almost 24 hours and held up pretty good. My make-up. I look tired. It's all a bit cakey and matted. I take out some face wipes and begin to remove the layers. My face actually feels better without the pores clogged so much. I start next on pulling hair pins out. One after another until I can't feel any more. I stand up and realize that I can't get out of the dress. "Nick, can you come here?" I call out and he immediately comes to me. "Can you help again?" I ask, motioning at the dress.
"Sure." He says quietly as he gets it much quicker than the first time.

"Hey, uhh, all your stuff is in boxes out in the garage, you've got clothes out there if you want to shower and change." I stare at him, still wearing the tux looking completely disheveled a day later.

"Oh, thanks, I can go look while you are in the shower?"

"It's your stuff, do what you want." I say absently as I hold my dress up and head into the bathroom.

I let the dress slip off me and start the water. I get in and just let the water run over me. I don't want this shower to end. I begin to shampoo my hair and repeat this cycle twice to get rid of all the hairspray that's in there. I complete washing and continue to stand there turning the water hotter and hotter. Eventually I feel numb and get out. I shut the water off and exit, grabbing a towel and beginning to dry off. I glance over at my closet and then to my bed. I just want to crawl in and go to sleep. I slip on a pair of form fitting jeans and a light sweater and begin to finish drying my hair. I grab a pair of flats and set off to find Nick. I listen thru the house until I discover him in the garage.

"I think I found some clothes." He says with a pile forming surrounded by a few open boxes.

"Well, I'm done in the shower, so it's all yours." I reply back. "I have a couple of calls to make, I will be in the office." I reply and head back into the house. I reach my office and dial up Rob. He answers right away and I bring him up to speed about the doctor consultation.

"Ohhh, Rain, that is awful. I don't even know what to say." He is genuinely upset.

"There is nothing to say, it is what it is, I guess." I say blankly.
"You want me to come over?"

"No, not for this. I mean, you can if you want, but you don't have to. I think this should be just us." I really don't know if I want him there or not.

"Well, are you driving there or is your brother picking you up? You really shouldn't drive alone." He says sympathetically.

"Well, I guess Nick will drive." I say.

"About that, so are you two, uhh, back together?" He asks carefully.

"No." I respond quickly.

"Are you sure about that? You look back together. Does he know you aren't?" He asks carefully.

"Rob, I swear, I got out there and wanted nothing to do with him. At first, everything was kinda snippy and we called a truce so that it didn't ruin the wedding then next thing you know, we were getting along. I got the phone call and he just kinda came out here. On his own. He helped me get to the hospital and now he is just sorta here. I'm not sure what my family thinks. It seems to make my mom at ease, you know, so I'm just leaving it alone for right now. Ya know?"

"But how does it make you feel?" Rob asks.

"Honestly, there were moments I could have pushed him off a cliff, but there were moments that felt good. This very moment? I haven't slept more than a few hours at a shot since Thursday night and am dealing with so much right now so I don't really care unless he pisses me off." I say.

"Got it. Well, you let me know if you need anything. My mother was going to send some lasagna over to the hospital for you guys. I will tell her what's going on when I get up, where are you all going when you are done there?" He asks.

"Done?" I ask as the words settle in my brain. Done. We are saying good-bye to my father forever. Done. I begin to cry.

"Oh my god Rain, don't cry. I didn't mean it...I'm sorry, I..."

"Rob, it's not your fault. I just can't do this. I can't even comprehend any of this. Why?" I continue to cry as I try to compose myself. "I have to go, I will let you know what's going on, ok?" I say as I almost have it together.

"Rain, text me if you need anything. Love ya." He says as he hits end.

I take a moment to go make some coffee and pour myself a cup. I dial up Doug next. It begins to ring. Shit, time change. He answers as I go to hit end.

"Rain, how are you? What do you need?" He asks immediately.
"I could be better." I sigh. "It's so much worse than I ever thought." I begin.

"Nick has kept me informed. I know. I am so sorry." He sounds sad. "Jen feels awful. She has all your things cleaned and packed. I will be overnighting them back tomorrow."

"Oh." It takes me a minute to realize what he is even talking about, my stuff in the hotel room. "I honestly don't care right now. Not even a blip on the radar." I reply.
"I know, but just letting you know." He says.

"Did you say anything to Tony and Lisa?" I ask.

"Well, I told them that you had an emergency, that you were fine, it was your family, but nothing else. Do you want me to tell them?" He asks.
"No, they are leaving for Europe this week, I don't want this to mess up their trip." I say.

"Rain, they can go anytime. Lisa is going to be upset when she finds out. I'm just being honest here." He says.

"Ehh, I will think about it." I say. "So, I guess there will be a funeral at some point this week. Would you come out for it?" I ask, sounding emotionless.

"Of course, I will be there, Rain." He says.
"And I expect you will bring Jen." I continue.

"If you want me to." He replies with hesitation.

"What's the deal, why are you so secretive?" I ask.

"Ehh, it's not the time." Doug replies hesitant.

"What? Why?" I ask.

"Look, Nick got all weird about Jen after that night and then got even weirder about people bringing their girlfriends around after everything happened. Jen used to date Todd. He doesn't want drama around at all." Doug says.

"Ohh." I say, thinking through this statement. "You know, I kinda like Jen, in a weird way. She kinda grows on you." I say.

"Tell me about it." Doug interjects as I hear the smile in his voice.

"Nick can get over himself." I reply. "He can deal with it. I said its ok." There is silence.
"I am inviting her to my house as my friend, he has a problem, let him take it up with me." I finish.

"Uhh. OK. I guess I will look into it. I'll find a hotel close. When do you want us to arrive?" He says, sounding a bit unsure.

"No! You will stay here. Whenever you arrive is fine." I say, not even sure of what I am saying.

"Are you sure? You have so much going on. We can stay at a hotel, Rain, it's not a big deal." He replies.

"NO. Nick is staying here, why shouldn't you two? At least I invited you guys." I say beginning to think about the fact that he really did just sort of assume.

"You don't' want him there? Tell him!" Doug says.

"No, it's fine. I just, I don't know. It's all coming at me a bit fast, is all." I say, sounding tired. "Whenever you get here is fine, just let me know. OK? I have to go." I say.

"Just text me if you need anything. I am so sorry, Rain" He says.

"OK, see you soon, goodbye." I say as I hang up the phone. I listen to the silence and realize the shower has stopped. I can hear his footsteps down the stairs.

"You good?" he asks, leaning into the doorway.

"You have a problem with Jen?" I ask.
"Huh?" He sounds confused.
"Jen. Todd's ex-girlfriend. Do you not like her?" I ask, motioning him to come take a seat.

"Uhh, I don't know." He replies, I can see him thinking.

"I like her." I state.

"Ohh, Jen. I have no problem with her. Why?" he asks.

"She was at the wedding, she is flying out here to stay with me." I say, studying for his reaction.

"Huh? Jen, Todd's ex-girlfriend? Why?" He asks, taking a seat.

"Are you aware that her and Doug are dating?" I ask.

"No." he immediately replies and I can see him thinking.

"No way! Really? Doug and Jen?" He asks.

"Nothing but the thought to hide his happiness. He is dating Jen and he seems to think he needs to hide it from you. Why?" I ask.

"Ahh. After everything happened, I said that there was to be no more girlfriend drama from anyone in the band. She was sort of hooking up with Todd. And they probably assumed whatever." He says.

"Well, whatever assumptions were made, I like her, Doug and her are actually together, I'm ok with it, and they are staying here, coming out soon." I say, waiting for him to challenge me.

"OK, whatever you need." He says.

"Need? What is that supposed to mean?" I ask.

"Nothing, I mean, whatever you want." He says

"Whatever, you ready to go?" I ask.

"Whenever you are." He replies and I get up to leave the house. I go get my purse, taking notice that it's still the same wristlet gift from the wedding. Ahh, to go back to that moment in time. I head into the garage and get in my truck.

"Want me to drive?" Nick is following me, in the garage.

"Nah, I'm good." I say, as we get into the truck and I start it up.

"Just let me know what I can do." He says quietly. My patience is beginning to wear.

"Do? What do you expect to do? What do you think you can do for me?" I ask, reaching maximum patience. "You know what you can do for me? Turn back time. I don't want to be here; can you do that for me?" I ask, on the brink of another meltdown.

"Rain." He says.

"Stop saying my name. You think that makes me feel better? It doesn't." I say.

"I'm sorry." He says as I continue.

"I'm sorry Nick. But I don't know what you want. Everything is shit. And you can't fix it. There is not a goddamn thing you can do." I say sounding exasperated. "What do you have to say to that, besides 'Rain'. I blurt out as I am driving.

"I will do anything you want me to. I don't know what to do." He says. I am so frustrated. Why is he here? He is trying to be helpful. Well, why is he trying to be helpful? We drive the rest of the way in silence and arrive at the hospital. I shut the truck off and sit there. Not ready to do this. Not wanting to go in. I pull out my phone and text Tony and Ty and ask where they are. Tony still on his way.

Ty and my mother are inside. I guess that I should be in there with her. I get out of the truck and Nick follows suit and we head in. I arrive at the room and my mother is going thru some documents with the doctor. Apparently, my father had his wishes expressed out in writing a long time ago. I can hear the doctor tell her that she can take as long as she needs. I begin to slowly cry again.

"Rain, you're here." She takes notice of me. "Nick, I'm so glad you came with her through all this." She looks at him. How is she so goddam calm? "We are each going to take as long as we need alone with him and then I will come back in and we are going to do this together." She says matter of factly.

"OK." Is all I can get out. I look to Ty and he is just standing there, staring at my dad.

My phone buzzes again in my pocket and I look to see that Tony is parking the car and will be here in a few minutes.

Tony arrives with Melissa and she is big, I swear I saw here a week ago and she wasn't that big. "You look tired." I say to her as its all I can think to say and should say something.
"Ehh, I'm good, I hope the little guy wants to come a bit early." She replies rubbing her stomach.

What a contrast I think to myself. A baby about to be born as we stand here to say good bye to my dad. Holy Shit. This little man will never meet his grandfather. Bella will probably have some clear memories, but those will eventually fade more as she gets new ones. I see Tony has become upset and I can tell my mother has just explained the process. She comes over to me and says that to take as long as I need and to just come get her when I'm done and they all leave the room. I take a seat next to my father and take his hand. I feel Nicks hands on my shoulders.

"What are you doing in here!?" I turn around.

"Your mother told me to stay." He seems surprised at what I have to say. "He was a great man. Not that it makes a difference what I think, but I liked him...a lot." He says solemnly.

"Nick, what the hell do I do? I can't not have a father?" I begin to cry harder.

"He will always be your father, you aren't not going to have a father. He will just be somewhere else. He is still with you." He says, hugging me. "I will wait outside." He gives me one last squeeze and heads out. My mother follows immediately in.
"Honey, let it out. Don't be like this. Express your feelings. Not what you think you should say. Say what you feel." She puts her arms around me.

"What I really feel? I'm mad, I hate everything right now, and this isn't fair. He didn't deserve this, I didn't deserve this, and you don't deserve this. None of us do. Why?" I scream out.

"Honey, I'm just as upset as you." She is calm. "But, this is life. That's what your father would say. And, you are your father. I will always have him around whey you and Tony and Tyler are around. I have that." She hugs me. "I think we should let Tony and Melissa come in." she says as she gets me to my feet and walks me out of the room. She leads Tony and Mel into the room and comes back out. "Nick, can you take me to go find some water?" She asks and Nick is immediately at her side and they walk away.

I look to Ty, "How is she so fucking calm?" I ask him. "Valium. The doctor gave her valium. Not sure how much she took, but it's probably best for her." He says, continuing to stare out the window.

"How you doing?" I ask, fearful of his reply.

"I don't know what to think, Jesus. I still can't even believe it's all really happening. I just keep wanting to wake up."

"You and me both." I say as we go back to silence. A few minutes later Nick and my mother return with vending machine coffees for all of us. I stare at my mother, jealous a bit of her valium. Maybe I should look into that.

"I should head in and check on them." She says as she knocks at the door and proceeds in. Melissa exits and leaves Tony with my mother. I instinctively give her a hug.

"Ohh, I can't believe we are about to do this. Tony is so upset and there is nothing I can do." She begins to cry. My mother and Tony exit the room a few moments later. "Ty, let's go, your turn." My mother gestures at him. Tony seems to have himself pretty together, I guess, better than I do right now. My mother does not exit like with the rest of us and stays with Ty. They are in there for about five minutes or so and the door opens. "Nick and Melissa? Can you go find Dr. Roberts?" My mother asks. Nick and

Melissa seemed shocked but agree and head to the nurse's station and my mother motions for Ty, Tony and myself to join her in the room. We circle around the bed and Nick and Melissa come back with the doctor. We say our prayers, kiss him on the forehead. I hold his hand and the machines are slowly shut off.

I stare at the machine slowly watching the heart rate line intermittently stop jumping. The beeps progressively get slower and eventually fade to flatline. He is gone. He is actually not here with us anymore. Final. Oh, I begin to shake uncontrollably and start to sob. My mother is talking with the doctor and motions for Nick.
"Rain, come here." He says as he tries to keep me on my feet. I just want to sit, lay on the floor, whatever. He gets me in a chair and goes over to my mother and the doctor. They are talking, but I hear nothing but the sobs coming out of me.

The doctor comes over to me. "Rain, I can write you a script for what I gave your mother, a small dose of valium, it will help take the edge off of the situation a bit. Maybe for the next few days? It's up to you, but I can have the nurse go get you one now if you like." He says so calmly. I realize how hysterical I probably am and just shake my head. Nick comes up and begins to rub my shoulders. "It might help. Whatever you want." He says.

"It's fine. How long do we have to stay in here?" I ask, having the sudden urge to no longer want to be in here. I want to be home, on my couch, curled up with a drink. Never so badly have I just wanted to lay down and close my eyes.

"Uhh, we can go whenever you want, I guess. Don't you want to stay here with your family?" He asks.

"You know what, that's what I think I am supposed to do, but that's not what I want right now. I want to go." I say. Tony takes notice.

"Uhh, why don't you bring Rain back to my mothers...uh, mom? You want us back at your house?" He asks her.
"We can go to mine, it's no issue. I don't think I'm ready to go back to the house yet." I say, realizing that we would all be there and Dad won't. Dad will never be there again. I have to get out of here. Now. "I am heading back to my house, you guys can come over, I will get food and stuff." I say as I grab my jacket. I kiss each person good bye and leave. The nurse is catching up to me in the hallway.

"Rain? Rain Brady?" Oh what the fuck now. I turn around and the nurse has a pill cup and a small cup of water. "Doctor Roberts has this for you." She hands them to me and I swallow the pill with the water. "He has this, too." She pulls a script out of her pocket and hands it to me. Looking at Nick, "Don't let her drive on them. Just take care of her. My condolences." She says and heads right away.

"Rain." He starts.
"Here, take 'em." I hand him my keys out of my pocket and we head out of the hospital to my truck.

Nick really is comfortable driving my truck. The valium is starting to put me in a haze and I am watching him. He notices me staring at him. "How you feel?" he asks.

"Not as bad as I did in there. But I understand how my mom handled it now." I say.

"Huh?" He asks.
"Doctor Roberts gave her some, that's why she held it together so well." I say. "I feel so bad for her. We have so much to do over the next week." I say.

"Whatever you need me to do." He says.

"This seems like a Doug kinda thing." I say, not even sure why it came out of my mouth. I swear I only thought it.
"Really?" Nick sounds shocked.
"I didn't mean that." I say quickly.
"No, I mean you are probably right, I'm sure he would do anything you ask him to. If that's what you want." He says.

"Ehh, we will see. I am sure my father has this actually all planned out already anyways." We continue the rest of the drive in silence. I text Rob on the way home to tell him that we are all going to my house. He informs me his mother has a tray of lasagna and she will be coming with him to see my mother. The tiredness is truly hitting me with the added valium and I go in the house and just crash on the couch.

"Want me to do anything? Get you anything?" Nick asks while covering me up with an afghan that had been thrown on the back of the couch.
"I'm not sure if I want a cup of tea, coffee, or a drink." I say.

"Well, you probably shouldn't drink on them until you know how it hits you." He says. The condescending look on my face must have said it all. "How about a cup of coffee with some Kahlua in it? Compromise?" He smiles at me.

"Sure." I reply beginning to fall asleep. "If I fall asleep, wake me up when people get here." I look at him and feel the veil of darkness take me in quickly.

Chapter 20

 "Rain, wake up? Rob is here. Here, bring her this." I start to open my eyes. Who is talking, where am I? I realize that I am on my couch at home and Nick is talking to Rob. I sit up and Rob sits next to me. He puts a cup of coffee on the side table and hugs me.

"I am so sorry, whatever you want, need. Just say it." He says. "There is food! My mother brought a tray and has taken over your kitchen. Now's your chance, go have her make you whatever you want." He is trying to cheer me up.

"Thanks." Is all I can muster.

"You really need sleep." He replies as I drink my coffee. Spiked. Thank you, Nick.

"Maybe tonight, doctor Roberts gave me valium." I say, sounding oddly proud.

"Take it easy, lady." He smiles and gets up and heads to my kitchen.

I sit and enjoy my coffee for a moment and eventually head to the kitchen. I see Melissa and Tony, Rob and his mother, Corinne, and Nick all standing around. "Where is my mother?" I ask.

"She will be here in a few, they are on their way. She had some more paperwork to sign at the hospital." Melissa replies.

I can smell the lasagna and I am starving, but feel like my tiredness is going to win this battle. "You guys enjoy, I am going back to the couch. Wake me up when mom gets

here." And I lay back down. I can't even get myself back to sleep and I feel Ty actually lay down next to me.
"Move over." He says.

"Are you kidding me?" I ask as I try in vain to shove him off. "Did the doctor give you stuff too? Get OFF me!" I push him with my feet.

"Just checking your mood." He says as he hops off the couch and me and takes my coffee and begins to drink it. "Holy crap? Really, Rain!" he says.

"Ohh, like you aren't gonna go get one yourself." I say, smiling back at him.

"Nope, I'm just going to finish yours." He says, smiling back at me.
"Mom out there?" I ask and he nods.
"Rob's mom is taking care of her, she is eating." He seems distant again. "You know, we actually don't have much to do, Dad literally already took care of everything, funeral home, casket, right down to the flowers and music. All mom has to do is find 2 pall bearers."

"Huh?" I ask.

"Two from the list don't live around here and mom says she ain't calling them." He says.

"Huh?"

"Seriously, she found a folder and it has everything spelled out, sounds like something you would do." He laughs. "You are Dad."

"Oh my god." I say with disgust. "Well, I guess it's good for mom. She won't be overwhelmed." I say, thinking it through as I get up to head to the kitchen. Rob and Corinne rush to hug me.

"Rain, my parents are on their way over, I hope that it's ok?" Melissa looks afraid to ask me.

"It's fine, do they have Bella?" I wonder, what an awful thing to have to tell a 4-year-old. She won't even understand.

"Yeah, I think she will come home with us for the next night or two, at least until we have a schedule." She says, sounding as tired as I am.

Melissa's parents arrive with Bella. Conversation is plenty around the table and mom gets tired and Ty leaves to bring her home. He decides he should just stay with her until things get easier. Melissa's parents filter out and then Tony and Melissa gather up Bella and leave.

Corrinne insists on cleaning my kitchen top to bottom and won't hear about just leaving it. Eventually, when my kitchen is way cleaner than it began the day, Rob and her leave. I return to my place on the couch.
"You good?" Nick sits down and placing my feet in his lap.

"As good as I'm gonna be." I say. "Look, can you call Tony and explain everything? Let him decide if Lisa should know or not, I really don't want to ruin the honeymoon, but I don't want her to not know, either. And call Doug and tell him he should probably head out? I told him I would tell him. Him and Jen can stay here. And a cup of tea?" I say.

"Anything else?" Nick sounds sympathetic.

"I'm sorry." I begin to cry again. "I didn't…. I will take care of it. I didn't mean to lay it all on you." I say as I start to get up.

"Rain, I want to help, this is literally the first things you have asked me to do." He says as he gets me to lay back down. "Tea first." He gets up.

A few minutes pass and he brings me a cup of tea and I sit myself up enough to drink it. "I spoke with Doug, he says he will be out tomorrow sometime. He will let me know more specifics later. I got Tony's voicemail and I'm sure he will call me back. Uhh, I told my parents. They want to come up." He sounds extremely nervous. "I will have them stay at a hotel. I guess they were kind of pissed off yesterday, they thought I just sort of chased you back home. They feel awful after I explained what happened."

"That's fine." Is all I can say.

"Why don't I run you a hot bath and then you can just go to bed?" He asks, looking at me. That sounds wonderful, but I don't think I even have the energy to get into and out of the tub.

"I think I'm just going to go to bed. What time is it?" I ask.

"2:30."

"In the morning?! Is it a full moon?" I look out the windows.
"No, in the afternoon."

"What day is it?" I ask.

"Still Sunday." He says. Holy Shit! It feels like it's been a week since the wedding.

"I can't sleep now. I am so fucked up." I say as I start to panic for some reason.

"OK, what do you want to do?" He asks.

"I should probably get this filled." I say as I pull the prescription out of my pocket. "Can you do that for me?" I ask him realizing that I don't want to actually go anywhere.

"I'm not sure they will let me get that for you." He says. "Come on, let's get you out and about. Maybe it will be good for you." He tries to smile at me.

"Well, let's go." I say as I get back up and head to the door. We go to the shopping center and I get my prescription filled at the pharmacy.

"Hungry at all?" He asks when we are finished.

"No, but I assume you are." I say.
"Why? I can eat later."
"I just assume you are always hungry." I almost laugh.

"Whatcha in the mood for?" He asks.

"Ice cream? Like a hot fudge sundae or a banana split. If you really want to know." I say.

"I think we could figure that out." He replies and starts playing on his phone. He finds a place that has both and heads there. We order and have our ice cream. "You should probably take one of those." He points to the pill bottle sticking out of my purse. I comply and sit staring at the empty sundae dish.

"How the hell did I end up here?" I say.

"What do you mean?" He asks.

"I mean, Jesus, I was partaking in a wedding, and I haven't even got a night's sleep and I'm getting ready to bury my father. I just, I guess I am, I am just tired is all." I say with heavy heart.

"Well, it's 4:30, want to head home and go to bed?" He asks.

"I really should try to stay up to at least 8? I don't even know what time it is now. I feel like I haven't slept in days."

"I kinda think you haven't." He is staring at me.

"Well, I guess we should probably just head back to my house." I reply and get up.

He follows me out of the restaurant and we drive back to my house.

"Which bedroom do you want?" I ask him as I head upstairs to the linen closet.

"Huh? You can have yours." He replies.

"Obviously, Doug and Jen will be here tomorrow? Which one do you want? They will have the other one." I reply.

"Ohh, either one, I guess I can take the one next to yours, I brought my stuff in there before to change so, you know." He says as he takes the sheet pile from me. "Let me get that. Go relax." He says.

"Jesus Christ, I don't want to relax. I just need to be...to be productive right now." I'm frustrated as I pull the pile back.

I go into the other bedroom and begin to make the bed. He leaves me be. It only takes a few minutes and the bed is made. I head back to my bedroom and change into some running clothes as I look outside, still daylight.

"I'm gonna go for a run." I say as I head out the door. I begin to head down the street. There is a nice 5-mile loop around my street and the one intersecting with mine. I begin to pick up the pace and think thru the events of the last few days. Planning a wedding, Lisa, all her happiness. My dad, holy shit! My dad. How did this all happen. I run through things in my head. Making lists, work, the bar. Nick. What the hell is up with Nick. A week ago, he wasn't even a thought in my head. I arrived in Vegas ready to ignore him entirely. Now, here he is, staying in my house. Why? Is it his guilt? Is he trying to get back to me? Is he just genuinely feeling bad for what I am going thru? Not the time to figure all this out. I pick up the pace to a full run and am heading back toward the final half mile to my house. It's getting dark anyways.

I arrive back and head in to my house a sweaty mess. "I'm going to take a shower and head to bed." I shout out and start the water in my bathroom. I take my shower and wrap myself in a robe when I get out and head downstairs to find Nick watching TV.

"Tired?" he asks me.

"Yeah, just getting a drink and then going to bed. I have a feeling tomorrow is going to be a long day." I reply, heading into the kitchen with Nick following.
"I talked to Tony, he said they would come if you want

them to, in a heartbeat, but it was up to you." He replies. "Nick, I'm too tired to figure out what other people should do. Tell them to enjoy their honeymoon. No worries." I say as I tip back my glass of orange juice. "I'm going to bed." And I head upstairs to bed.

Chapter 21

I wake up feeling groggy, but look outside and see that there is full sun. How long did I sleep? I look over to the clock, 10:30, ehh, not too bad seeing I haven't' slept in days. Did the last few days really happen? I grab my phone off my nightstand, 17 text messages and 5 missed calls. Yup, everything has happened. No voicemails so nothing scary. I scroll thru the numbers, Tony, Ty, Lisa, Rob and Tony's office. He went to work?

Text messages were from random workers at Tony's shop offering their condolences. By Text? Really? Rob texted, Corinne wants to know what I want for dinner. Ha.

Doug texted that Jen and him would be arriving around dinner time.

Random text from Ty in the middle of the night asking if I was up. Ahh, he can't sleep. I feel bad.

I send Tony a quick text to call me when he gets a chance. Obviously, I'm the last one up and he can get me up to speed. I head downstairs wishing I had made the coffee the night before and arrive in the kitchen to Nick making eggs.

"Coffee." He hands me a cup and as I start to drink it, he continues. "I made eggs, I couldn't find any bacon or anything. You need to get some food." He points out. "Ty was staying here while I was gone. I'm sure there are ramen noodles and spaghettio's in the cupboard."

"It's ok, want to go out for breakfast?" He asks.

"No, I'm actually pretty good most days with just my coffee." I reply watching him move thru the kitchen like he owns it. "There is some lasagna in there, if you really need something beyond the eggs." I say smiling. My phone rings and I see its Tony.

"Hey, what's up?" I ask him.

"How did you sleep?"

"I slept, which is good enough. What's the plan for today?" I ask.

Tony goes on to explain that we need to head to the funeral home and do all that stuff with mom. He will pick me up in 45 minutes to head over there. I end the call.

"Well, Tony is picking me up in like 45, so I got to go get ready." I say and retreat to my room with my coffee.

"You want me to go with you?" Nick asks.

"I think it's just my brothers and my mom." I say as I continue up the stairs. I change into something appropriate and head to my office. Jesus, I have a lot of things to get in order.

Nick appears in the office with a cup of coffee for me.

"Doug and Jen will be here around 5ish. He just rented a car at the airport. You mind if I use your truck while you are gone?" He asks.

"You could just use the car, it's still registered and insured. It's your car." I reply as I log into my email.

"Really? Why?" He is confused.

"Ehh, I paid the insurance for the year and then just paid

the renewal bill, not really thinking anything of it. Ty drives in around the block once every week or two, he seems to think that it's good for the engine. I think he just likes to race around the neighborhood. Keys are hanging in the garage." I say as I scan my emails.

There is a knock at the door as I hear it open. "I'm in the office." I yell out and Tony momentarily joins us in the office.
"You ready? This is going to be rough." He sighs.

"Maybe you should take your pills with you?" Nick chimes in.
"Yeah, maybe you should take one now." Tony replies.
"What, you think I can't contain myself?" I ask.

"You might as well not deal with reality to its fullest, if you don't have to." Tony puts his hand on my shoulder.

"Fine, let's get this over with." I reply as I get up to go.

We head to the funeral home and meet my mother and Ty there, Dad really had everything planned out. Only problem was the reception after the funeral. The banquet hall he intended is under renovation and closed for another few weeks.

"Why don't we just close down the bar and have it there?" I volunteer.
"Rain, that's a big commitment." My mother chimes in.
"No, I hire a caterer and close it to the public. Not a big deal at all." I huff.

"Mom, the place usually has more people in it than the funeral will have, it's probably easiest." Ty offers.

"Yeah, you know dad was really proud of the bar and Rain." Tony adds.
"Fine, just take care of it." My mother replies and we can tell she is done with this process. Obit will start running in the paper the following morning. Thursday will be the wake, Friday is the funeral and one week later it's over, beginning to end. Tuesday and Wednesday are to prepare. Prepare, uggh. The way the funeral director said it, you think we were preparing for war or something. I guess he meant for out of town guests to arrive or whatever, but it annoyed me anyways.

"You guys want to come over for dinner? Doug and Jen will be here tonight, I think Rob's mother is sending more food over." I offer.
"Melissa's parents are taking us all out to dinner." Tony replies staring at me then my mother. "But I'm sure they wouldn't be offended that you aren't coming."

"Fine, so who is driving me home?" I say simply.

"You sure you ok?" Ty asks.
"I'm fine." I say.

"You're acting like a bitch." He says and I glare back at him.
"I will take you now." Tony hesitantly gets up. We all say our goodbyes and head out.
"Want to stop by the office on the way back? I saw some emails about stuff Mel asked me to look at." I offer once we are in the car.

"You better work this shit out in your head, Rain. We are all upset, but Ty called it correct." He says, trying to take my hand.

"Look, I'm just trying to keep up with everything. You want to let shit slip for a week, it's gonna be a mess when you get back." I say.
"There is nothing that can happen in a week in there that should take your attention off Dad." He says and I can hear his frustration gaining momentum.

"Whatever. Let it pile up. What do you suggest I do then?" I ask and there is silence. "Should I let my feelings run the show? Should I just collapse into a sobbing mess?"

"Nope! Just keep being a bitch." He says as he steps on the gas a bit harder. We ride in silence for a while. "Rain, I'm sorry. I don't know what's going through your head. You know, this is probably exactly how Dad would act. I can't fault you for that." He is trying to apologize.

"Believe it or not, I have a lot on my mind. I still don't think it's real. I mean, fuck, one minute I'm dressed like a showgirl participating in a wedding, then I get a phone call and everything is gone. Jesus Christ, he's gone. Forever." I begin to cry.

"Rain, I'm sorry. Do you want to stop at the office? We can if you really want to." Tony says.
"No, just bring me home. I guess I will start calling some caterers, get everything in order for Friday." I say as I slowly stop crying.

We reach my home and he says he will call me later tonight. I head in the house and flop onto the couch. My house is quiet. I don't remember the last time I sat in my house in silence. Nick. Where the hell is he? I go out to the garage and the car and truck are there. I check upstairs and he is not there. I text him. He replies that he is in the basement and I head down.

"Ehh, just making some use of some free time." He says from the tiny recording studio. "I cleaned up a bit down here and decided to play. Any special requests?" He asks as I just stare at him. I have the urge to just yell at him to get out of my house and I hear both Ty and Tony calling me a bitch in my head.

"No, no special requests. I need to go work in my office for a bit." I simply say and head back upstairs.

I head to my office. I really haven't gone through my emails in a week. I would occasionally skim them and flag things, but I decide to go back to the last day and go one by one. I finish them all up and begin to check my accounts and look at my trading portfolio. I move some things around and then pay some bills. I have a list of companies I need to cross check in the news, but decide to move to the bar. I need to close Friday night. It seems to be a regular open mic night. Thankfully, that's not too bad to cancel. At least it wasn't a big band. I call the manager and explain and tell them to update the sign right now, call the bands that already signed up and let them know and see if any staff want the night off. The ones that were counting on the shift can work and get paid. See, I'm not a bitch. I call a few caterers and request info and explain the situation of time. Quotes will be emailed to me. I make a few more calls and then begin to do the research on some companies and I hear Nick call for me. I come out of the office to see Doug and Jen standing in my living room. Jen runs to me to hug me and begins to cry.

"I am so sorry for you, I feel so bad." She has tears running down her cheeks.

"Thank you." I say calmly, patting her on the back. "How was the flight?" I look to Doug.

"Probably easier than yours was." He replies. "If you had just given me 10 minutes to think, I would have got you on a direct flight." He sighs.

"Ehh, I'm here now, that's all that matters." I say as he hugs me.

"Uhh, you guys have a room upstairs." I say as I lead them up there. "The wake is not till Thursday and the funeral on Friday. We are having a reception afterward at the bar. Let me know if you guys need anything in here. I don't think that I have too much food right now, but I think Rob's mom is sending over some more food." I make a mental note that I have to go to the store, soon, as I head back downstairs.

"You ok, Rain?" Nick is following me.

"Yeah, I'm fine." I reply while heading back to my office.

"You have been in here for hours. Are you sure?" He asks.

"Nick, this is what I do, every day. I work on things, then I head to the bar at night, then I come home and go to bed and repeat the entire process over and over. What do you think I do?" I am sitting back at my desk.

"I don't know, isn't it kind of lonely?" He sits in the chair across from the desk.

"Nick, I don't like the attention, never have. I enjoy this, and right now I need to stay busy." I say as I dial the phone to reach Rob.

"Hey, just checking in. Is your mother actually sending over more food?" I say.

"Shes kinda busy, but I'm sure if I ask her, she will make whatever you want." He replies.

"Nah, I have Doug and Jen here now and was just kinda figuring out dinner." I say back. "Don't bother her about it. The lasagna was enough. I guess I should go shopping." I pause. "Hey, want to go with me? Just the two of us? I could use some alone time." I ask.

"Quality time at the grocery store, couldn't think of a better plan." He says.

"You want me to pick you up or you want to come here?" I ask.
"Ehh, whatever. Why don't you just come get me, I have to change anyways." He says.
"Be there in half an hour, thanks." I say as I hang up the phone and look up to see Nick still sitting in the room.
"Alone time? You ok?" He asks.

"Nick, I just need to get my mind straight. I haven't hung out with Rob in over a week. He is my rock and I need food and you certainly aren't going with me. I don't need to be mobbed at the store." I say. "Hang out with Doug and Jen and I will bring dinner back."

"Jen. How am I supposed to hang out with her?" He says quietly to himself.

"I'm sure a great entertainer like you can figure it out." I say a bit snarky as I get up and grab my keys. "I will be back in a few hours."

Chapter 22

I get to Rob's house and head in. Corinne meets me with more hugs and condolences. I tell her where and when the funeral will be and that it will be in the paper and head to Rob's room to get him. We head to the store and just shop and talk about life more. He says that the guys from our old bowling team will be going to the funeral and some other people I know from his job. It's amazing how much of your past comes back when someone passes away.

"So, what's the deal with Nick? You guys back together or what?" Rob asks as we continue to shop.

"Nick?! No, he just sort of followed me back from the wedding." I say.

"Ohh, kinda seems like it."

"Uggh, it might seem, but it's not. I assure you." I say with a huff.

"Stressing you out?" Rob stops to see watch me as I reply. "You know, I can't tell. There is enough things stressing me out right now, I can't really label what's causing what." I reply. "Where's the life advice, Rob, I could use it right about now."

"Hey, you never wanted to talk about anything when you two broke up." He begins and I interrupt. "And that is still not up for discussion."

"Well, this is how I see it, you looked a hot mess when you got back, you obviously made your point to him, Jesus, he went to rehab....And you knew what you were getting into when you started with him." Rob is carefully choosing his words. "I'd hate to see what she looked like when you were done with her." He tries to get a smile out of me.

"Rob, stop." I say realizing that everyone assumed I had some catfight with some bitch he was cheating with. My head is beginning to hurt. "I lost, trust me." I say hoping we change the subject. "And we are done discussing it." I say with finality.

"Whatever you say. Think we have enough stuff?" he looks at the food cart.

"Yeah, I will get home and realize what I forgot, I should have had a list." I reply absently as we head to the checkout. "Ahh, I actually need to bring something for dinner tonight. I really don't want to cook."

"Let's just pick up some pizza and be done with it." Rob says as he pulls out his phone. He orders pizzas while I pay for my stuff and we head home.

"Look, I don't know what happened when you two broke up and I'm not going to push you, but he is staying in your house, are you sure he knows you two aren't together?" He asks while I drive.
"Look, I hadn't seen him since the night it all happened. We saw each other at the wedding, I was there for Lisa and that was it, we talked and called a truce to just be civil to each other and then my dad...and then he just followed me back here. I didn't ask or expect him to. I guess he is really just trying to be supportive? He can't think that this

will bring us back together? Could he?" I am thinking out loud now.

"Look, I don't know him that well, I have no idea." Rob replies, a bit shocked. "You said Doug is here, have you talked to him?"

"No, but that's not really a Doug kind of conversation anyways." I wonder what Doug would say.

"Did he bring his girlfriend with him? I thought I heard you say that." Rob asks.

"Yeah, Jen. I know her, she is very innocent." I say.

"You aren't that innocent, missy." He laughs back.

"Whatever, you will meet her." I reply as I go inside the pizza place to get dinner.

We make it back home and head in to find Jen cleaning my kitchen. "What are you doing?" I ask.
"Oh, just keeping busy. Nick and Doug are in the studio in your basement and I didn't really feel like I belonged. I figured I would just stay busy until I got back and figured you had so much going on, I would just clean a little to help out." She says, wiping down a counter. I glance over at Rob waiting for him to acknowledge my earlier comment.

"Hi! I'm Rob. Rain's friend." Rob says to her and extends a hand.

"Hi, I'm Jen. I'm here with Doug, but I'm Rain's friend, too." She says proudly as Rob glances back at me winking.

"Rain, your house is amazing. I hope there is a chance I get to see the bar while I'm here, too." She beams.

"I'm sure you will, we are having the reception after the funeral there." I say.
"Rain, I am so sorry. I can't imagine what you are going through. If there is anything I can do while I am here please tell me. You looked so upset that night and I felt so bad for you. Everything always goes wrong for you." She says and I cut her off as I am not sure how far she will push her thoughts.

"It's fine, Jen, I'm glad you were able to make it out for this. I'm glad you're here. Do you want to go get Nick and Doug? I have pizza for us all." I say and she nods and heads to the basement.

"Well, she is bubbly." Rob grins at me.

"Yeah, but she is sweet. Be nice." I glance back at him.

"I always am, I'm gonna unload your truck." He says as he heads outside.

Nick and Doug return to the kitchen with Jen. "Sorry guys, I had no urge to cook tonight, I was kinda sick of looking at food with all the shopping." I say as I pass out paper plates.

"Absolutely fine, you ok?" Doug asks.
"Yeah, Rob's here and bringing in the stuff. I'm good." I say.
"I can go help him." Nick interjects and immediately heads out the door.

"What's up with him?" I look to Doug.

"We can talk later." Doug glances seriously at me.

"Great, let me find my bottle of valium first." I sigh.

"Valium? Really?" Doug seems shocked.
"Yeah, my doc thinks they will help with the next few days. I guess they are, a bit." I sigh. "Kinda wish I had them on arrival in Vegas, things might have gone smoother." I look at him seeing if he catches my subtleness.

"Not now, we will talk later." He does.

All the bags end up inside and Rob helps me put everything away since he is really the only one who knows where everything goes and we all eat pizza. We chat about the flights back and forth, we chat about the bar and the arrangements for the reception being held there. Doug volunteers to take over coordinating it to take it all off my plate. We finish and clean up and Rob heads home.

"So what do you all want to do tonight?" I ask.
"Whatever you like." Jen replies.

"I apologize for not really having anything planned to keep you occupied, you've seen the basement if you guys want to hang out down there or stay up here and watch tv or whatever. I honestly think I just need to go to bed." I say, realizing its almost 9pm and I am still trying to catch up on sleep.

"That's fine, if you are tired, rest. We are fine." Nick says, staring at me with a concerned look on his face.

"OK, please don't hesitate to wake me up if you need anything, I will see you all in the morning." I say and head upstairs and change and get into bed.

Chapter 23

I wake up feeling more refreshed than I have in over a week. I grab my phone and no missed calls, no texts. Maybe this was all a nightmare. I get up and head downstairs in my robe to see Jen, Nick and Doug in the kitchen.

"Coffee?" Nick is extending a cup in his hand and I take it. "What do you want? Eggs, sausage, bacon?" he has been cooking.

"Meh, nothing. Coffee is fine. I am going to head outside with this if you don't mind." I say and head to the patio and close the door behind me. It's a beautiful May morning, it feels like it's going to be warm today, it's probably already 65 degrees outside.

"You ok?" Doug asks as he joins me on the patio. "It's freezing out here." He replies.

"Haha, you are too west coast, this is beautiful to me. Sit." I say as I gesture at the chair across from me and he takes a seat. "What did you need to talk to me about?" I ask him.

"Ehh, Nick is uncomfortable." He is studying me for a reaction.

"Are you kidding me?" I don't even know what else to say. "Am I not rolling out the welcome wagon enough for him when he followed me back here to watch my Dad die. I dare him to say it to me. In fact, go get him." I am pissed.

"Rain, calm down. I kinda pointed all that out to him already. I told him he is not in charge of this situation. He is a spectator and whatever happens, he cannot interfere with it. Plain and simple." Doug is trying to calm my nerves.

My hands begin to tremble. "Can you go find that bottle of pills for me?" I ask him.

"Uhh, sure, where are they?" He gets up.
"On the desk, in my office, I think." I say as I try to just take deep breaths.

Doug returns moments later with the bottle and hands me one to take with my coffee.

"Doug, if you explained all this to him, why even tell me?" I look at him.

"Cause I'm not sure what you are doing. I need to know what you want?" Doug replies.

"What do you mean, what I want. What I want is for my Dad to be here with me having coffee, what I want is for my life to be back to the way it was. But I don't think you can do that for me." I say, staring ahead blankly.

"I mean, with Nick and all." Doug looks fearful of what I might say back.
"Really? Is that all he is concerned with? You know, I got to Vegas and wanted nothing whatsoever to do with him. I was ready to stab him in his sleep at one point and then it all sort of calmed down and he kinda grew on me a bit, but

then…everything changed. My Dad, ohh. I can't do this." I begin to cry.

"Rain, I'm sorry. It's awful. It sucks and I know there isn't anything anyone can do to bring him back. But we are all here for you to try to make you at ease." He says rubbing my shoulders.

"Except fucking Nick, who thinks that I am supposed to take him back because he is acting like some knight in fucking shining armor here." I am still crying but it's turning to anger.

"Don't worry about him. He should know better. I just think he cares about you so much, he doesn't get it. He doesn't get it why you don't feel the same way is all." Doug is trying and Jen opens the door.

"Oh, Rain, what's wrong? I was coming out to tell you that your boxes are here. The stuff from your room at the wedding. Are you ok? Can I get you anything?" She looks very concerned.
"Actually, some more coffee and a couple of napkins?" I smile back at her.
"Sure." She takes my cup and brings it back in the house.

Nick returns a moment later with a full cup of coffee and some napkins and sits down at the table. "What's wrong?" He says.
"Lots of things are wrong, Nick, I'm about to bury my father and am not ready to." I say flatly.

"Rain, I would fix it if I could. I would do anything to see you smile." He says and takes my hand.

I glance at Doug and then to Nick.

"I'm sure I will smile at some point, it's just not going to be right now." I say and see that my reply has been approved by the look on his face.

"Is there anything that you need to do today? Anything that you want to do?" Nick asks.
"Well, I have some things to do in the office and I guess I have to find something to wear the next few days and I have to check in with my mother." I reply.
Nick and Doug seem to be communicating without talking as they stare at each other.
"I guess I will head into the office and get started." I say and head back into the house. I go into my office and settle down to begin sifting through emails and other mundane tasks. Tuesday has begun.

I am researching companies when my desk phone rings. Caller ID says its Lisa's cell phone.

"Hello?"
"Rain, oh my god! Tony just told me. Why didn't you call me? We just landed in Europe." She exclaims.

"Lisa, I didn't want to ruin your honeymoon." I say.
"Jesus Christ, it's just a vacation. We've been here before." She sounds exasperated.
"Lisa, it's fine." I say.
"You didn't even say good-bye in Vegas." She sounds upset.

"Now that I completely apologize for, I honestly was out of my mind when I finally picked up my phone. I just needed to get home. I am sorry." I say, realizing I hurt her feelings.

"No, don't be sorry. I feel awful about you." She says.

"Don't. Just enjoy your honeymoon, enjoy being married. Everything that night was beautiful, you know. It was like a storybook. Magical." I say, thinking about how perfect it really was.

"Yeah, until you took off like Cinderella. I heard your prince Charming followed you back home, too." She laughs. "How is that going?" Her voice changes to being serious.

"It's going. Prince Charming is actually the last thing on my mind. Jen and Doug are here, too. And family and friends will soon start arriving. It's surreal, it's about to turn into a parade of everyone who ever crossed our family's path. Not looking forward to it." I say.

"Jen and Nick are both in your house together?" She sounds bewildered.
"Yeah, why?" I ask.

"I really shouldn't say anything." She replies.

"Well, you already said something so...." I am curious.

"They just don't get along, is all. Maybe you should talk to Nick about it. I'm not even sure if Doug knows so you didn't hear it from me. Listen, I really needed to check in with you, but I am at an airport and trying to get thru customs so I will check in with you soon and you call me if you need anything at all." She says.

"I love you Lisa, enjoy your trip!" I say.
"Love ya too, sweetie." She says as she ends the call.

I wonder what the hell is the deal with Nick and Jen? And how can Doug not know, Doug knows everything. Whatever. This is not the time for me to be figuring out Nick's issues. I look up at the clock and its 2pm. Wow! I look at the things I still need to do and apparently the mall is one of them. I go find Jen to see if she wants to go with me. They are all sitting on the couch watching some mundane documentary on the 70's metal scene.
"Jen, want to take a trip to the mall? I have to get something to wear to the wake and funeral. Maybe get out of the house for a bit?" I offer.
"We could all go, if you want." Nick offers.

"Well, I really have no urge to have the four of us go clothes shopping for me. It's really kinda weird." Is he actually serious?
"Actually, the suit Doug brought me doesn't really fit like it's supposed to anymore, I think I need a new one." He says.
"Well, there is more than one car out there, you two can go anywhere you like. We are going shopping." I say as Jen stands up. "Truck or Mercedes?" I ask her.

"I think the Mercedes sounds nice." I can tell she has no idea what to say.

"See you guys later." I say as we head out the door. We get situated in the car and head to the mall. "So, tell me about you and Doug." I prod.

"Well, we've been dating for a little while. Keeping it to ourselves a bit." She says.

"I know that, how did it happen? Weren't you with Todd?" I ask and feel bad as soon as I hear the words.

"Yeah, Todd and I were ok. I think I was just there for him. He wasn't bad. Then after everything that happened with you and Nick, Nick didn't like Todd bringing me around so much and we kinda grew apart." What the hell is that all about?

"Did you want to be with Todd?" I ask.

"You know? Not really. I think I just served the purpose of being a girlfriend, like anyone would do, just as long as he had a girlfriend. Does that make sense?" She replies.

"Yeah, I get that. But how did you and Doug get together?" I really need to know now.

"Well, I was always asking him about you when he came into the club. I really needed to know that you were ok, and wanted to know what was going on. Lisa would probably have fired me if I asked her, she is kinda protective over you so I would always ask Doug. And then he started coming in more and more to see me and eventually we went out on a real date and we just sort of grew on each other." She is smiling. "I guess you could say that you brought us together in some weird awful twisted way."

"Well, every cloud has some sort of silver lining, I guess." I say, not wanting to think about it all over again. "I'm glad you two are together, you both seem really good for each other and really make each other happy." I say truthfully. We continue to the mall and head in to begin looking for something funeral appropriate. We get a few outfits for myself and I buy her a black pantsuit to go in as well. She seems forever grateful that I got it for her and I am happy to do it. We chat about mundane things. Antidotal stories from working at the Storm. Meeting Doug's family and all sorts of things. I look at my phone and it's almost 5pm.

"Hey, mind if we stop at my mom's house? I should really stop in today." I say as I start the car.
"Ohh, I don't mind at all, are you sure I should go with you?" She asks.
"It will be fine." I say as I head out of the mall and head toward my mother's. We reach my parent's house and I see a lot of unrecognizable cars in the driveway. I pull onto the edge of the grass as there is no place to park and we head in. "Don't be nervous, besides, not even sure I know everyone in there myself." I say, trying to make her comfortable. It makes me laugh a little that in this situation, I am trying to make her feel better. We head in and lots of people I kind of recognize start to say hello. 2 people my dad worked with and a distant cousin I probably haven't seen since that last funeral. My mother is sitting at the table with coffee.

"Oh, Rain, I wasn't expecting you. Here, have a seat." She begins to get up.
"Ehh, I was just stopping by on the way from the mall." I

say. "This is Jen, my friend from California, she just flew out for the funeral." I introduce her.

"Shopping at the mall, that seems fun." My Dad's co-worker chimes in. Not sure why this statement rubs me the wrong way. I had to go, I'm not some ditz that takes solace shopping.

"Well, I guess I had to look presentable to bury my father." I say. My mother glares at me and I wish I had just said something else. "I'm sorry, mom, it's just been a long day." I apologize.

"Well, I'm sure you are under some stress, would you like me to fix you something to eat?" She replies.

"No, you have guests, I should get going anyways. I have a lot of work to get done." I reply and nudge Jen toward the door.

"Nice meeting you all." Jen offers as I force her out.

"Well, that was just peachy." I say as we head back to the car.

"What's wrong?" She is concerned.

"I don't know, I'm just being judgy a little bit. Taking comments wrong, I guess." I say as we get in the car and head for home.

"How is your mom handling everything? She seemed pretty good." She asks.

"She is taking valium, same as me. Same doctor wrote it, in fact." I laugh.

"Why is that funny?" She replies.

"Not sure, my mom and I are kinda opposites, I think this is the first thing we have really had in common." I laugh a bit more.

"So you are more like your Dad?" She laughs too. And it all comes crashing back again. I am like my Dad, and now he is gone. No one will really every get me again. Not like my Dad did. My laugh turns into a bit of a cry and I try to contain myself.

"I think I need a drink." I say tearing up.

"OK, where do you want to go?" She asks.

"We can go to my bar. I should really check in anyways." I say and pick up the pace in the car a bit.

"Ohh, that's great! I really wanted to check it out." She says. I drive to the bar and head into the private parking and pull into my spot directly next to the back door. We head in and most of the people behind the bar are shocked that I am there. Lots of people are offering their sympathies. I sit down at the bar and ask for a shot of Jack and immediately a glass and the bottle appear. I offer Jen one.

"Uhh, No, I shouldn't drink, you go ahead though. Probably be good for ya." She side hugs me and orders a soda.

I drink and focus on the music. It's all sound system tonight as a Tuesday does not warrant a live band. The place is less than half full and everyone is eating and drinking. I have a few shots and feel a bit woozy, thinking back to the valium I had earlier. I take Jen on a tour of the entire bar and show her my private office. She is in awe of the entire place and has lots of questions. I enjoy her company.

I sit down at my desk and stare at the picture collage on the wall. The last time I sat here I was planning a barbeque with my father. We were trying to coordinate a family vacation. Ohh, I miss him. I have the bottle on my desk and take a few more swigs and begin to cry.

"Oh, Rain, don't cry." I look up at her. "Actually, let it out, sweetie, you need to." She is sweet. I just want to go to bed and go to sleep. I just need to get thru the next few days and then restore order to my life.

"I think I want to go home." I announce. "You need to drive." I hand her my keys and we head out to the car.

"Oh, shit, Rain." She says in the driver's seat. "I can't drive a stick shift. I didn't know, I thought it was an automatic."

"It's fine. I will call a taxi." I say, about ready to just sleep in my car.
"No, I can call Doug. He always knows what to do." She says. I think she has called Doug for help before and this thought makes me giggle.

"Doug is going to call a cab for us sweetie. We can call a cab ourselves." I say, sounding as drunk as I feel.

"No, I'm calling Doug. I don't want anything to go wrong again." She sounds worried.

"Huh? Whatever." I say, closing my eyes. I hear her talking on the phone but it sounds like background noise.

"Doug and Nick are coming." She is trying to wake me up. "Whatever, Lets go back inside." I announce and get out of the car. I stand up and realize that I am wobbly. The cool air hits me and brings me back to life a bit more and I head in.

"Rain, wait, let me help you." She takes my arm and we head back in and I sit back down at the bar.

"I'd like another drink." I announce and see the bartender look to Jen and shrug their shoulders. They place a drink in front of me. I take a sip and realize that it's a Jack and Coke this time. I'm not in the mood to argue, so I just drink it. Jen continues to make small talk with me and I keep drinking.

"Hey, someone need a ride?" I hear Nick.

"I guess." I reply and attempt to get off the barstool and fall to the floor. I feel Nick help me up and I lean on him.

"I'm so sorry, I didn't think she drank that much but she mumbled something about the pills in her purse and I realized she took them. I should have stopped her." I hear her continue at a mile a minute and can't understand the rest of what she is saying.
"It's fine, Jen, let it go." Nick says. "Why don't you and Doug just head home." He sounds angry, what the hell is he so mad about.

"Are we taking my truck home?" I ask.

"Yes, Rain, we should go now." He says in a much nicer voice to me helping me up and out the door.

"I think I need to stop." I say as I immediately get sick on the pavement.

"Jesus Christ, are you ok?" He asks.

"Why are you mad at me? No one asked you to come." I say as I sit down directly on the pavement.

"Rain, you should know better, those pills? You shouldn't be drinking." He is rubbing my hair back.
"OK, you are the expert on drinking and drugs, aren't you?" Did I just say that?

"Rain, stop."
"Well, it's not like you haven't carried me home drunk before." I laugh maniacally.
"That is true." He smiles.
"Except you won't be delivering me to my Dad this time because he's dead." I say quietly and start to cry again.

"Rain, we have to get you home. Do you feel ok?" He sounds concerned.

"I need water." I command.

"Sit here for a minute, can you stay put?" He asks and I nod and he heads into the bar and comes back out with a few bottles of water. He opens and hands me one and I begin to drink.

"I'm good. Help me up." I say as I scramble to get up and he helps me to the truck and places me in and puts my

seatbelt on. As he is leaning over me, I sigh. Him brushing up against me brings a flurry of memories.
"God, I wish this could work." I say out loud. Why did that come out of my mouth? I'm not even sure I thought it.

"What could work?" he asks as he leans back out of the truck.

"Nick." I say. What am I doing?!?

"Rain, what?" I see his face change as it hits him what I meant.

"I don't know. Nick, I don't know what I am thinking. Just forget it." I say as I put my head back and begin to fall back asleep.

Chapter 24

I wake up feeling groggy and in my bed. How the hell did I get here? I get up and realize that I am still in my clothes. I undress and put my robe on. I grab my phone and head downstairs. Nick is in the kitchen and hands me a cup of coffee. This is beginning to feel like that movie 'Groundhog Day'.

"Can we talk?" He asks.
"Where are Jen and Doug?" I look around.
"They went out to breakfast, what happened last night?" He asks.

"Well, I guess I forgot I took valium and had a few drinks." I say. "Live and learn." I lift up my cup of coffee and take a drink.

"You really need to be careful, Rain." He replies. I am not in the mood for drinking advice from Nick. "Do you remember anything?" He asks.

"I remember getting sick. I remember getting there in the car and leaving in the truck. Jen can't drive stick? Doesn't surprise me." I say. He is too quiet. "What? What happened?" I ask and he remains silent.
"Nick! If something happened last night you better tell me." I am getting mad. "What did I do? Tell me!"

"Jesus, Rain, you didn't do anything. It's what you said to me." He says solemnly.

"What did I say?" I ask, having a sigh of relief at least nothing happened.

"You said you wished we could work." He is looking at me. I try to replay the night. Why did I say that? Do I?

"I don't know, Nick, there are moments that sometimes I do, but, holy shit, my mind is all over the place right now. I have to bury my Dad in two days. I can't handle this conversation right now." I am getting upset thinking about it. "Why are you doing this now?" I begin to cry. I need to get this shit under control. I drink more of my coffee and head directly back to my room and get in the shower.

I do my best to wash away the drama. I stay in there till the hot water begins to run out and finally get out and dressed. I head immediately to my office and start working on emails.

"Hey, I brought you a cup of coffee." Nick enters.
"Fine, put it down." I say, not looking away from the screen.
"Listen, if you want me to go, I will." He sits down in the chair.
"Nick." I look at him and then put my head in my hands. "You don't have to go, I know, I think you mean well. But I don't have the mind right now to be sorting out anything other than my Dad. I can't. Not right now. It was confusing enough in Vegas, dealing with you, but now...I just can't. I'm sorry." I say.

"So that's what it is? Dealing with me?" He asks.
"Don't. You know what I mean." I say.

"Actually, I don't know what you mean." He pushes.
"Then I can't help you." I stand up from my seat.

"Rain, wait. I'm sorry." He says.

"I need more coffee." I announce.

"Let me get it for you." He takes the cup and exits the office returning with a filled cup.

"Thanks" I say. "Look, I'm sorry. I just can't handle this right now. I can't handle anything." I say as I put my head back into my hands.

"Whatever you need, whatever you want, just say it." He says.

"Plans for today?" I ask, trying to change the subject.

"Not really, I could take you out for dinner tonight." He offers.

"I think I got a text from Ty that him and I are taking my mom out." I say, looking thru my phone.

"Oh, well, you want me to go?" what a strange question.

"Uhh, no, but you might cheer up my mom. You can come if you want, I guess." I realize how awkward it sounded coming out of my mouth. "What about Jen and Doug?" I ask.

"You know it's not your job to entertain her." He says.

"What's that supposed to mean?" I ask.

"I don't know. Hey, I got a suit yesterday." He says, changing the subject.

"All by yourself?" I smile.

"Well, Doug helped a little." He smiles back.

"Of course, he did." I laugh. "I have some things to get done here."

"I'll let you be." He says and exits.

I continue to work in my office for a few hours until I hear a knock at the door as Doug enters.

"Hey, I took care of the catering for Friday night. You ok?" He says as he sits down.

"Where's Jen?" I ask.

"She went for a walk. She will be back later." He says as I look curiously at him. "She has never been out east, she thinks everything is scenic." He laughs. "You sure you're ok?"

"No, I'm not, but under the circumstances, I think its ok." I say. "I'm getting sick of people asking if I'm ok. You know?" I finish.

"Sorry. I know." He says.

"I kinda just want it all over with, you know, so it can get back to normal and I can deal with it myself." I stare at him.

"I get that." He replies. "It will be soon enough."

"It's like Vegas all over again, just a more twisted version." I look at him as I take the pills out of my purse.

"Be careful?" He looks to them.

"Yeah, no drinking, figured that one out." I say as I take one. "You know, if Jen knew how to drive stick, it all would have been fine." I laugh.

"Don't start blaming her." He says.

"You know I'm kidding. I felt awful. I puked. I didn't even drink that much. Jesus." I say.

"Yeah, I heard." He smiles. "I should let you get back to work. Want me to get you anything?" He asks.

"A cup of tea would be spectacular." I say and he nods and leaves.

I get back to my work and Doug brings me a cup of tea after a while. I continue to lose myself in working. Research, numbers. Hours later Ty comes into the office. "Mom's waiting, you joining us or blowing us off again?" he hops up on the desk.
"Holy Shit! What time is it?" I look for my phone. "Fuck, 5! Just let me get my purse and we can go. Want to take my car or yours?" I ask.
"We are taking mom's car, I'm driving. She's sedated, shall we say." He smiles.

"I understand. Don't let me drink or you will really see sedated." I laugh. "Oh, shit, I think I told Nick he could come with us." I say, vaguely remembering the conversation from earlier.

"He's out in the kitchen with mom. She really likes him." He nudges me. "Maybe more than you do." He laughs.

"Maybe?" I laugh along with him. "Let's go."

We head into the kitchen where Nick and my mother are engaged in conversation. "You all ready?" I ask and we head to the car.
Nick and I are in the backseat and Ty is driving with my

mother in the passenger seat. "I really feel like any other seating arrangement would have worked here, why is Ty driving?" I laugh.

"Well, at least it's not his car we are in." My mother cracks a joke and we all laugh. The four of us head to dinner and all enjoy ourselves. It's really just a relaxing evening and there are finally a few hours of no drama. Tony is with Melissa who isn't feeling well. Her nerves coupled with the fact that she has less than a month to delivery isn't really a good combination. Tomorrow is the wake and we decide to head home early to all just get some rest. The inevitable begins tomorrow. Ty and my mother drop off Nick and myself. I head into the kitchen and find a note that Jen and Doug went to dinner and a movie and would be home later.

Chapter 25

"Well, it's just us tonight, want to see what's on tv?" I look to Nick.

"Whatever you want. Want a glass of wine?" He heads to the fridge.

"Not sure if I should drink." I say.

"Ahh, one glass won't hurt. You're home and I will watch you." He smiles as he gets a glass and pours some wine. "Head out and see what's on, I will bring it for you." He says and motions me out of the room.

"Umm, are you spiking my drink? I can carry it myself." I laugh.

"Just trying to be nice." He shakes his head and hands me the glass and I head out to the couch. I look thru the guide and give up, there are so many channels and appears to be nothing on. Nick joins me and I hand it to him. "Nothing interesting, remote's all yours."

Nick begins to flip thru the channels himself.

"Sit down, here." I pat the space next to me on the couch. He sits.

"How about this?" he settles on some sci fi series.
"It's fine, Rob is obsessed with this show. I don't get it." I reply, stretching my legs out.

"I'm kind of getting into it." He pulls my legs over on to his lap and begins to rub them.

"You don't have to do that." I say, hoping he doesn't actually stop. It feels really good.

"You need to relax. You want me to stop?" He asks.

"No." I say as I rearrange myself to sit better. I drink down the rest of the glass of wine.

"Want more?" He watches me.

"I don't think I should." I say.

"I'm here, you can have another. Maybe a bit slower this time?" He removes my legs and takes the glass. He comes back a minute later with a refilled glass. "Slower." He hands it to me.

"Fine." I say as I slide my legs back onto his lap.

"See, I knew you liked it." He smiles at me and begins to rub my legs again.

He watches the show and continues to rub my legs and I slowly finish the glass of wine. Darkness begins to set in and I feel myself shift on to him, leaning in and he places his arm around me. I feel at peace for the first time in a very long time as I fall asleep.

"Rain, Rain, you have to get up. Come on, let me help you to bed." I feel Nick nudging me. "Come on, or I can just carry you."

"Fine." I am too tired to get up. "Or just leave me here, I'm comfortable." I say, half asleep.

"You will be sore tomorrow and it's gonna be a long day, come on, I'll carry you." He picks me up and carries me to my bedroom.

"Stay." I say, still half asleep.

"Rain." He replies.

"Please? It felt nice on the couch." I say.

"Whatever you want. Let me go change and I will be right back." He says.

Chapter 26

I wake up fully clothed with Nick wrapped around me. What the fuck? But it actually feels nice. What the hell do I do? Why? I recall last night. Shit, I asked him to stay. I begin to wiggle to get up.

"Rain." He turns over, continuing to wrap himself around me.

"I have to get up." I say and he releases me. At least he has shorts on.

"You ok?" He asks.

"I'm fine, have to pee." I say and head to the bathroom. I can't remember the last time I slept with that much peace. Especially in the last two weeks.

"Want breakfast? I'm going to go make you some coffee." He says. I wonder what's going thru his head. He seems to want to get out of here fast enough.

I decide as long as he is gone to just shower. I make it quick and throw on a tee shirt and loose skirt and head down to the kitchen. Jen and Doug are already in there eating.

"Sorry I didn't make it till you two got in last night." I apologize. "I have really been the worst hostess ever with you two here." I mean it.

"Rain, this isn't about that. We should be the last thing on your mind." Doug replies as Nick hands me a cup of coffee. "I've enjoyed the trip." Jen joins in.

"Hey, not sure how you want to coordinate today, getting there and all, my parents are getting to their hotel about 2 and I have to bring them." Nick says.

"No big deal, I can drive there." I say.

"You can't drive yourself. Jesus, Rain." Doug says.

"We can all go together and Nick can go with his parents." Jen offers as Nick looks shocked to hear her speak.
"Yeah, whatever. I guess its fine." I say, realizing that I don't want to go. I don't want to say goodbye.

"Doug could go get my parents and I could drive you?" Nick says.
"Nick, they are your parents. You should really go get them." Jen seems bewildered at this idea.

"So, they are my parents but Rain is my...." And he trails off.

"You're what, Nick. Go with your parents, I can go with Jen. It's fine." I say, making myself clear that it's not up for discussion. "I think I will have my coffee outside." I get up and head out to the patio. I hear a heated discussion after the door is closed and soon Nick is joining me on the patio. He sits down in silence.

"Sorry about asking you to stay with me last night." I offer.
"Rain, last night was, well, I've, well, it was great." He says looking for words.

"Huh?" I ask.

"It made me feel great to have you ask me to stay with you." He says.

"Nick, it was a moment of weakness, yeah, it felt good and I really feel lost and lonely. It did feel good." I say hoping this doesn't become another discussion. "Hey, can you go get my phone? I'm sure Ty or Tony have texted me."

"Sure, where did you leave it?" He asks.
"Purse, bedroom? Not sure." I am trying to think.

"No worries, I'll find it." And he leaves.

"Hey, what's up?" Doug joins me on the patio.

"Nothing, Nick went to find my phone." I say.

"Nick was with you last night?" He asks.
"Do you question everyone Nick wakes up with?" I look back at him as he is shocked at my words. "Nothing happened, I just needed a really long hug. It's been a bitch of a week." I say. "It felt good. I slept good, OK?" I am waiting for him to answer.

"I just don't want you to do anything you will regret later." He says.
"Fair enough." My voice calms a bit.

"Here is your phone. It was shoved in the couch." Nick appears.

"Thanks." I say as I check thru multiple texts and missed calls. "Looks like I have to be to the funeral home at 1:30 to 2ish." My hands start to shake.
"You ok?" Nicks asks.

"Stop asking me that. No, I'm not OK. I am not prepared for this. Sorry." I say with a huff and head into the house. I can hear Nick and Doug following me.

"I know you're not ok, I meant your hands were shaking." He stops me and turns me to face him.
"Yes, Nick, I am so shot right now that my hands are shaking, that's how bad I feel. You can't fix it, you can't make it stop, you could stop asking me if I'm ok." I look directly at him.

"Maybe you should take one of those pills. It's only going to get worse today." He says while rubbing my shoulders.

"You're probably right. I think I left them in the office." I say and walk away.

I take my valium and head to the kitchen and pour a glass of wine.

"What time do we need to be ready?" Jen appears.

"1:15." I reply.

"You want me to do your hair?" She asks.

"Huh?" I ask.

"I can do it for you, hair and make-up, I'm going to school back home. I could play around with it, if you want. I mean you are beautiful the way you are, but I could do it for you." She is nervous and talking quicker.

"As long as you keep my glass full, why not." I reply and we head up to my bedroom. I change into what I am going to wear and check the clock, its 11am. Have to leave in 3 hours anyways. Jen plays with my hair, curls it, chatting away about mundane things. She really wants to work in a salon, she is tired of waiting tables. She goes on and on about her classes and, in usual Jen fashion, any other time or place I would be annoyed but it's just a pleasant distraction right now. She really is sweet.

"There, I'm finished." She announces. It actually looks quite nice, she spent forever with a straightener and then curled it on the side. Nothing too flashy, my makeup is there but looks quite natural but with the perception that I have a healthy glow.

"It looks amazing." I tell her. I think she might tear up. "How about you hurry and get ready and the two of us will go to lunch." I offer.
"Really? What about Doug?" She asks.
"He can join us or go with Nick. What do you want?" I ask her.

"I'd like to have lunch with you but I don't want Nick to be more mad at me." She says fading off at the end.

"What? What does Nick have to do with this?" I ask.

"He just, I don't know. It's not important." She fades out again.

"Whatever! If you want to have lunch alone with me, that's what we are doing." I smile at her. "Can you be ready in 15 minutes?" I ask.
"Sure, I will be right back." She says.

I head downstairs. "Change of plans you two." I announce and Nick and Doug look up at me. "Doug? Jen and I are going to lunch, she should probably drive so we can take your rental? You can just go with Nick." I wait for a response and almost simultaneously they reply together. "That's fine." Doug says.

"What? Why?" Nick says.

"Because I would like to have a nice lunch before I get there." I simply say.

Jen hurries down the stairs and we head out.

"Where to?" she asks as she starts the rental car. I give her directions to a restaurant close and on the way to the funeral home. I send a few texts to Ty and Tony on the way and we arrive.

Lunch is peaceful. We keep the conversation light. I talk about college and how I shaped into me and she talks about what made her into her. We eat and then head to the funeral home. She parks the car and I see Tony's car and my mother's car already there. I am just not ready to do this. I sit in the seat, staring at the building and wishing I was anywhere but here.

"Rain, you need anything?" She puts her hand on mine. "Like coffee or a water or something? I'm sure they have it inside for you, but I could go get you something, anything else." She says.

"No, I guess I should just go in." I say and exit the vehicle. "You want me to wait here or go in with you?" She asks.

"Actually, why don't you go get 2 coffees and two hot teas for us and bring them back, no rush. I think it's just us for a bit in there." I realize that this is a bit family and personal. She has never even met my father.

"I can do that, text me if you need anything else, I'll be back." She says, fidgeting in the driver's seat.

I slowly walk to the door and begin to open it. There is a man on the other side that finishes opening it and offers to take my jacket and shows me the way to the private waiting area where my mother and brothers are.

I walk in and my mother, all dressed in black, has her head in her hands and is crying. Tony and Ty are in full suits and sitting on either side comforting her. They all slowly look up at me and I begin to cry, myself.

Tony goes to get up to comfort me and I motion at him not to as I walk toward them.

"Here, sit here." Ty begins to get up and I motion at him to stay as well. I grab the chair next to Ty and pull it directly facing my mother and sit down facing her and just hug her and cry.

"Oh, my god, I did not expect it to be this awful." I moan. "Mom, I love you so much." I continue to cry and the four of us are just quiet after that.

About 20 minutes later a man comes in and takes us to see my father. He is laying in the coffin all spiffy and nice, except he isn't really him. He looks like some wax figure of my father, like really close, but just not him. I am done crying and just staring at him.

Melissa has joined us and is with Tony and my mother and Ty comes up and stands next to me.

"Rain." he starts.
I immediately interrupt him "If you ask me if I'm ok I will kick you." I say a bit too loudly.
"Rain, seriously." I hear my mother huff.

"Sorry." I say.
"Please don't start you two." I can hear her smiling a bit.

"She started it." Ty takes his queue, knowing this is cheering her up in a weird way.

"You never care where you are or what you say, do you?" Tony comes up and puts his arm around my waist.

"Not particularly." I laugh.

"You are your father's daughter." My mother laughs and I join her trying to hold back tears of my own.

"Where's Nick." Ty looks around the room. "I just realized he's not here."

"Just now? Really?" I say with a bit of annoyance in my voice. "He had to go get his parents, they flew in and Doug went with him. Jen brought me here." I say.

"Then where is Jen?" Melissa asks.

"Ehh, she didn't really belong in here for this. She went to get coffees and teas for us." I say.

"Oh, there is nothing that would make it better right now than a chocolate milkshake." Mel says.
"Oh, crap, I can do that for you! Let me text her." I tell Melissa and pull out my phone.
"Ohh, don't bother her." She says back.
"Trust me, she loves helping and nothing would make her day better than making someone else's day." I say as I text her.

The funeral director comes back in and takes us on a mini tour of how things will work tonight and then back here tomorrow before the funeral.

I think to myself that a week ago, I was running thru a dress rehearsal for a wedding. I thought how odd that weddings and funerals were kind of alike and laugh out loud and get a weird look from the man.

"Sorry." I say and realize that I cannot handle myself appropriately and ask to excuse myself to go have a cigarette outside. I enjoy my cigarette when I see Jen pull in and walk over to help her with the trays. I tell her to head in. I take my coffee to wash down a valium and stay outside and have one more cigarette before heading back in.

"I'm pretty sure you've met everyone, Jen, my mother and brothers and Melissa, Tony's wife." I say as I point to everyone.
"Yes, your family is so nice. This isn't going to open up to

the public for another 30 minutes or so, do you want me to wait in the car?" She replies.

"No, Jen, it's fine that you stay here with us." My mother offers.

We take our seats and make idle chit chat for a while. This is the most awful I have ever felt in my life and in a few minutes there are just going to be a bunch of people parading in that I may or may not know just telling me it's going to be ok. The doors open and I see its Rob and his mother. The go up to pay their respects and make their way down the line talking and hugging each of us. Corinne talks with my mother and tries to comfort her.

Slowly people start trickling in, each stopping to hug and offer condolences to each of us. A line is beginning to form. I need to get outside and get away from this. I need a cigarette and to just be away from this crowd. I ask Jen if she will join me and she obliges and we head out the back. "Do you smoke?" I offer her one and she shakes her head no.

"Is there anything I can do?" She asks.
"Maybe some coffees for everyone?" I ask. "You really don't have to, if you don't want to leave." I say.

"No, I can go get them again. You want me to get another milkshake for the pregnant one? I'm sorry, I can't remember her name." She says.
"It's Melissa." I laugh. "And you would probably be her favorite person if you did." I say. "Do you need money?" I go into my purse.

"No, it's the least I can do." She says getting her keys out and turning. "I will be back in a little bit."

I am left outside to enjoy my cigarette and feel guilty for being out here and head back in. I see Nick's mother hugging my mom. His father is speaking with Ty and Tony and Nick is talking with Melissa. I begin to walk over and Nick takes notice of me.

"Where were you?" He asks.

"Just outside having a smoke." I say. "Jen just left to go get coffees and a milkshake." I giggle a little at myself.

"You should have texted me, I could have stopped on the way." He says as his parents walk up to us.

"Rain, dear, this is just awful for you." His mother hugs me. "How are you?"

"I'm doing ok." I slip out of her hug.
"Well, I'm glad Nick is here to help you." She looks at him beaming with pride.

Nick's father and I make eye contact and he rolls his eyes at her statement.

"I'm sure Rain is getting by with support from everyone." He says and pats me on the shoulder.

"Yeah, it's been a whirlwind since the wedding, but everyone is really offering their help." I say.

"Well, we are going to take our seats, we don't want to occupy all of your time." Nick's father gently nudges his mother away. I do feel a kinship to him.

"How was the ride over?" I ask Nick, not sure what else to say.
"Actually, my dad got his own rental, they flew in from Vegas and are just going to drive back to Jersey. I rode over with them and Doug just followed us. So, I also don't have to drive them back after tonight." He looks at me. "Why don't you sit?" He looks from me to the chair. The line is really getting packed and I really want that coffee.

"So we meet again." Doug is standing in front of me.

"Ahh, I just want to go to bed." I say, hugging him. "Jen just left to get us some coffee." I say. "She should really be here any minute."
"It's fine, I think I will just go sit with Nick's parents." He says. He acknowledges the rest of my family and heads to take a seat.

People continue to stop and hug and kiss on the cheek. Some are co-workers and have anecdotal stories of my father and some are friends of the family. Tony's friends, Ty's friends. My mother's friends. Jen arrives with my coffee and passes them out. Melissa is in her heaven with the milkshake. I head outside to enjoy my coffee with a cigarette and take another one of the little pills.
"How are you doing?" Nick asks me.

"I've been better." I sigh.

"Did you guys eat?" He asks.

"Not since lunch. Not sure what the plan is. Why?" I ask, squishing out my cigarette with my shoe.

"Let me take you all out after it's over." He states.

"Ehh, I will check with them. Not sure of everyone's plans." I say as we head back in.

I take my place next to my mother and Ty moves over a seat to let Nick sit next to me. People continue to come thru, some more recognizable than others. The guys from Rob's bowling team make their way and chat with me for a few minutes. I think they are a bit shocked to see Nick with us. They knew we broke up and he was really never mentioned again. About two hours in, our pastor comes in and we have a small prayer service and then the line continues. Some people stay and chat with others and some immediately leave. My mother wants to go outside and get some air and I join her, along with Tony and Ty. I mention that Nick offered to take us all out to dinner and Tony points out that he has to get back to the babysitter. My mother just wants to go home and go to bed and Ty decides its best to stay with her. We return back inside when my mother is good.

"Nick, they appreciate your offer, but my mother just wants to go home and Ty is taking her. Tony needs to get Melissa home and take care of Bella." I offer.

"What about you?" He asks. "You said you haven't eaten since lunch."

"I guess we can go. Are Doug and Jen or your parents joining us?" I ask.

"No, just the two of us. Let me take care of you." He rubs my back.

"That's fine." I say.

The line continues for another hour and a half or so and the valium is serving me well. The people that work at the funeral home usher all but immediate family out and we are left alone once again. The four of us, my mother, Tony, Ty and myself take one last trip to the casket and say our goodbyes. We all split off and leave. I go outside with Nick and he opens the car door for me. I look at my phone and see that its 8:30 already.

"Where do you want to eat?" I ask.

"I have reservations. Some Italian restaurant. Private table in the back." He says and starts driving.

We arrive at a small, pleasant looking place and head in. There is a quiet table in the back set up for the two of us. "Do you want a glass of wine?" He asks.

"It might put me to sleep." I reply as I glance over the menu. "I think I just want a Caesar salad with chicken."

"You always do." He smiles at me.

The waiter comes and he orders my salad and a chicken parmesan dinner for himself. He orders a glass of wine for me along with an iced tea.

"One day left, then you can settle back to your routine." Nick states.

"Yup, this really feels like the longest two weeks of my life." I say. "Thank you for being so…" the words trail off. I don't even know what to say.

"I'm trying." He understands and takes my hand.

"I know." Is all I can say.

The waiter brings our food and we eat in silence and head home. We head upstairs and I enter my room. I feel his presence at the doorway. "You can come in." I just don't want to be alone.
I go into my bathroom and change into a teeshirt and get into bed.

"I can go change, I'll be right back." He is staring at me in bed.

A few minutes go by and I feel him get into bed behind me and wrap his arms around me. I just begin to cry as I feel him kiss the back of my head. "Princess, don't cry." I hear him whisper and slowly I fall asleep.

Chapter 27

"Rain, I brought you coffee." I hear Nick as I sit up in bed.

"I already ate, I assumed you didn't want to but I can get you something if you want." He has way too much energy. "Give me a minute?" I sit up as he hands me a cup.

"You've got an hour to be ready." He sits on the edge of the bed next to me. "How did you sleep?"

"It was peaceful." I say being honest.
"Good." He kisses me on top my head. "You need anything from me? I have to go get ready."

"Nah, I have to get in the shower." I say as he exits.

I wash and then just stand under the water contemplating that the hardest and final part will be over today. Then just back to normal. What is normal at this point? I shower until the hot water is gone and head out to get ready.

I quickly dress in a form fitting black dress and heels and head downstairs to find Doug, Jen and Nick cleaning the kitchen.
"Want more coffee?" Doug asks.

"Sure, and a pill, I guess." I say.
I take my cup and pill out to the patio and Jen joins me. "I think Doug and I are going separate from you and Nick. He said he would drive you back there today." She says.

"That's fine, I think that we are taking a limo to the cemetery anyways. I can't really believe this is actually happening." I say.

"Rain, it will get better. You are the strongest person I've ever met." She says with this endearing quality.

"How?" I ask, a bit confused by her statement.

"Everything you've been thru?" She questions me.

"Jen, I am about the most boring person you will ever meet." I say.
"Well, I certainly don't see it that way." She replies.
"Well, then you need to get out more!" I laugh as Nick joins us.
"Hey, I have to go get ready, I will be down in a few minutes. Kitchen is all back in order for you." He says and heads back in.

I continue drinking my coffee in silence until he returns in his suit. He is so clean and proper looking. What a contrast to when I first met him so long ago. I sit back and just stare at him.

"What, is something wrong?" He asks, looking side to side and down the front of him.
"No, just such a difference." I say and get up to head in.
I gather my purse and jacket and we head out to the funeral home.
"You gonna be ok today?" Nick asks.
"Not sure, never done this before." I say as I begin to tremble.
"Rain, you can get thru this." He takes my hand. "I'm right here for you."

I begin to cry. "I don't want to do this."

"Rain." I can tell he does not know what else to say.
"It's not fair. Why the hell did this happen? Jesus Christ,
I'm not ready to not have him here with me." I am balling.

"Baby, come on now. You have to be strong for your
mother today." He says.

"Why the hell do I always have to be strong? I can't do
this! I don't want to." I am still crying.

"Did you take your pills?" He sounds concerned.

"Yes, I took the fucking pill. I don't think that it's really
stronger than me anymore." I say.

"Do you have them with you?"

"Yeah, in my purse." I say, gaining a bit of composure.

He pulls off the road into a coffee shop and tells me to
wait. He returns a few minutes later with a coffee and
hands it to me. "Why don't you have another one? I don't
think it could hurt." I oblige and we go the rest of the way
in silence.

Tony and Melissa are there and he tells me that Ty and my
mother are going to be there in a few minutes. We all
head back in. There is a private room and we get to see
him again. Pallbearers begin to arrive and things are
becoming a bit more real to me.

I see them take my father and place him into the hearse to
head to the church. The six of us climb into the limo. It is
pure silence again. The church service is quite packed and
long. The valium is taking its toll on me and I seem to just

be leaning on Nick the entire time. After the service we then head to the cemetery and begin the process again. I am beginning to feel sick and groggy and wish I had not taken the second valium. We eventually make our way back to the funeral parlor and climb back to our respective cars to head to the bar. I feel numb.

"Do you want to talk at all?" Nick asks.

"No." I say flatly.

We arrive at the bar. It is surreal. I remember bringing my father here when we first opened and now we are here again saying good-bye forever to him.

There are two police officers standing outside.
"What the fuck now?" I ask out loud.

"I'm not sure, stay here." Nick gets out of the car.
"It's fine, Doug got them here to kind of ensure that its only friends and family that come in. Kind of a security detail." He says, patting my hand. "He really thinks of everything. Why don't we go in? Your mother and brothers just pulled in." He says, trying to coax me out of the car.
I sigh and get out of the car.

Inside are employees all offering condolences, food is spread out across banquet tables and everything has been re-arranged a bit to seem more intimate and less like a concert venue.

"Doug really did a nice job." I say as I walk in and am greeted by Rob.

"You need a drink." He says and I begin to cry again.

"Don't do that." He says back, smiling at me.

A rum and coke appears at my table where I sit with my mother.

"Dad was pretty popular." I say as I look around at the hundred or so people in the bar.

"Rain, you doing ok?" She asks me.
"Are you?" I ask back.

We are interrupted by people coming by to talk with my mother. Lots of people all stopping at the table to make her feel better. A few people that I went to school with are there. Lots of dad's co-workers. I giggle out loud thinking that there is no one working at his big office building today. The drink is numbing me a bit and I get up to get another one. I get my drink from the bar and head to my office to find solitude.

Sitting at my desk, seeing 2 weeks' worth of work piled up actually calms my nerves a bit, thinking of sifting thru it all and tuning everything out. I just sit at my desk and light up a cigarette and enjoy my drink.

"Rain, are you in here?" I hear Jen and contemplate not answering.

"Yeah, come on in." I say.
"I think Nick and others are looking for you." She says.

"It's ok. They will survive for a bit. I just need a minute." I say. "Want a drink?" I ask her.

"Nah, I'm good."

"I kinda do." I say, looking at my empty cup.

"Oh, I can get you one. I will be right back." She takes the glass and leaves.

Nick returns with a fresh drink. "You might want to slow down a bit?" He says.

"Are you the expert on knowing limits?" I ask him.

"Rain, I just don't want to see you get sick." He says.

"But you brought me the drink." I say.
"And I'm just asking you to take it slow." He says.

"How long are these things supposed to last?" I ask.
"I don't really know, till everyone goes home?" He has no idea. "But I think you are supposed to be here to the end, and by here, I mean out there." He points.

"Why? So everyone can pat me on the head and feel bad for me?" I ask him.

"They just feel bad for you, they are trying to be nice." He says.

"Fine." I say and get up, feeling a bit unsteady on my feet at first.

"You need help?" He asks.
"No." I say and head back out to the big room. I play nice

for the rest of the night and people start to filter out until, at last, it's just Doug, Jen, Melissa and my brothers, Rob, my mother and myself.

"What time is it?" I ask.

"6:30." Ty says.

"Holy Shit, you could have said 2pm and I wouldn't have questioned it." I am shocked.

"For real, though."

"Rain, I have to take off, you call me tomorrow?" Rob says and gives me a big hug.

"Jen and I will take care of closing everything down here, you guys. We got this." Doug offers.

"Oh, you guys don't have to, I can get it." I say.

"No, you guys shouldn't be worrying about it." He says back and Jen smiles at me.

"Thank you so much for getting this all together for us." I say.

"I think mom wants to go so we should probably get going, too." Ty says.

"Yeah, Bella is with the babysitter and Mel really needs to rest."

Moments later, everyone is gone and it's over.

"You want to go?" Nick asks.

"No, I want a drink. I want to drink till I can't remember today." I say.

"You can't do that." He says back.
"Why?" I ask.

"Why don't you just go home and go to bed?" He asks.
"Cause it's not even 7?" I say and motion for the bartender to leave a bottle on the counter. I take a swig.

"What are you doing?" He looks at me.
"What are you doing?" I shoot back.

"What do you mean? I'm trying to prevent you from getting sick." He says reaching for the bottle.
I pull it away and take another drink. "Rain, don't."

Doug and Jen join us at the bar.
"What do you two think? Should I get drunk if I want to?" I direct my question to the both of them.

"I'm staying out of this." Doug laughs and heads into the back again.

"I think, if she wants to drink, she should." Jen offers.
"I'm not asking you." Nick sounds irritated with her.
"But I was." I look at him. "Whatever, just bring me home." I say and get my jacket.

We reach the car and get in. "What is your problem with her?" I ask.
"I just don't like her is all." He says. "Can we talk about something else?"

"Like what, burying my father?! What the hell is the deal with you and her?" I ask and as soon as the words come out he doesn't even have a chance to answer. "You slept with her! Didn't you!?" I blurt out.

"NO! Oh, hell no." He yells back and his answer shocks me.

"Then what?" I ask again.

"Just forget it." He says and we ride in silence the remaining way back to my house. It's weird that its finally empty.

"Would you like a glass of wine or something?" He offers.

"Sure, and I would also like to know what the deal with you two is?" I say calmly.

He brings me the glass on the couch and sits down next to me. "Listen, I just don't like her." He says.

"What did she do? Did she do something to you?" I am so confused.

"No, it's you. If she had just stayed with you that night, helped you to the bathroom and all, none of any of this would have ever happened." He is speaking quietly and taking my hand in his. I feel enraged by his statement.

"Are you fucking kidding me?!" I stand up slamming my glass on the coffee table.

"Rain, calm down." He stands up with me.

"Are you fucking kidding me? You blame her for that night? After all this time? That's how you worked this all out? You blame her? So, let me get this shit straight? If she had just helped me to the bathroom then I never would have seen you cheating. You never would have lost your temper with ME for catching you cheating. In turn, you never would have hit me. Holy shit. You are fucked."

He is trying to take my hand and it's not going to happen.

"Don't you fucking touch me." I shout. "And you have to

do this now? Today?" I begin to cry, I sit down on the couch and just cry. "Holy shit, I don't think you have any fucking remorse for what you actually did to me. After the last two weeks, you think it's all ok? It was her fault. Oh, my god." I have my head in my hands and I am sobbing.

"Baby, it's not like that." He tries to put his hand on my back.
"No, it is. Tell me how it is then" I say. "If she had taken me to the bathroom, I would never have caught you and everything would be business as usual? How many times did you fucking cheat when we were together? Huh?" I ask.
"Rain, it was only that night, I swear, and it wasn't me. I was so fucked up that night, it wasn't me." He says.

"So who fucking hit me? Who broke my fucking ribs, who beat me into a fucking coma? Please tell me? You know you have never once acknowledged what you actually did. And now I know why! Holy Shit! God, I cannot handle this right now. Why are you doing this right now?" I am screaming.

"Rain, I am sorry." He says, sinking back down on the couch.
"Sorry for what?" I spit out. "Do you even know what you actually did to me?" I ask.

"Mostly." He has his head hung. "I know it was bad."

"And that's how you worked it all out? Blame someone else? Then just buy my silence with a bar? Is that how it works?" I ask.

"What? What are you talking about, I had bought the bar before, it was going to be your wedding present." He is mad.

"And what the hell? Why the hell would you ever buy me a bar as a wedding present?" I pause. "Just a way to keep me occupied while you go off getting serviced from the fan base?" I am pissed.

"Rain, I heard you and your brother talking and you were upset that you couldn't buy it, I was doing it to make you happy." He says.

"What?! Oh, holy hell. I can't believe...He wanted the goddamn bar, I was just going to help him. I couldn't. I felt bad for him. Next thing you know, I get the fucking deed. Yup, sorry for beating the shit out of you, here is a bar, hope we are even now." I say.

"It's not like that." He says.

"Then fucking explain." I say.

"Look, I know I did awful things. And that's why I went to rehab. I never wanted to take a chance of hurting you again. But she was supposed to take care of you that night."

"So you could go find a blow job, we are over that fact." I spit at him.

"No, I should have never done that either." He says.
"But you did." I say.

"I didn't blame her at first. But I guess every time I played it over in my head, that was the first thing." Nick says a bit quieter.

"This is all bullshit, all bullshit." My hands are in fists at my side. "Why is this fucking happening?" I cry as I look up.

"What do you want me to do? To make it better? How can I fix this?" He says back to me.
"I need a drink." I say.
"I'll get it for you." He stands up quickly.
"No, I don't need you to get it, I can get myself a drink." I pick up my wine glass and head to the kitchen. He begins to follow me. "No, just leave me alone." I finish.

I go into the fridge and take stock of what is in there and settle on a bottle of beer. I open and drink the contents, leaning against the counter. I get another one and open it and head back to the couch.
"There is nothing you can do to fix this." I look at him.

"What?! What do you mean 'nothing'?" He has a look of shock on his face.
"Nick" I sound much calmer now. "I think I thought something different about all of this, but if you are actually blaming anyone but yourself for any of this then I was wrong about all of it." I sit down on the couch and stare at the wall, nursing my beer.

"Rain. Rain, talk to me." He says changing his seating position to the coffee table to face me.
"I said what I had to say. I just can't. I can't handle any more shit in my head right now." I refuse to look at him.

"Rain, I'm sorry. I'm sorry for everything I did." I finally look at him.

"What did you do? What are you taking responsibility for?" I ask.

"I should have never gone that far that night, I over did it. I never should have met up with Lucy, shit, I should have had her banned from the bar. And I never should have....Jesus Christ." He is frustrated.

"Should have what?" I dare him to answer me.

"I never should have hit you. I never should have hurt you. Oh, my god Rain, please forgive me. I am sorry, so, so sorry." He is beginning to break down, I can hear it in his voice.

"I think I need to go to bed." I say and begin to get up.

"Do you want me to leave? I'll understand if you do." He looks at me.

"All I wanted was for you to be a friend these last two weeks." I say and begin to head upstairs. "I slept last night, for the first time in a long time, I actually felt at peace."

I head to my room and change into a tee shirt and lay down under my covers. I hear him come up the stairs and head to his room and I begin to softly cry. A few minutes later he is at my door and I am trying to not be heard. I feel him come closer and get under the covers.

"Rain, my princess." He says as he wraps his arms around me and kisses the top of my head.

Chapter 28

I wake up alone. Where the hell is Nick? Did he go home? I get up and put my robe on and head downstairs to find Doug in the kitchen.
"Hungry?" He asks.
"No, I just want some coffee. Where's Jen?" I look around.
"Nick and her are out there." He points outside.

I see Nick and Jen sitting at my patio having a discussion and head toward the door.
"Rain, don't." Doug stops me. "I'm not sure what is going on out there, but let 'em be."
"Yeah, ok. How did clean-up go last night? Everything good?" I ask.
"It was fine, we went out afterward, checked out some of your competition." He laughs and I look at him. "You have nothing to ever be worried about. You good from yesterday?"

"Yeah, we just had it out. Probably a long time coming." I say as Doug looks confused. "Oh, my god, the funeral. Yes, it's all good. Holy Shit, it was a bad day." I say.
"What do you mean 'had it out'?" He is staring at me.
"Ehh, just finally had a discussion that we should have probably had about a year and a half ago." I say.

"Right after your father's funeral?" Doug asks.

"It was my doing." I say, glancing out at the patio.

"Does that have anything to do with it?" He asks, looking out along with me.
"Yup." I say, sipping my coffee.
"Oh, boy."
"I think things will be better." I say.

"You know, you are the only one that has ever gotten to him. Shit, he didn't see you all that time and as soon as he did, he was right back in the palm of your hand." He is still staring out the window

"What?!" I ask, looking away from the window at Doug.
"Oh, nothing bad, I mean it in a good way." He says.

We see Jen and Nick get up from the table and begin to head in. Doug busies himself at the counter and I turn to face him and not the window.
"Rain, Jen and I just had a long talk and I think we are good now." Nick announces.

"Good with what?" Doug asks.
"Nick has blamed me for things for a long time and finally realized he was wrong." Jen offers.
"Completely wrong, and it won't happen again." Nick adds looking at me.
"Well, I cleaned up from breakfast, we have to be at the airport in a few hours so we should go pack." Doug announces and waits for Jen to join him heading back to their room.

"Rain, can we talk?" Nick asks.
"Can we go outside?" I ask.

"Of course." He heads back out following me. "How did you sleep?"

"I slept good." I say. "And you?"

"Not good." He is looking at me. "I can't lose you."

"Lose me? Nick, You don't have me." I say realizing how harsh it sounded after it came out.
"Rain."

"I didn't mean it that way. I mean, we are not together anymore, I've literally been talking to you for, what, two weeks total since everything happened. I need time to, I don't know how to put it? Time to trust you? Be comfortable again? Does that make any sense?" I ask him.
"I can do whatever you want, Rain." He takes my hand.
"Can we just be friends now?" I ask. "Maybe just be normal friends, and live our own lives and just be happy when we are together?"

"Rain" he beams "I guess I can settle on that for now. You will see, I can grow on you."
"I know you can, you've done it before." I look at him and he smiles at me and I smile back.
"So you want me to stay for a few more days?" he asks.
"You can if you want." I offer. "But I have a lot of work to catch up on. You don't have anything to do back in L.A.?"

"No, the whole month is kinda nothing, Lisa and Tony are gone so we just kinda all do our own thing." He shrugs his shoulders.

"So what are you going to do here?" I ask.

"Hang out with you? I don't know, I have to work on some new stuff I'm trying to write."

"OK, well, I am gonna go take a shower and get dressed." I say and head up to my room.

I come back out prepared for the day and Jen and Doug are in the living room with their luggage packed. Jen gives me the biggest hug she can muster and thanks me profusely over and over for everything. Doug offers to help with anything that comes up and I insist that they need to visit soon. Together. Doug and Nick talk for a few minutes and then they are off. I head to my office to see what awfulness awaits me there.

Going thru emails and such, I realize that I am not that far behind. I move some items in the brokerage account around and shift some money. I take care of some invoices for the bar. I send a few 'thank you' texts to employees that worked last night and text Rob to call me. The phone rings instantly.
"I figured you would call me on your lunch break." I say.

"Well, its Saturday, so I'm not really at work." He laughs. "Wow, you are really messed up."

"Doug and Jen headed home, Next week, things will be back to routine." I say. "What are you doing tomorrow?"
"Coming over to watch 'Sentenniel'. Like I do every Sunday." He says.
"Shit, if today is Saturday, then tomorrow is Sunday, you're right."

"Rain, go back to bed. I will see you at the bar tonight, Chris and I will stop in for a drink." He hangs up.

How messed up am I. I go back to check my accounts as I realize that nothing actually moved, it will all pend until Monday morning. I need to get back into my routine. I don't even know what day it is. Jesus. A week ago, I was in a wedding. Ahh, Lisa, I send her a quick text that it's all over and I'm doing ok. I look to the clock and see that its almost 1 and head out to the kitchen to get myself a salad for lunch. I glance over and see the basement door is open and head down with my bowl of salad to find Nick in the studio playing guitar. I tap on the glass and he looks up and heads out to the main room.
"Lunch?" He looks at me.

"Yeah, made it all by myself. Want some?" I offer a forkful of lettuce to him.
"Nah, I can go find something." He replies. "What time is it anyways?"
"About 1. I gotta admit, I did not realize it was Saturday until a bit ago. I have to go to the bar about 8ish until close tonight. If you want to join me." I offer.

"Sure. Anyone playing tonight?" He asks.
"Not even sure, no one big is all I really know. I guess you will find out." I say. "Want me to make you a sandwich or something?" I look at him.
"Sure, I will be up in a minute." He says and starts shutting down the equipment in the studio and I head back to the kitchen.
He arrives in the kitchen as I complete his lunch. "Perfect timing." I say and push the plate toward him on the

counter. "What were you working on?" I ask.

"Oh, just some songs that have been rattling around for a bit." He starts eating.

"Well, I am gonna lounge on the couch for a bit, rest up for tonight." I say and put my bowl in the dishwasher and head to the other room.

"Can I get you anything?" Nick asks upon entering the room.

"Nope, I'm fine." He joins me on the other side of the couch.

I flip thru the channels and settle on a documentary and doze off. I wake up to my phone ringing and answer it. It's Mel checking in with me. We chat for a while and we agree to take my mother out to lunch next week. I look over and Nick is sleeping on the couch. I contemplate waking him up out of my boredom but decide to just let him sleep. I head back to my office and go thru some research data.

"Hey, whatcha doin? I guess I was tired." He sits down across from the desk.

"Yeah, I let you sleep. I have work to get done." I say, not looking away from the monitor.

"How long till we head to the bar?" He asks and I look at the clock.

"Maybe hour, hour and a half." I say.

"Do you normally eat dinner before you go? I can make up something." He offers.

"That's fine." I say, looking at him. "I forgot your constant eating habits. I usually just have a salad or something before I go."

Nick heads out of the office and I spend the next half hour getting more work done and head out to the kitchen.

"Steak?" he has pans all over the stove.
"Maybe a small piece." I look around. How can he eat this much all the time? I set the table and he puts food on plates and we sit down to eat.
"This is nice." He says.

"Yes, it kinda is."

"Do you really eat alone all the time here?" He asks.
"Not all the time, sometimes Ty is here, sometimes Rob is here. Sometimes I just eat at the bar." I shrug my shoulders and begin to clean up.

I change into a pair of form fitting jeans and boots and a dressy blouse before we head to the bar. The place is getting crowded when I get there and more employees are greeting me to pay their respects about my father. Nick immediately draws attention when he gets there and we need to head to my office to escape the mob.

"This is crazy. I don't miss it, that's for sure." I say to him.
"What do you want me to do?" He asks.

"I don't know, what do you normally do." I ask.

"Go on stage, settle everyone down?" He offers.
"It's too early for that." I reply. "Look, I don't care really

what you do, I guess I will go talk to the band and get back to what I do." I say and leave the office. I go speak to the local band and let them know that Nick is here and offer for him to go on with them. They seem elated and agree. I head back out to the manager and have them announce the band and they head on stage. The place seems way more packed than normal. Thank you social media. Everyone in here probably told someone else that Nick was here.

The band plays their cover songs and a few originals that no one appears to know and then Nick joins them on stage for a few Heavensent songs and the place is madness. At the end of the song, he calls me on stage and wants everyone in the place to give me a round of applause for being the owner and a close personal friend of his. We exit the stage and the band goes back to its setlist.

"That was fun, it's been a while since I sang in front of a crowd." He says while grabbing a beer.

"Well, thanks for packing the house tonight." I say, grabbing a beer of my own. "The guys out there should really be about done and the place will be closed in an hour." I should go start register paperwork." I announce and head to the bar. I start my normal tasks and answer a few questions about Nick and the hour flies by. I return backstage to see Nick drinking with the guys in the band and generally having a good time.

"It's all closed down out there, just waiting for the clean up to finish." I announce.
The band thanks me for the opportunity to play at the bar

and thanks Nick for joining them and heads out.

"Tonight was a blast." Nick says.

"Yeah, every night, it's a blast." I say with sarcasm.

"You really don't like the bar?" He asks.

"Ehh, it's kind of grown on me, it was a challenge at first, and I enjoyed it, but it is really not for me. None of this is my lifestyle." I say, grabbing my folder of paperwork to bring home. I double check the safe in my office and we head for home.

"Is it turning a profit? It has to be." Nick continues.

"Well, yeah, it's not the money." I say.

"You could hire someone to manage it full time, take it off your plate." He says.

"Ha, I have thought about that, a. I would have to trust them fully and b. I moved everything off my plate to get it running in the first place. I've thought about asking Ty and Rob to maybe do it, but I'm not sure about Rob leaving his real job for this. I trust Ty but he is kinda immature sometimes, not on purpose or anything, he's just, you know, Ty." I laugh while driving.

"Maybe you should talk to Rob? Who knows, maybe he would be interested." He pushes.

"Ehh, maybe, something to think about." I say and we drive the rest of the way in silence.

I head immediately upstairs upon arrival and get in the shower. Out of the shower and to bed.

Chapter 29

I wake up alone and get up and head downstairs in my tee shirt to get coffee. I sit out on the patio enjoying it and contemplate asking Rob to run the day to day stuff at the bar. What would he even think, would that be too close for our friendship? Maybe I can bring it up to him. Ty would jump at the chance but would require his own babysitter until I could trust him. How the hell does Nick always plant an idea in my head. I finish my coffee and head back in to find Nick making himself eggs and bacon at the stove.

Glancing at the clock, it's almost 10:30am. Rob will be here in a bit.

"Nice outfit!" Nick smiles at me and I remember I am wearing only a t-shirt.

"I have to go get dressed, Rob is coming over to watch his show." I say.

"Does he not have a tv?" He looks at me weird.

"Yes, he has a tv, but he is obsessed with that show "Sentennial' that you were watching the other night, the one I can't stand? Well, he comes over every Sunday and makes me suffer through it." I say.

"I love that show." Nick smiles.

"I know." I say flatly. "I don't get it, I don't' want to get it, but Rob seems to think that if I watch enough, something will click and I will love it, too. Or maybe at least understand it." I feign annoyance. "I guess today, there will be two of you to annoy me." And I head upstairs.

Returning to the kitchen in actual clothes I ask Nick what he will want for food.
"What do you guys normally eat?" He asks.
"Takeout, always takeout." I say.

"Want me to make something?" He offers.
"No, I think it might kill the mood." I laugh.

I do some general cleaning in the house, stripping the linens from the room Doug and Jen occupied. I start some laundry and Rob arrives.
"You will never believe who enjoys your stupid show." I laugh as I answer the door.
Rob and I sit on the couch catching up over the last few weeks of my absence and we settle on Chinese food for dinner.

There seems to be a mini marathon of the show on and we get to watch the last few weeks of episodes in succession before the new one is on. Rob and Nick talk and prod at me through all of them. A few times I get up to go do something elsewhere in the house only to be brought back by one of them as if I had escaped some sort of punishment. After 3 hours of the show, Rob heads home. Overall, it is a nice Sunday.

Monday morning, I am up early and working in the office, I then head over to Tony's shop to get that office in order and then back home. Nick has a salad waiting for me.

"I think I'm gonna head home at the end of this week." He announces.

"Oh? You sick of me finally?" I smile at him.

"No, I have some meetings with the label and stuff." He sits with me at the table.

"Oh, ok. Well, life has to get back to normal at some point." I say in return.

"You could come with me if you want?" He asks.

"And do what? Plus, I am just trying to get back to normal myself." I say.

"That's fine, but when will I see you again?" He asks. "Would you come out and visit me?"

"Nick, I'm not sure what's going on around here. I've been promising Lisa I would come out and visit her, so maybe we can have dinner or something if I'm out there." I offer.

"I could come back and see you." He replies.

"I guess? If you're out here or something, don't need to make a trip just to have lunch." I say. I finish eating my lunch and head back to my office. The rest of the week is going smoothly. Nick spends time playing in the studio, working on whatever he is working on, I try to play catch up from being missing in action for two weeks. I had dinner mid-week with Melissa and my mother. It was nice to check in with her. She has been busy with insurance companies and gathering things to settle my father's estate.

Friday as I'm getting ready to head to the bar Nick comes in to join me in the office. "Want to go out to dinner? Just the two of us?" he sits.

"Nick, I have to get to the bar." I say.

"Do you really have to go this early? I head to the airport in the morning." He points out.

"I guess we can have dinner. Anywhere in particular?" I ask.

"Whatever you want. Seafood?"

"We can do that; do I need to change?" I stand up and look at my outfit.

"Rain, you always look incredible. Let's go." He says and we head out.

Arriving at the restaraunt, we get a few looks from people that recognize him and head to a quiet booth in the back.

"So, you need me to take you to the airport in the morning?" I ask.

"Flight leaves at 11 so I should be there by 10, I can take a cab if you don't want to get up." He says.

"I can get up and bring you, you've done enough for me." I say.

"I haven't really done anything for you." He says.

I take his hand. "You know, you really have. I don't know what I would have done this week without you here to...to distract me." I smile.

"I'm a distraction?" He smiles back.

"Let's be honest, the last 3 weeks weren't exactly bliss with each other, but I think we are in a good place now." I say.

"And what place is that?" He stares at me.

"Friends? Nick, we talked about this." I sigh.

"Yes, I know, I know. But there is hope?" he is holding both my hands.

"There is always hope." I say.

"No matter what happens, I will always love you, Rain." He says.

I feel tears welling in my eyes and do my best to hold them back. "Nick, Don't."

"I'm just saying. I don't want to upset you, I'm just letting you know." He says.

"Do you want to go to the bar tonight?" I ask him.

"Sure." He says.

"I was kinda thinking that I might just go home and curl up on the couch all night." I say back.

"We can do that, sounds much better." He says as he signals for the check from our dinner.

Back at the house, we just curl up on the couch and watch tv all night, mundane entertainment. I fall asleep on the couch and feel Nick's presence next to me and I just curl up next to him.

Chapter 30

I wake up on the couch curled up in Nick's arms. "Nick, wake up." I say.
"Can we just stay like this?" He asks sleepily.

"What time is it?" I ask as I free myself from his grip and look for my phone. I check and its 5:30am. "Ahh, for a bit longer." I say as he wraps himself around me and I play with the phone setting an alarm for 8.

The alarm goes off and I realize I am alone on the couch. "Coffee?" Nick comes into the living room with a cup in his hand.

"I might miss this the most." I say as I take it.
"I woke up and got packed a bit ago. Want breakfast?" He asks.
"Nah, just coffee is good." I say contemplating truly having to take care of myself once I drop him off.
"You sure you don't want to just get away for a bit?" He asks, sitting next to me.

"I have been away from reality for a few weeks, I need normal now." I say.

"Well, if you change your mind, you can call me." He says with hopefulness in his voice.

"We'll see." I say with a tone to just put it off for later.

We eventually head to the airport in his car, having another discussion about what to do about the car and he insists that I just keep it here. We reach the airport and Nick wants me to walk him in so I park.
"Rain, you sure we are ok? I mean, I feel like I'm not going to see you again." He seems fidgety.

"Nick, I, I have a life here." I realize I have no idea what's going to happen after he leaves. "We can be friends. I think that's what we need to be right now. Don't you?" I ask.

"You promise you are going to stay in touch?" He asks.
"You can always call me, you know." I say.
"I eventually gave up when I did that." He replies.
"Nick." I sigh. "I think it's different now. Jesus, you're sitting here with me, aren't you?" I ask.
"You promise?" He takes my hand and looks at me.
"I promise." I say to him.

"You promise what?" He is still looking intently at me.
"I promise we will see each other again." I kiss his hand.

"I love you." He whispers as he kisses my hand.

We sit in silence just holding the moment until Nick checks his phone. "I can't miss my flight, you don't need to walk me in. I'll text you when I land, ok?" He says.

"Sure, that sounds good." I say and he gets out of the car and I head home.

Chapter 31

Driving, I think that he is actually gone. This whole whirlwind of madness that began with me heading to Vegas is over. I head home and back to my empty house and realize I don't know what to do with myself. I head into my office and begin to work. I then head to Tony's shop and handle the office there. I head home, eat by myself and begin the same routine over and over. Thursday, Friday and Saturday nights are spent at the bar and Sunday Rob comes over and watches his show with some fast food. This routine begins to calm my nerves from the loss of my father.

Sprinkled in are some texts back and forth with Nick. Lisa and Tony returned from their honeymoon in Europe and we have talked on the phone. She has been busy with her job and dealing with married life, as she put it. Jesus, she lived with him for about a decade, how much could possibly be different.

Sitting in my office, I check the calendar for upcoming dates and see that Rob's birthday is in 2 weeks. The big 25. I should really do something. I send some texts out to our mutual friends and clear out the back room at the bar for that night. Spontaneously, I decide to invite Nick. Not sure why, but him and Rob have always been fine together and I decide to extend an olive branch. I get an immediate text back double checking and asking if the date is set in stone. I call him and he immediately answers.

"Hey, you got my reply?" He asks.

"Yeah, what's wrong with the date?" I ask him.

"I'm booked to do some guest work on a friend's song, and that is the same weekend." He says.

"It's kind of his birthday and I already sent out invites. Not sure what to do. I don't think he is going to be offended if you can't make it." I say, wondering why this is becoming what it is.

"I just really want to see you, and this is as good a reason as ever, how about the weekend before?" he asks and I look at the calendar again. I guess I can send out an update to everyone, I literally just sent them out.

"Ahhh, I guess. So I assume that this is your rsvp? I will move the entire party up a week so you can go, you are going to fly out here?" I ask.

"I can come in, uhh, Friday afternoon and leave Sunday morning, if that's ok?" He seems to be checking some papers.
"Since you are asking me if its ok for the weekend, I assume you are staying here?" I laugh.
"That's what friends are for, right." He laughs.
"It's fine, Nick, I will see you then. I have to get back to work." I say and hang up.

I resend all the invites and change things around at the bar. I realize that it's this Friday. I send an email to Mike and Chris that he works with and get them in on surprising Rob. The promise they will take care of it and let me know it was pretty smart to do it the week before his birthday so he is not suspicious. Nick the Rockstar to the rescue again. I have to laugh. They are actually right about it.

I get back to work and run my usual routine all week until Friday when I am in the office and hear a knock at the door. I head out to answer it.

"Hey, wasn't sure if I should just walk in." Nick is standing there.
"What? How did you get here? I thought you were going to text me to pick you up?" I say in shock.

"Ehh, I wanted to surprise you." He says as he hugs me.
"Well, you sure did that." I say. "Come on inside. I'm just getting some last-minute work done before heading over to the bar. I need to pick up the cake on the way."

Nick brings his suitcase up the stairs and I head up to fix my hair and makeup for the evening. He comes in to my bedroom and stands behind me while I sit at my vanity.
"You are so beautiful." He says as he plays with my hair.
"Stop." I say and brush it back down.
"No, Rain, I mean it. Have you missed me?"

"You do have an effect on me. I'll say that." I say as I finish up and head back downstairs

"What's that supposed to mean?" He asks as he follows me.

"We aren't doing this. Not tonight." I say as I reach the living room and turn to look at him. "If I didn't miss you I would not have invited you. If you didn't miss me you would not have come. Leave it at that." I smile and get my purse, checking the contents. "Let's go." And we head out to the car.

We drive to the bakery and I realize how big a full sheet cake is. Nick puts it in the trunk because I might have dropped it. We continue to the bar and it is pretty busy for a Friday night at 5.

People take immediate notice of Nick and most actually don't react too crazy. I guess he is becoming a normal sighting around here. I have a waiter bring the cake to the room and go in to check on decorations and stuff. I remind some of the wait staff that this is Rob's party and to not run a tab for anyone. I double check everything again and some of our friends begin to trickle in. I let them know that Rob should be there about 6ish. Everyone is having a great time. Tony and Melissa even make an appearance. Melissa is still really pregnant. She is due any day now.

Mike and Chris send me a text that they are in the parking lot bringing Rob in and I shut the lights off in the room so we can all yell surprise when he comes in. Rob is shocked and elated.

"Oh my god, how did you even?!" He hugs me.

"I had to, it's your birthday......in a week." I hug him back.

Everyone mingles and chats and the party is a complete success. People are eating and drinking end enjoying themselves. Tony and Mel head out as she is not feeling well. We sing happy birthday and cut the cake. Lots of people have gifts and cards for Rob and he begins to open them.

"Oh, my god, are these what I think they are?" He seems to squeal like a teenage girl and we are all curious.

"What is it?" I ask.

"Nick got two tickets to the Sentennial convention at the casino next weekend." I look to Nick.

"What? What even is that?" I am confused.

"Look, I know he loves the show. It's this whole comic con type convention dedicated to just the show. The producer and writers are doing sit downs, the actors will be there in costume, it's a whole thing." He says.

"Are you serious?" I laugh.

"Rain, these are like front row seats with the actors and writers. Do you know what a big deal these are?" Rob joins in, while inspecting the tickets. "Shit, and it's on my actual birthday."

"Did you do this on purpose?" I look at Nick suspiciously.

"No, Rain, I swear. Someone was talking about flying out for it and I know he loves the show, so I made some calls." He says.

"Are you going with him?" I find this absurd.

"No, I can't, I'm in the studio, I told you that. You can go with him, make a weekend of it, my treat." He says.

"Come on Rain, you will love it." Rob is pleading with me.

"You've got to be kidding me, Rob, anyone else you want

to go with?" I smile.

"Nope, you!" He says as he hugs me.

Nick and Rob are laughing and watching me as I feign sulking and walk away.

The night continues and people gradually start to leave. Chris and Mike help pick up and pack Robs gifts up. The bar will be closing soon and I check on the office and get ready to leave with Nick.

"Rain, this is the best birthday ever. Thank you so much." Rob is happy. "And, Nick, I don't think you really understand how cool this will be." He is still holding the tickets.

"I do, man, I swear that if I wasn't booked, I would be going with you." He says and shakes his hand.

Rob leaves with Mike and Chris.

"You ready?" I look to Nick and we head to the car.

"You really didn't need to do that, especially making me go with him. But apparently you did good." I pat his arm.

"Rob's a good guy, and he is a friend." He shrugs his shoulders.

"Yeah, well I'm your friend, too. But don't ever get me tickets like that." I say, laughing. "Ehh, it will be a fun weekend, just the two of us. Thank you." I say.

"I meant it about picking up the tab, just let me know, ok?" He says.

"Yeah, I think I can handle a weekend at a casino." I laugh and we arrive home.

"Anything you want to do tomorrow?" I ask.

"Just thought maybe hang around here if you want. Watch tv or just lounge on the couch?" He asks.

"That's what the Rockstar wants to do?" I laugh.
"With you? Yes!" he smiles at me.

"I think we can do that until I head to the bar. Want a beer or something?" I head to the kitchen to get one.

"Sure." He replies and I head back with two beers. We sit quietly on the couch and drink them, just enjoying each other's company.
"I think I'm gonna go take a shower. You want to wait here? I will be back down." I say.

"Sure" He replies and I head upstairs.

I take my shower, letting the water hit me and think about the day and how well it went as I shampoo my hair.
"Rain, quick, the phone!" Nick startles me.

"Holy Shit! What, I will be right there." I say as I quickly rinse off the shampoo in a panic.
"It's Tony, Melissa is in labor and they are headed to the hospital." He is now in the bathroom with me.
"Oh my god, I will be right there." I step out and reach for a towel realizing that he is in the bathroom and I am completely naked, trying to wrap myself up and take the phone at the same time.
"Tony! Is everything ok?" I ask, in a panic.

"Yes, but we have Bella with us, can you come get her?" He says.
"Sure, I will be right there." I say and hang up and trying to

dry off quickly.

"I have to go get Bella, she is there with them." I say and begin to get dressed.

"OK, I can drive you, I'll go start the car." He says and leaves. I quickly get dressed and head to the car and we leave for the hospital arriving within 25 minutes. I am directed to the room they are in and knock quietly and head in. Melissa is in labor, but it seems really calm. "Want me to stay for a bit?" I ask.

"The doctors think it's going to be a while, just take Bella to your house and we will call and update you." Melissa says. I look over and my niece is in her pajamas asleep in a reclining hospital chair. Nick carefully picks her up.

She wakes up a little. "Am I a big sister yet?"
"Not quite yet, we are gonna sleep at auntie Rain's house and bring you back when you are, ok, Bella?" Nick says to her.

"Hey, her car seat is in my car, I gotta run down with you real quick." Tony seems flustered, looking from us to Mel.

"It's not gonna happen in 20 minutes, go!" Mel says and we all head down to get Bella's car seat and back to my car.
"Good luck, Tony. Call me if anything...." I say and he runs back in.

I fumble with the car seat and eventually secure it in the back of the Mercedes and Nick places her in and we make sure she is buckled in and we head back home again. It is almost 3:30am when we arrive back at the house. Nick

carries her in and puts her on the couch.
"Should we just leave her there?" He asks.

"She sleeps over once in a great while, usually upstairs, but it's almost morning, it's fine." I say and sit back down. "Never a dull moment." I laugh.

"Wow, we just saw her earlier." Nick seems surprised. "Yeah, she did say she just felt uncomfortable, that's why they left early. I think her actual due date was a few days ago." I say. "A little boy, I can't believe it." I am so happy for them. "Well, at least you will have someone one to eat breakfast with you in a few hours. She prefers pancakes." I look to Bella and smile.

"I'm sure I can do that." He says.

"Well, now I am really tired, I think I'm just going to crash here so she is ok when she wakes up." I say.

"Ohh, ok, I guess I will see you in the morning." Nick says and heads up the stairs.

I wake up to Bella staring at me extremely close. "Uncle Nick is making pancakes." She says.

"Uncle?" I ask her.

"Yeah, I asked mommy if he was my uncle and she said yes, like Uncle Rob. Do you want pancakes?" she asked.

"Umm, No pancakes for me." I say as I begin to tickle her. "But I do need coffee." I laugh and head out to the kitchen.

"I kinda like 'Uncle Nick', don't you?" He says.

"Yeah, just like 'Uncle Rob'" I laugh.

"I'm an only child. I think this is my only shot." He says, flipping pancakes.

"Im guessing no phone calls?" I say.

"Not yet." He replies as I grab my phone and text Tony. I wait a moment and no reply.

Bella joins us in the kitchen and begins to ask all kinds of questions of Nick. What do you do? Why do you live so far away? Just your random typical 4-year-old questions. I sit with my coffee and enjoy watching the banter between Nick and Bella. My phone buzzes and I check it.
"Bella, your brother was born!" I exclaim as I am texting back.
"Can we go see him...now?" She asks.
"Why don't we have breakfast first and then we can go?" I say. "Give mommy a few minutes." I laugh.

I watch as Bella picks at her pancakes and tells us all about how life with her new brother will be. I get her cleaned up and find some clothes she left here that still fit her and get her changed.

"Do you want to stop and get your brother and mother something?" I ask her.
"Yes, who doesn't want presents, do I get one?" She replies back.
"I think, maybe." I tell her and we head off, stopping at the mall. She picks out a stuffed toy for her brother and some

flowers for her mother. Bella picks out a new dress and we are headed to the hospital. She decides she must change into her new dress in the bathroom before we see her brother.

"Hey everybody!" I announce as we head into the room. Melissa looks tired but happy. The baby is being held by my mother. I lean down to kiss Mel's head and congratulate her and hug Tony.

"Meet your nephew, Donald." My mother beams. They named him after our father. I begin to cry. Nick shakes Tony's hand and gives Melissa a kiss as well.

"So glad you are here for this." Tony says to Nick.
"Just glad for you guys." He says back.

Bella wants to hold the baby and give him her present and Ty begins to play with her. She gives her mother her flowers and all in all it is really just a perfect moment. Such contrast from a few weeks ago when we were all in the hospital room before.

My mother decides that Bella will stay with her for a few days and we visit for a while and eventually have to leave.

"Mel looks good." Nick says as we are driving home.
"Mel is gonna have her hands full when she gets home and Tony goes back to work." I laugh.

"Someday." Nick says.
"Someday what?" I ask.
"Someday, I will have kids of my own." He looks at me.

"Ya know, up until last night, I could never picture that, but you are actually pretty good with them." I smile. "Always shocking me!"

We arrive back at my house and it is already 4pm. I really need to start sleeping better. "So much for hanging on the couch all day, I'm sorry." I say as I start the coffee maker. "I have to head over to the bar soon."

"It's ok, I think this was all a little more important. We can hang on the couch anytime." He says.

"You hungry? Nevermind, you are always hungry." I say. "What do you want to eat?" I ask looking through the refrigerator.
"Want to go out? Then we can head over to the bar?" He offers.
"Sounds good, let me go change." I say. I am skimming my closet and come across the white lace up shirt I first wore when I met him. I pair the shirt with a tight-fitting pair of jeans and heels and head downstairs.
"Wow! You're killing me." He is studying me.
"Nick! I'm just heading to the bar." I say.
"Yeah, but...." He gives up and we head to a restaurant. We have light conversation over dinner. He tells me about his plans for the following weekend and laughs about mine. We head to the bar after dinner and it seems to be the same scenario as the first time. He gets mobbed upon entry, we hide in my office, he plays a few songs with the band and we close up shop. We head home after the bar is all closed down and I head upstairs with him at my heels.
"Want me to join you?" He says, longingly.
"Nick, why do this? You are going home tomorrow." I say.

"I could stay for a few more days." He offers.

"You know, this is so hard for me, it messes with my head." I say.

"Goodnight, princess, I love you." He kisses the top of my head and heads to his room. Like I will sleep now.

I get into bed and lie down thinking about Nick and I. This is not possible, I should have known better in the beginning and look what happened. Somehow, he is back and waiting. Ehh, put it out of your head Rain. Go to sleep.

Chapter 32

I wake up and head to the shower. I get out, get dressed and head downstairs and Nick is making pancakes.
"I forgot how much I enjoy these." He says with a smile.

"I wonder how little Bella is doing today, I think I will stop by there after I bring you to the airport." I say.

"That would be nice for her. She loves you, you can tell." He says.

We have breakfast and then head to the airport. This time is quicker and less dramatic than the previous drop off. I pull up to the loading area and he says to have fun with Rob and he is off. I head over to my mother's house and visit for a while. It still seems surreal that my father is not here, but Bella seems to occupy the loneliness a bit. At about 5, I head home. Back to my empty house again. I spend a bit of time cleaning and settle down on the couch at about 7.

Monday morning, I head to my home office and get some work done and then head over to Tony's shop. I plan to spend some extra time there since Tony will be out all week. I stay busy all week, running Tony's jobs and doubling up on work for the bar since I will be out all weekend, again. Thursday night at the bar, Rob comes in and we go over his itinerary for the weekend. He really has all this planned out. We decide to drive down on Friday after he gets out of work. He will meet me at my house.

Friday afternoon, Rob arrives at my house all antsy about our trip. Everything is booked, two adjoining hotel rooms. Spa service for both of us, club passes. Dinner reservations, and of course the convention. Dear God, the convention. We get to the hotel at about 7 and have dinner reservations for 745 so we head to our rooms to unpack, there is a connecting door between us and Rob is loving it.

Dinner just the two of us is nice, we catch up. It's been a long time since we had any real undivided attention. I bring up how Nick suggested he run the bar and Rob has a lot of pros and cons and promises he will think about it some more, but is still ready to cover for me anytime.

After dinner, we head to a club. I manage to get us to the VIP area and Rob swears that every other person is in the show. I can't tell how you would know and I don't pay enough attention to bother but Rob is seemingly in his glory with all this so I am happy for him. It's so much different to be in an actual dance club than the metal music that seems to surround me so much these days. We are dancing and drinking and having a good time until Rob decides it's time for bed. This is his weekend and I am just here to follow along and oblige.

The next morning, he joins me in bed.

"Breakfast?" He asks.
"Just coffee, what do you want, I'll order it." I say.

"So is this what life is like with Nick? Room service in bed every morning?" He asks, looking at the menu.

"A, not quite and b, we are actually not together." I say.

"Yeah, ok." He elbows me.
"We are about as together as you and I." I laugh.
"Come on, Rain, I know you." He says.

"Nope, just friends now. It's all good." I say.

"OK, so you're game for some blind dates then?" He asks.

"Not a chance in hell!" I elbow him back laughing.

"You don't think I could find you someone?" He giggles.
"Well, your judgement is probably better than mine." I say and then we order breakfast and coffee.

The room service cart comes and we chat while we eat, afterwards we get ready for the first part of the convention. Rob gets all dressed and comes back into my room while I finish getting ready.
"What's going on first?" I ask.
"We have a meet and greet with the writers and producers at a lunch thing, then back to the hotel for massages and then the q & a thing with the cast and writers. There is a costume contest thing tomorrow, but I'm not gonna push my luck on that one." He says.
"Costumes? Are you kidding me? Are we here with children?" I ask.

"You have no idea how seriously people take this show. I mean I like it, but people are obsessed with it, it's kind of a cult following." He is serious.

"Well, I will do whatever, but I draw the line at dressing up." I smile at him. "Let's get going." I say and we head to find the convention area we need to be at. We find our table and take a seat. I wonder who else will be seated here with us? I also have a bizarre curiosity how much something like this costs to attend.

We are apparently seated with 4 other regular people and 2 actors from the show. Rob is elated. Before we eat, he is all over the room and talking with people and trying to figure out who is who. We take our seats to eat lunch and introduce ourselves around the table. The 4 other people are all from California. Wow, I could not imagine travelling all this way to do something like this. They are obsessed with the show, just as Rob described. I have a few glasses of wine and check my phone, periodically checking on Rob. I'm not sure he would even notice if I left, but I would not do that to him anyways.

"Rain, you have to meet this guy." Rob has a man standing next to him with a glass of champagne in his hand. "This is Len Feldman, he is the creator and producer of the show." Rob seems like he is introducing me to the president. I stand and shake his hand. This guy is wearing jeans and a white button-down shirt with a blazer over it. Very nice looking. He really does not belong with this crowd, never mind being in charge of the whole thing.

"Very nice to meet you. I hear it's an amazing show. You seem to have quite the followers." I say.

"You hear? You've never seen it?" He seems taken aback.

"No, I've seen it, I seem to watch it every Sunday." I look

and smile at Rob. "I just don't quite understand it the way he does, I guess." I say and watch as this guy does not know how to respond to me so I continue. "I'm not saying I dislike it, I guess I just don't 'not' dislike it." Oh, my god, I'm digging myself a hole here. Rob begins to grip my arm to make me stop. I don't have a clue what to say. "Well, I love the show. I am quite a fan." Rob interrupts.

"Well, it was quite interesting to meet you both." Len replies awkwardly and leaves for another table.

I sit down. "That was fun." I say sarcastically.

"You really know how to make an impression, don't you?" Rob says. "Well, this is about over, want to head up for our massages now?" He asks and we head back to our rooms.

We get our massages and enjoy the early afternoon. I don't really make conversation with him as we are both enjoying ourselves and soon the interrupted bliss is over and it's time to get ready for round 2 of the 'Sentennial' fun. I decide on a simple pair of black palazzo pants and a form fitting white long sleeve shirt. I slip on a pair of black heels and we are off.

Back to the convention room and there are tables set up on the stage and singular metal chairs lined up, there must be seating for a thousand people in here. We have front row seats, looking at the tables that seem to be a few feet away. There are projection screens overhead to give those at the back a better view.

The place is slowly filling up and we take our seats on queue when the lights dim. There are spotlights on the stage and the writers and producer and actors come out and take their seats at the tables set up. I look up and have a direct line of sight to Len. He introduces himself and the place erupts into applause and I am in shock. As he goes down the line of people it seems to get louder and louder.

They seem to have an agenda to meet, talking about the production of the show, thanking the fans, thanking each other. I am becoming bored to death. It oddly feels like an award acceptance speech, except it's been going on for about 45 minutes. I look over to Rob and he is fully engaged and interested. I am jealous for a moment that there seems to be nothing besides work that I am this interested in.

They shift gears and begin to take questions from the audience. Rob has his hand in the air and Len makes eye contact with us and comes over with his mic.
"How long do you expect the show to continue?" he asks.
"Well, as long as the networks keep renewing it, we will be here. As long as the fans love it, the networks will continue to renew it." He says and the fans again stand and cheer.

"Do you have a question?" he asks me.
"Uhh, me? Uhh, no, I'm all set." I feel my face get hot and he is smiling at me.

"Who is your favorite character?" He smiles at me and I begin to panic.
Rob leans over in front of me "Its Petra!" he answers for me and squeezes my hand as I scowl at Len.
"Who else likes Petra?" He says and more cheering and he moves along to a different part of the audience.

"Why? Why did he do that? You know I really hate this show now." I sulk.

"Ahh, he was just having a little fun with you. I think it was awesome." Rob replies. "Don't take things so personally, jeeze!" he hugs me from the side.

"Fine, I guess it would be funny from his perspective." I reply.
"And mine, I will have to tell Nick about this!" He laughs.

The questions continue for another hour. Oh, dear lord let this end. I kinda feel like they are speaking a foreign language in a way. My thoughts start to wander and I begin to wonder if I could force myself to actually understand the show. Like just binge watch it until I became part of it. I am wondering if it could be used as some form of torture to make spys talk as well and Rob snaps me out of my train of thought.
"Rain, it's over." He smiles. "Are you happy?" He asks.

"Oh, that soon? It seemed like it just started." I try to seem aloof about the whole thing.
"That is a pathetic attempt, but I still love you and of course thank you for coming here with me." He kisses me on the cheek.

"Am I interrupting?" Len is in front of us.
"Uhh, no." I seem startled.
"I just wanted to let you know, I meant no harm earlier. It was all in jest. I hope you aren't offended." He offers.
"No, its fine." I force a laugh. "I guess I should at least know the show if I show up to something like this." I say.

"I'm actually curious about that. You managed to get high end tickets to both main events. How did you manage that and not even want to be here?" He says.

"They were a birthday present for me and she's my best friend so I insisted she come with me." Rob offers an explanation.

"Well, I really feel bad for putting you on the spot like that, I was shocked at how you panicked. Let me get you two a drink to make up for it, sound good?" He offers and I can instantly feel Rob's grip tighten on my hand.

"We'd love to." He answers instantly.

"Well, come on, let's go." Len replies.
"Holy Shit, can you believe this?!" Rob whispers at me.
"Calm down, Rob, he's just a person." I say.

We reach the bar and the three of us sit at a table and Rob is occupying the conversation talking about the show. Len seems to be making quite a bit of eye contact with me. He seems genuinely nice.
"Well, I think we have taken up enough of your time." I announce at the end of our second drinks.

"Yeah, while this was amazing, I'm sure you have other people to meet." Rob says.

"So you two have plans for this evening?" He asks looking between the two of us.

"We are going to hit up the club. Karma, I think it's called?" Rob replies.

"Ohh" He replies slowly. "Well, I was going to see if you two wanted to go out for dinner. But if you have plans, that's ok." He replies.
"Rain can go!" Rob replies.

"What? I thought you wanted me to go to the club with you?!" I am shocked at his answer.

"Well, I know you really didn't want to go, and you can have a nice dinner and you've already done so much with me this weekend." He has that look. I know that look. I've seen it before when he thinks he is flirting for me.

"Well?" Len asks.
"Uhh, I guess its fine, dinner and then I can meet up with you later?" I look from Len to Rob.
"Sounds like a plan." Rob replies.

"When?" I look at both of them. What is going on?

"Dinner in an hour? Meet me back down here?" Len replies.
"Do I have to change or is what I have on ok?" I ask, still a bit confused how this is all happening.
"You look amazing right now. See you in an hour." He says and walks away.

"What the hell is going on?" I look at Rob.
"He likes you, oh my god, Rain. He asked you out to dinner and you stood there and I answered for you." He is laughing. "I can go to the club, and hopefully meet someone, too. You can meet me there later. Enjoy dinner, Jesus. You really are clueless....and difficult." He says, looking at me more seriously.

"Difficult? You think I'm difficult." I ask him, feeling hurt.

"Well, why can't you just be open to things once in a while, you can have dinner without getting hurt you know, it's just dinner." He says. "And holy shit, it's Len Feldman. I wish he asked me to dinner." He says.

"He did, you could join us." I reply.
"Just have dinner." He says and we head to our rooms. Rob spends forever getting ready to head out to the club and I sit down checking emails and text messages. One from Lisa catches my eye. She wants me to come out and see her. I reply back that I will check my schedule. I have some text pics of my new nephew. My mother checks in and the manager at the bar checks in as well. I flip on the tv and find the news and watch until Rob comes in to tell me it's time to go.

We head back to the bar and Len is waiting for me.
"Wasn't sure if you were going to show up." He says.
"Don't worry, I would have dragged her back if I had to." Rob buts in. "Well, you kids enjoy yourselves, I'm off." He says and heads out.
"I have a table ready." Len says as he walks to the back of the restaurant.
"Thank you." I reply as I follow.
The table is in a more private part of the place and is set with a white tablecloth and a single rose on it. It appears to be the only one of its kind in the place. There is a little table set with a chilled bottle of wine and as soon as we take our seats a waiter appears to fill our glasses.
"To Sentennial" He lifts his glass.

"Really?" I reply as I lift mine which causes him to laugh. "You know, I attend these things and everyone knows every detail about me that google can provide, it's nice to sit with someone who isn't obsessed with it."

"Well, that would be me!" I say. "All this craziness, why do you have this in Connecticut?" I ask.
"I grew up here, the season is wrapped up and I come back home, my parents still live in Greenwich. Do you live around here?" He replies.

"Glastonbury."

"Ahh, so you're local." He says.

"Yeah, born and raised." I reply back.

"We have something in common. Ever been out to California?" He asks.

"A few times, I have friends out there." I say. "Do you go back and forth?"

"Once filming wraps up, I kinda congregate out here." He points out. "What do you do?"

"That's a loaded question. I am a day trader by choice, I also run the office at a construction company and in my spare time...I own a bar." I look to see his reaction.
"Is that all?" He laughs. "Seriously?"

"Sadly, yes." I say with a sigh.

"What bar?" he asks.
"Nor'Easter, in New Haven." I say.

"Oh, my god, I've been there! I thought you were gonna say some dive bar hole in the wall or something. You're shitting me, you own the Nor'Easter?"

"Yup. You've really been there?" I am a bit taken back. "Yes! I'm not kidding, I saw a jazz show there about 6 months ago, it was amazing. How do you always have headliners in there?" he asks, genuine in his curiousness.

"I have friends in California, The Storm?" I say.
"I've been there, too! Well, everyone's been there, but...wow. This is amazing." He says with excitement.

The waiter comes and takes our order and we continue to discuss the differences in California and Connecticut. We talk about growing up and what we've accomplished. He seems to be careful not to talk about his show too much. We talk about music and some of the shows that I've had. We seem to really be having a great evening. Drinks, chatting. My phone buzzes and I have a text from Rob looking for me. I check the time and I have been sitting here for 3 hours.

"Everything ok?" Len asks.
"Yeah, my friend is looking for me." I reply.
"Do you have to go?" He looks at me.
"I really should, it's his birthday weekend. I should also kinda make sure he doesn't get into trouble." I say and see his smile fade. "You can come with me if you want!" I suggest.
"Karma?....Only if you dance with me!" he offers.
"Deal, wanna go now?" I ask him and he settles the check and we head to the club.

I text Rob that I am on my way and to be outside the ladies' room in 5 minutes and Len and I head in.

"How are you ever going to find him?" He asks.

"I told him to wait by the ladies' room. He will be there." I say and we find our way there.

"Rain! O. M. G. Len is here!" Rob is drunk. "This is Scott, he is my birthday dance partner tonight." He slurs. Scott seems maybe a bit more sober than Rob, but not far behind him.

We decide to find a table in the VIP area past the velvet ropes. I begin to speak to security there, trying to work my magic and Len pops up behind me and handles it.

We reach the table and get our own bottle girl who seems to take a liking to Len, maybe she knows who he is, or maybe she can tell he is the only one at the table interested in girls.

"So tell me more about Rain." Len asks Rob. This is going to end badly. Rob has had too much to drink.

"What do you want to know?!" he laughs.

"Tell me something about her she wouldn't have told me." He says.

"She's afraid of relationships." Rob blurts out. Holy Fuck. Why? How much has he drank? The answer seems to even take Len by surprise.

"Well, that was way more personal than I expected, I'm sorry Rain." He looks to me.

Scott seems to size up the situation and asks Rob to head back down to the dance floor leaving Len and I alone.

"Well, now it's really weird. Remind me to thank him for

this later." I say with annoyance.
"He is drunk, let it go. It's fine. Don't be mad at him." He says.

"I'm not, he thinks he's helping, hell, my brother would have said way more." I laugh.

"Is that why you work so much?" He asks.

"Are you trying to diagnose me?" I reply in a matching tone.

"Look, I just got out of a really long relationship, this is all sorta new to me." He says.

"I'm not mad, bewildered maybe, not mad." I reply.

"How long are you here for?" He asks.
"I leave tomorrow morning." I reply.

"Back to work?" He asks, smiling.
"Always." I say.
"Maybe I will stop in the bar? Will you be there?" he asks.

"Thursday, Friday and Saturday nights, I'm there from dinner to close. Stop by!" I say.

"Well, I hate to do this, but I have things early in the morning and need to get some sleep. I really had a nice dinner with you." He says and gives me a half hug and heads out.

I look at my phone and see its 1am. I should find Rob and get him back to the rooms before I have to carry him.

I find him and Scott on the dance floor and tell him it's time to go. It appears that Scott is joining us to head back to our rooms. Whatever, Happy Birthday Rob. They head into Rob's room and I head into mine.

Chapter 33

I get dressed and head into Robs room through the connecting door and see that him and Scott are still asleep and retreat back to mine. I text him to see if that wakes him up, then try to call. He is out and will probably have a hangover when he wakes up. I order breakfast for the three of us and have it delivered. I take mine and push the cart into his room and shout to wake up and go back to mine. I finally hear movement in his room.

I scroll through my phone and send Nick a text 'All future presents for Rob need to be pre-approved by me'. Within minutes, my phone rings.

"Are you ok?" He asks.
"I'm fine, Nick."

"Saw Lisa yesterday and she is really bugging for you to come out here." He says.

"I know, I got a text from her. I said I would check my schedule." I tell him.

"Well, you can stay here if you want." He says and I do not respond. "Or with Lisa, she'd probably love that." He adds.
"I'm just trying to find my routine, the last month or so....it's wiped me out." I say. Why the hell did I text him.

Rob and his new friend, Scott, come in the room and thank me for breakfast.

"Is that Rob?"

"Yes, Nick, it's Rob." I say.

"And Scott, Hi, whoever you are!" Scott shouts.

"Who the hell is that?" Nick seems defensive.

"Rob met a friend last night." I giggle. "Like you've never woken up with someone you just met. Seriously!" I say.

"Ohh, Rob's friend, well tell him I said Hi." He says with a complete change of temperament.

"Alright, I will, I'll talk to you later." I say and hit end on the call. "He says to say 'Hi'" I say.

"Who?" Scott asks.

"Nick Stone!" Rob replies.

"No way, that was really Nick Stone? From Heavensent?" He seems in awe.

"Yeah, he actually gave me the tickets for my birthday." Rob is embarrassing when he is trying to impress someone.

"Dude! Len Feldman last night, now Nick Stone? This is pretty wild." Scott says.

"It's really not like this all the time, I swear." Rob's ego comes back into check a bit.

"But still!" Scott is clearly starstruck.

"Well, I already ate, why don't you two go eat, Rob, we should really get ready to check out and head home." I announce, hoping he will notice I want to go home.

"Scott, I should really get going, you're gonna call me this week? Dinner, maybe next weekend?" Rob is waiting for a reply.

"Sure. I should get going anyways." He replies and heads back into their room.

"What is all that?" I look at Rob, trying not to laugh.
"Oh, shut up! He actually lives about a half hour from me. And he is really nice." He says.
"Unlike you last night. What the hell, Rob?" I ask.

"What?" He asks with a bit of confusion on his face.
"You told Len that I was afraid of relationships? Are you kidding me?" I begin to pack my stuff.
"I was drunk, I kinda remember saying it, but wasn't sure it actually came out. I'm sorry." He says.
"Ehh, its fine. Happy Birthday." I shake my head. "And him?" I look to Robs room.
"I, unlike you, am not afraid of a relationship. We'll probably have dinner, see where it goes." He says and heads back to his room to pack.

40 minutes later, valet is bringing my car to the portico and we are packing our bags to head home.

"You aren't mad, are you?" He asks as I drive.
"No, of course not. I'm glad you had a good time. But the bar has been set for my birthday, that's for sure." I laugh.
I drop Rob off at his house and head for mine. All alone again. I do some laundry and clean up a bit and settle down on the couch to find something on tv. 'Sentennial' is a re-run and I leave it on the channel. I can't. It's just so intolerable. I settle on a nature show and fall asleep.

I wake up and check my phone, its 5:30 in the evening. Jesus, I just need to get back into my routine. I seem to be up at any given hour of the day or asleep at any given hour of the day. This can't be good. I prepare for Monday morning and skim through some emails. I send some texts and decide to head over to Tony's house to stop by and see my new nephew.

The visit is great, I hold little Donnie a bit and play with Bella and clean up the kitchen for Melissa. I go over a schedule with Tony since he is going to stay home a few more days with Mel and the kids and I head home around 10pm. I head straight to bed saying a prayer that I would like no drama for the next week.

Monday morning comes in and I get my coffee and head to my office to go over accounts. I make some trades and settle on some low risk moves as I will be busy with Tony's shop mostly this week. I wrap up paying some bills and head to the shop. Ty is working in the garage and says 'hi'. Now there is someone that I need some quality time with soon. It seems we mostly pass each other now. I head into the office and take care of incoming and outgoing invoices. I check that all the jobs are on schedule and move some things around. I seem to be done about 2pm and decide to go visit my mother.

I visit with her and have a late lunch. She started volunteering at the library to give her something to do, she tells me all about the different things she is doing there and how much they appreciate her. It's good for her to have something to do. I head home at about 5pm and make myself dinner and settle on the couch, eventually heading to bed.

Tuesday and Wednesday follow the same routine and I feel at peace, finally. After dinner on Thursday, I head to the bar and begin paperwork there, invoices out, payroll out. I check the schedule and see that there is a pretty popular band inquiring about playing and call their manager to negotiate. I take care of other mundane tasks and then head out to the bar to get a drink. I watch the band playing and then eventually close the bar. Friday and Saturday are a repeat. Sunday, I have my family over my house for a big dinner and we all soak up some baby and Bella time. Everyone has a good, relaxing time.

The following week is the same, except that Tony is back in the shop most days. Saturday night, we have a pretty popular band playing and the place is packed. I am in my office trying to call for an extra off duty cop to pick up a shift for security.

"Rain, there someone here asking for you?" a waiter knocks at my office door. No one asks for me, people ask to speak to who is in charge and that is handled by the manager on duty.

"Who?" I ask.

"I don't know, Len something?" He says.

"Huh? Hang on, I will be there in a minute." I say stacking up my papers and heading into the bar.

"Told you I would stop by." Len Feldman is standing there with flowers in his hand.

"Holy shit, you are!" I exclaimed. "Grab a drink, we can go in the office, its quiet in there." I say and he grabs his beer and follows me.

"You know, these are for you." He hands me the flowers and I'm not exactly sure what to do with them so I lay them on the desk.

"I can put them in a vase back at my house." I say, unsure. "So what are you doing here?"

"I told you I would stop in. I really like the guys playing tonight. I was busy the last few weeks and finally had a chance to come by." He says.

"How's your friend. Rob, was it?" He asks.
"You know, he is still seeing that guy he was with. Who would have guessed?" I laugh.

"Really! Good for him." He says.

"So you're here to see the band? Want to go meet them?" I ask.

"Well, I'm here to see you, but I'd love to meet them." He says.
"Me? Really?" I ask.

"Sure, I told you I would stop in." He says, taking a drink from his beer.
"OK, well let me go introduce you before they go on." I offer and lead him into the back area where the bands get ready.
"Hey, guys." I call attention to myself in the room.
"Rain, it's great to see you again." The singer comes up to me.

"I just wanted to introduce you to Len Feldman. He is a fan." I step away so they can see him.
"Aren't you that producer?" One of the guys asks.
"Yeah, that's me." Len extends a hand. They continue to have a conversation bouncing from the band's music to the show and this goes on for a few minutes.

"Well, I'll let you get ready to go on, Rain, we can go." Len says to me.

"You want me to put you at a table up front?" I ask as we head out to the hallway.
"Where do you usually sit?" He asks.
"In my office? Sometimes at the end of the bar." I say.

"You really don't watch and enjoy the show?" he seems shocked as we reach my office again.
I sit down at my desk and he sits across from me. "Want another beer?" I ask, buzzing the front on my phone.
"Sure." He replies and I ask the bartender to send in two beers.

"I'm not completely into the rock scene." I say, feeling like I admitted some big secret.
"But you own a bar?" He seems shocked.

"Kinda funny, eh?" I look at him.
"You are odd, in a good way, but still pretty odd. Why would you buy a bar if you didn't want to run one?" He asks jokingly.
"Someday, if I know you much better, I can explain. But it's not for right now." I say.
"Shit, you should write for the show. I bet you have a pretty good storyline." He laughs.
"Believe it or not, I strive for boring." I say.

"Is that your quest?" He laughs again.
"I guess you could say that. Always so close, yet never there." I try to sound dramatic.

"Are you free for dinner sometime this week?" He comes right out and asks.

"Early in the week, I'm always here the latter." I say.

"Tuesday? Would that work for you?" He is checking his phone.

"Sure, that's fine, any place in particular?" I ask. Things seem to be easy with him. I enjoy this.

"I will take care of the details, want to meet here?" He asks.

"I can manage that." I say. "Want to head out to see the show? I'll even sit at a table with you if you want." I giggle.

"That would be perfect." He says and we head out to the bar. I instruct a small table to be put up front and sit down with him. We enjoy the show and he heads home when it's over. I wrap up the bar, head home and go straight to bed.

Sunday is a day of rest, I clean and go grocery shopping and lounge on the couch most the day, Rob comes over and we order pizza. He brings me up to date on him and Scott, it seems to be progressing nicely. He brought him home to meet his mother. I mention that I am having dinner with Len on Tuesday and Rob is shocked.

"Are you fucking with me?" he asks.

"Nope, he stopped by the bar last night and I said I would go. It's just dinner, right? Those were your words." I look at him.

"You like him! I can tell." He points at me in an accusatory manner.

"Yeah, a little. He seems nice, he is not full of himself, he just seems, I don't know. Harmless?" I say, searching for the right word.

"Good for you!" he says. We finish our pizza and chat a bit more and he heads home. I decide on a bath for myself and head to bed.

Monday morning is the usual and Tuesday rolls in and I hurry to get everything done early. I head to Tony's shop and rush thru everything to get home to head out to dinner.

"Hey, want to come over for dinner tonight?" Ty sticks his head in.

"Can't, I have a date." I say.

"You could just say no, you don't have to make shit up." He comes in the office.

"I do. I am having dinner tonight with someone." I say.

"Who?" he asks.

"Len Feldman." I say back.

"Why does that sound fami....bullshit...Tony get in here!" his voice becomes a yell at the end and Tony comes rushing in thinking something is wrong.

"What, are you ok?" He looks frantic.

"Rain here has a date tonight, not only a date, but with Len Feldman." He folds his arms and leans back as if he just got me in trouble.

"So, bout time you got out there." Tony clearly has no idea who he is. "Wait?! The Len Feldman?" He looks at me.

"Yes, is that a problem?" I look at them both.

"When did you meet him? How?" Ty asks.
"I met him at the casino that weekend, Rob's birthday? He came by the bar and asked me to dinner." I say.

"Leave her alone, Ty. Jesus, at least she is finally getting out there." Tony sticks up for me.
"But what about Nick?" Ty seems defensive.
"We are not together, we are friends." I say with a bit of attitude in my voice. "I have to go." I say in a huff and head out.

I head home to get ready and now I am in a bad mood. How dare he! I get home and hop in the shower and get out and begin to blow-dry my hair, I put some mascara on and slip into a form fitting sheath dress, it is almost July and its beginning to stay hot at night. I slip on some heels and head out in the Mercedes.

I pull into the bar and see that there is a black car in the parking lot, a bmw. It's Len. I park and get out as does he. "Nice car." He says and I feel an odd pang of guilt for driving here in Nick's car.

"Ehh, I have a truck, but it didn't really fit the outfit." I reply back.

"You look beautiful." He leans in and kisses my cheek. "Want to take my car?" He asks. Does he know how I feel about the car? I stare at him. "I can drive and I know where we are going so...." He finishes when I don't reply. "Sure, that's fine." I say and he comes around the car and opens the door for me.

He tells me he has a house of his own out here, but has been staying with his parents as work is being done on his. He explains how hectic it is staying with his parents. We chat on the way to the restaurant. I mention that I've had a house for about a year and a half. I let it slip in conversation that I just lost my father and he is apologetic. "I see why you want boring, seems like it's been pretty busy lately." He comments. We reach the restaurant and head in. It is a very nice place on the water. We have a table overlooking the ocean.

"This view is amazing." I comment, looking out the window remembering the last time I saw the ocean was in Malibu. "I love listening to the waves, its soothing."

"Watching you is amazing." He says, staring at me.
"Len." I say back.
"No, Rain, you are. And I really like you." He takes my hand.

"Aww, your making me blush." I'm not sure what to say.
"I mean it." He is insistent. "I want to see you more." He says.

"I think that would be nice." I reply back.
We have dinner and chat more about life and growing up. Our families, he has a sister. They get along. After dinner, we have dessert and coffee.
"This really has been enjoyable." I say. "I really do enjoy spending time with you."
"So are we like 'dating' now?" He raises his eyebrows at me.
"You didn't really ask me, but I guess we are! I feel like I'm

in middle school or something. I think I played it cooler in high school, yup, this is definitely middle school all over again." I laugh.

"Hold on, let me call all my friends and tell them I have a girlfriend." He laughs too.

We head back to the bar where I left my car and start to kiss while still in his car. This feels nice. We eventually decide it's time to go, I do have work in the morning. I head home a bit giddy and arrive, take a shower and go to bed.

Wednesday morning, I have a text from Len telling me that he had a wonderful evening and it was signed 'your boyfriend'. I laughed out loud in my bed. I start the day as always and later we make plans for him to join me on lunch on Thursday. The weeks pass by and we go out, movies, theater, mini golfing, a petting zoo. I am really having the time of my life.

The end of August rolls in and he is over at my house while I am grilling steaks outside.

"Hey, there is an award show coming up that I have to attend in California, I have to go out for about two weeks for meetings and stuff, but I'd love for you to fly out to go to see me get it." I almost drop the steak on the ground. California. Flashbacks of flying back and forth till we meet our demise. Stop.

"Uhh, when is it?" I ask.

"The weekend after labor day. It's up to you" He says nonchalantly.

"I guess I could?" I reply back.

"I'd love it if you did. I hate these things, but I'm being presented with some award for my donations to a charity and I'd love to have you at the table with me." He says.

"Sure, just send me the dates and I can set up travel arrangements." I say.

"I can take care of all that for you. You only have to come out for the weekend." He says. "The awards are on a Saturday night."

"Actually, I have to go see my friend out there anyways, I've put it off all summer, I can stay a few days and visit her." I am thinking out loud.

"Whatever you want." He is agreeable. "But I have to head out a few days prior and stay, so you'll have to fly out alone, sorry."

"Its fine, done it before." I say and we have dinner. He tells me about an animal hospital he helps fund and what it does.

The next week flies by. I settle on flying out Thursday and meeting up with Lisa, spending that day and Friday with her. Saturday will be with Len and then Sunday morning I will fly home.

Chapter 34

I dial Lisa's number from the phone in the office.

"Rain!" Lisa answers on the second ring. "What's up!?"

"What are you doing Thursday and Friday next week?" I ask.
"Not sure, probably at the bar, why?" she asks.
"With me?" I wait.
"Shut up! Are you for real or are you fucking with me?" She is in shock.
"I'm serious." I say. "I met someone and he is accepting an award or something Saturday and I'm actually coming out there."
"Wait? You met someone? Where? Who?" Her tone changes a bit. "Does Nick know?" she asks.
"No, what does Nick matter for?" I am becoming confused.

"Nothing, are you happy?" Her cheerfulness comes back.
"Yes, I am." I say.
"Then that's all that matters."
I give her my flight info and she agrees to pick me up at the airport. I will spend Thursday and Friday night with her and then head over to Len's house.

The next few days fly by and Rob is soon driving me to the airport. I board and fly and Lisa picks me up.
"Oh, I am so happy to see you." She embraces me. We drive to her house and we change and head out to the pool. We are talking and catching up and drinking.

"Is Tony here?" Nick walks thru the sliding glass door. "Holy shit, Rain? What? Is that you?!"

"Yeah, its me." I say.
"Why didn't you tell me you were coming?" He asks.
"Ehh, I wanted to see Lisa, I figured we would see each other tonight at the bar." I say.

"Ohh, Well, I guess I better make sure I head over tonight." He says. "What made you decide to fly out finally?" He asks and I contemplate why I feel so nervous saying I met someone.

"Nick, are you going to be long?" A woman appears, dressed like she belongs in a video. She comes up to him and puts her hand on his arm. "You promised you wouldn't be long."

"Why don't you introduce us to your friend?" Lisa says, clearly waiting to see how Nick will handle this.

"Uhh, yeah, this is Tanya." He stutters.
"It's Tandy." She immediately corrects him and Lisa stifles a giggle.

"Nice to meet you, Tandy." I stand up to shake her hand.
"You and Nick together?" I ask.
"Yeah, we are." Tandy is smiling like a toddler with a cookie and I swear I see Nick actually begin to sweat.
"Its fine, Nick. Friends." I say the word and it snaps him out of the trance he seems to have entered.
"Look, I needed to see Tony. Tell him to call me when he gets back." He says and shuffles Tandy out of the back yard.

"Well, that was fun." I look to Lisa. "The bar ought to be a blast tonight now." I don't know how to react.

"And you aren't' with someone?" she says calmly.

"We are friends, that's it." I say flatly. "Maybe I should bring Len tonight." I suggest.

"Len, tell me about Len." Lisa says and we get back to chatting and I tell her how we met and everything leading up to now.

"Maybe, let on you are seeing someone, and best not to bring him actually to the bar?" Lisa offers. "Let it sink in first? I think that will help." She says.
"Fine, when do we have to get ready." I say grabbing my phone to see what time it is. 4 texts from Nick.

'why didn't you tell me you were coming'

'im sorry'

'see you tonight'

'im sorry'

 I hand lisa the phone and she reads.
"Well, this is not going to be good." She hands it back to me.
"Maybe I should just go to Len's house and forget the bar." I suggest.
"NO! he knows you aren't together, shit, he always has someone with him at the bar. At least you are seeing someone seriously. I'd fucking tell him."

"But now it just seems like revenge." I say. "This whole trip was a bad idea." I say.

"I'm dealing with him right now." She picks up her phone and dials.
"Nick, yeah. Its Lisa….Yeah, she is right here…..no, listen to me…..the poor girl is dating someone and can't even tell you because she is so worried about hurting your feelings…..yeah, and you showed up at my house with whoever the hell you are with this week…..I told her to bring him tonight…….whatever…." She clicks end on the phone. "There, dealt with." She seems satisfied with herself and I seem mortified of what lies ahead.

"I'm not bringing Len tonight. He doesn't need to get intertwined into this." I say as we are getting ready.
"So, Nick thinks you are, so he will behave. That's all that matters." She says. "Rain, I am really happy for you, seriously. Don't let him get to you." She has her hands on my shoulders and she is lecturing me.

We head to the bar and head in straight to her office. She puts her headset on and calls Jen in.
"Oh, Rain! It's you, here! This is awesome." She hugs me with elation.

"Jen, keep Rain happy tonight? I have a feeling it's gonna get weird." She says and Jen looks at me.
"Everything OK? Is it Lucy? Cause she is banned, she can't come in, I think that security actually has a picture of…."
"No, it's not her. It's just stuff." I offer to calm her down.
We hang out in Lisa's office until she tells me I should go sit down around 8. She has to go into boss mode. I find the

table and Jen comes over with a burger and fries.

"Can you just sit with me?" I ask her.

"Lisa will get pissed, it's packed tonight." She says. "Doug will be here shortly, he can sit with you." She offers.

"That will work." I Say. I see her pull out her phone and send a text, presumably to Doug.

"He is coming in now. Want a drink?" she asks and I order a rum and coke.

"Holy shit it is you. I never thought I would see you in here again." Doug arrives with a smile and I stand up to hug him. "Nick know you're here?"

"Yes, and it's gonna be interesting." I reply.

"Huh?" Doug looks confused just as Nick stumbles in a bit drunk with Tandy at his side.

"Hey guys." He sits at the table.

"Hi again." Tandy says as Doug looks in shock.

"You all met already?" Doug asks me.

"They dropped by Lisa's house and Nick didn't know I was here yet." I say.

"And Rain came into town unannounced to her see her new boyfriend. Where is he?" Nick asks.

"Oh my fucking god." Doug says quietly and looks to me "New guy?!"

I lean over and quietly say to Doug, "I'm just sort of having dinner a lot with this guy, he invited me out to go to some awards show, I'm staying at Lisa's and he isn't even here tonight."

"Then what about Nick?" Doug asks back.
"Lisa got pissed cause he came strolling in with her." I say and Doug understands.

Jen shows up at the table with a beer for Doug and her eyes get wide upon seeing Tandy. "Uhh, anyone want any drinks?" She asks, looking immediately nervous.

"I'll have a beer and whatever the lady wants." He smiles at her and she instinctively rubs his arm like she is claiming ownership.

"So where is your new boyfriend?" Nick asks me.

"Not here, Nick." I say back not making eye contact.
"Lisa said you were bringing him. I thought it could be some sort of double date or something." He is drunk and not thinking clearly.

"He is just someone I've gone out with a few times, not really someone I'm ready to bring around my friends yet." I look up at him.

"But you are coming out here for him to see him?" He asks in an accusatory tone that's getting me mad.
"No, he asked me to come out here and I thought it was the perfect excuse to come surprise you, but I guess that was a mistake. I need to find a bathroom." I get up and head to the security area, hoping there are no problems. I speak with security and they let me through to use the private bathroom.

"Rain." I hear Nick's voice.

"Don't Nick, I will be right back at the table." I say.

"Stop, I want to talk to you."

"I'm actually going to the bathroom, I will be out in a minute." I yell.

"Well, I'm waiting." He says.

I exit the stall and begin to wash my hands. "What is your problem?" I look at him.

"My problem?" He asks.

"Please tell me what I did to deserve the Tandy show out there? You couldn't hold off for one night?" I feel myself getting upset.

"Lisa said you had a boyfriend and was going to bring him tonight." He is so blunt honest when he is drunk.

"So you did it because you wanted me to see you with someone, point made. It doesn't matter." I say and try to head out of the bathroom and he puts his hand on the door to stop me.

"Knock it off, Nick." I say.

"I will send her home." He says.

"So you will just hurt her feelings like that?" I ask.

"She doesn't mean anything to me." He says.

"Real nice." I say with a scowl and he has this sad expression wash over his face. "Let's just go back to the table."

"Fine" he says and escorts me back.

"Where'd you go?" Tandy asks.

We answer simultaneously. "To the bathroom." Which makes her a bit uncomfortable.

Lisa joins us and hugs me as she sits down. "How's it going? Everything good? Tony should be here soon."

"That's good." I say.

Conversation continues, awkward, but passes the time and Tony arrives.

"Lisa said you were here, but I wasn't sure if she was hallucinating." He laughs and hugs me. Nick and Tony engage in conversation while Lisa and I are chatting away, leaving Doug to talk to Tandy. Eventually the band takes the stage and begins to play. I look over to Lisa, she is really cut out for this. She is just so engaged in the music. I would just as soon go sit in her office.

The band eventually stops and calls Nick and Tony up on stage.
"Ohh, I've heard he calls his girlfriends up on stage and sings to them, I wonder if he might call me?" Tandy squeals.

"I wouldn't hold your breath." Lisa snarks.

Nick and Tony play for a bit and Tony stops to have everyone acknowledge his Wife, Lisa and there are cheers. He ends with telling everyone how much he loves her. I am so happy for Lisa. I look over and Tandy is very antsy in her seat waiting to see Nick's next move on stage. Nick takes the mic and thanks me for coming. A dedication to old friends being reunited and dedicates the next song and him and Tony play. Lisa elbows me so hard that it almost knocks me over.

"See that shit?" She shouts.

"Yes, standing right next to you." I say.

Jen has joined us at the table and its quite a song. Tony and Nick return after they are done playing.

"That was great." I exclaim.

"We've been playing with it a bit." Tony laughs. "But Nick thought it would be good tonight."

"It was!" I say as Nick takes his seat between Tandy and Tony.

"Guess I know what happened in the bathroom!" She says loud enough for me to hear and the table goes quiet.

"I think I should go." I stand up.

"Rain, don't." Lisa is tugging at my arm.

"No, I don't belong here, this was a bad idea." I say and my hands begin to tremble. "I really need to go."

"But the night's not over." Jen says.

"It is for me. Lisa, stay, enjoy yourself. I will find a cab home." I say and head to the door. Tony, Doug and Lisa follow me out.

"Come on guys, don't make me feel like this, just let me go." I say. "I swear I am having flashbacks. I have to get out of here."

"I'll take her back to your house." Doug offers. "Give me a minute to get my car." And he heads back into the bar.

We say our goodbyes and Doug and I head to Lisa and Tony's house. "This was never going to work." I say in the car.

"What? Oh, ignore the girl. It doesn't matter." He says.

"It shouldn't matter, but it does, and it pisses me off that it pisses me off, if that makes any sense." I say fidgeting my hands in my lap.

"Rain, you still care about him. That's all, it doesn't make you a bad person, it actually makes you a really good person, don't you see that?" Doug offers. "And Nick is a good person, too. He just has a streak of asshole in him, that as soon as it shows, he regrets it....at least with you anyways." He laughs a little at the end. "Shit, he did the same thing in Vegas when he thought you were with that stripper, remember?" He asks.

"Yeah, but I'm actually seeing someone now. What am I supposed to do?" I ask him.

"I don't have a fucking clue on that one, maybe give it some time?" He offers.

We arrive at Lisa's house and he lets me in. I text Lisa and let her know I'm there and gonna take a shower and head to bed. She texts back she will get me up in the morning.

Chapter 35

"Pretty good for a Thursday night?" Lisa laughs as she hands me a cup of coffee.

"Not sure if I can handle another night in there." I sigh.
"This was a dumb idea."
"What? Coming to visit me?" Lisa looks hurt.
"No, thinking Nick and I could be friends." I say.

"Rain, he's like a big dumb animal. He is hurt and he lashes out." She looks at me. "You can't tell me you don't know how he feels." She looks serious.
"Never said that, but I thought...I don't know. Are you expecting me to go back there tonight?" I ask her.

"Well, I'm supposed to be there, but I can see what I can do." She says. It's almost 10, get ready, we are going shopping." She says and heads out of her guest bedroom. I look at my phone and see Len texted his address for me to head over tomorrow morning. Ty texted me to say him and Rob did not burn the bar down. Rob texted to say that there was no actual fire and everything is normal. Nick texted me to see if I will have dinner with him.

I reply back to everyone but Nick and get ready for shopping. Lisa and I spend the next few hours shopping, she loves to buy clothes. I tell her that I need a dress for this awards dinner.
"Well, formal? Dinner? What do you need?" She asks.
"I don't have a clue. I wonder if we could google it to see what it looked like last year?"

"Seems legit, let's get some lunch and figure it out." She drags me to a diner for food.

We look through pictures of past events and decide on a semi-formal dress. Something sexy, she seems to think I need.

My phone buzzes again. "Do you need to get that?" She asks.

"It's Nick. He wants to have dinner. I am just ignoring it." I say.

"You two are supposed to be friends, why don't you just have dinner with him? Talk it out?" she prods.

"I'm visiting you." I reply.

"It's dinner, go!" She says. "Or else, Tony and I can take you out and invite him anyways. Then it will just be weirder." She looks at me with her 'checkmate' look.

"Fine." I tell her and send him a quick simple text 'pick me up at tony and lisas when you want to go' and we get back to our shopping. We find a perfect dress. It is form fitting at the top and is somewhat evening gown length with white and black layered sheer pieces. A slit on the right side that comes up to a high thigh point but you would really never know standing still at attention. It is really a beautiful dress. I get some white sparkly matching heels and we head back to her house. We head back out to her pool and are sipping drinks when Nick enters the patio.

"Hi Lisa, Rain." He announces himself.

"Hi Nick, so nice to see you again." Lisa says with sarcasm.

"Really?" He looks at her.

"Hey, don't get attitude with me, I'm the one that's making her have dinner with you." She smiles at him and heads into her house.

Nick comes over and takes her lounge chair next to mine. "Where do you want to go for dinner?" He asks.

"You're the expert out here." I say and then decide to tempt fate…. "Is your girlfriend joining us?"

"Is your boyfriend joining us?" He replies back immediately.

"No. Look, I'm sorry for last night." I offer the olive branch first. "I am seeing someone, yes, but we've just had dinner, lunch, stuff like that. He asked me to come out here and I thought I finally had a reason to come out and see you and Lisa and everyone. It was never supposed to end up like last night."

"So you really wanted to come see me?" He asks.

"Yeah, I haven't seen you since Rob's party. I wanted to see everyone. I haven't seen Doug and Jen since the funeral, Shit, I haven't seen Tony and Lisa since I ran out on their wedding." I think about all this as I'm saying it.

"Come on, let's go to dinner." He pulls me to my feet.

"I should really go change. I will be right back." I head in and slip out of my bikini and slip on a maxi dress and flip flops and head back outside. "Is this ok?" I ask him. "The heat is miserable out here in the beginning of September. I love the fall when it's nice and cool back east." I say.

"You look great. And, yeah, there is something about fall in New England. I will give you that." He says and we head to his car and to an Italian restaurant.

"I'm sorry about bringing her last night." Nick says as soon as we sit down.

"Its fine, everyone knows you aren't going to stay single for long." I say feeling the weight of my words.

"But I shouldn't have tried to antagonize you about it." He says and I think about his words.

"You are absolutely right." I say.

"Look, I'll try to be more....aware of what I am doing." He says.

"Oh, I'm pretty sure you were completely aware of what you were doing last night." I say with a laugh.

"Rain, I'm sorry. I really am." He says solemnly.

"I know." I say and we place our orders and eat and keep conversation light. We talk about Bella and her new brother. I show him pictures on my phone and he tells me about his guest appearance on a new album for some band. The conversation never touches on Len or any of his escapades.

"So what do you want to do now? We could go back to my place, watch tv? Or head to the Storm."

"Your place? Isn't it kind of far?" I ask.

"No, I'm staying at the LA house now." He says. Its 30 minutes from here."

"We can head to the bar, if you want. I think Lisa kinda wanted me there with her since I leave tomorrow." I say.

"Sure, let's go." He says.

We arrive at 'the storm' and head in the back entrance and go straight to the tables at the front. I realize that he probably spends way too much time here. We order drinks and watch the show. Lisa and Tony join us. Todd is also there, I realize I have not seen him since the wedding either. All in all, it's quite an enjoyable evening. I head back to Lisa's house with her and Tony at the end of the night and go right to sleep.

Chapter 36

Lisa and I have coffee in the morning after I have all my stuff packed. The dress for tonight is in a zip up plastic cover and I call a cab and we say our goodbyes.

I text Len that I am almost at his house and he says that he will open the gate and meet me outside, which he does. "How were your friends?" He hugs me after I get out of the cab.
"It was fun. Busy." I say and he helps with my luggage. I take the dress out and carefully carry it inside his house. It is a mansion. It is very modern. Steele and glass. He gives me a tour of the place and the views are amazing.

"Ehh, it's a lot of house for just me, but sometimes I have parties and it comes in handy." He laughs. "I know you are working thru some stuff and like to take it slow, so I had one of the guest rooms made up for you. Let me know if everything is ok." He says and shows me the room.
"Its fine, I'm just here for the night." I say, hanging the dress up.
"Is that for tonight?" he asks.
"Yeah, I went shopping with Lisa earlier." I reply.
"Ohh, I was going to take you out." He says.
"No more shopping for me for a while, that girl can wear you out." I laugh. "What time do we have to be ready by? I don't know where or when this whole thing is." I point out.
"Oh, I am so sorry. I should have sent you the info. We should leave here by 4, the limo will pick us up and there is a red carpet thing. Then we can head in. I think it's over by 10 or so? The limo will bring us back." He says.

I take out my phone. "Its 12 now. What do you want to do?" I ask.

"Want lunch? There is a little green bistro in town. It's kinda nice." He says.

"Sounds great." I say and grab my purse. We head to lunch and he tells me more about the animal charity and other charity awards that they are giving out. Apparently, there will be other stars there collecting awards for their charity work. We have salads and head back to his house.

"How long does it take you to get ready?" he asks, "Hour or two?"

"Uhh, I need to take a shower, blow dry my hair? Maybe 30 minutes total?" I am bewildered by this.

"Really? What about makeup and that stuff?" He asks, just as confused as I am.

"Silly, I don't wear any. Maybe some mascara, but that's it." This is weird.

"Maybe a little longer, I should probably pin my hair up with the dress that I have." I say, feeling like I'm somehow obligated to take forever to get ready.

"We have time for a glass of wine on the balcony then." He pulls my arm to follow him. The view looks over all of Los Angeles. It is beautiful. He hits a button and a gas fire in the fire pit lights. He heads to the bar and pours two glasses of champagne and hands me one. "To us." He says. "And to your award." I add and we drink. We remain on the patio for a while longer and he lets me know that I should probably start to get ready. I head to my room and take a shower and carefully dry off and begin to blow-dry my hair carefully. I get out some bobby pins and clips from my luggage and carefully pin my hair up. I pull some random strands out to frame my face and then slip on the dress, realizing that I cannot zip it up by myself and call out for assistance.

"You ok?" Len reaches the bedroom door.

"Could you offer a little help?" I ask and he zips up the dress to the back of the neck and I turn around.

He takes my hands and holds them out. "You are absolutely stunning." He pulls me in and kisses me. "And you might be the first woman in history to be ready early. I have to finish getting into my tux." He hurries out of the room. We head down the hall and have enough time to spare to have another glass of champagne on the deck.

His phone buzzes and it is to let him know the limo is in the driveway. We head down and get in. The traffic is horrendous, but the ride is nice. I opt for a bottle of water on the ride over. This is the last place I need to be tipsy. We eventually arrive and step out of the limo onto a red carpet and flashes are going off. Paparazzi are all asking him questions and I do my best to stay immediately on the outside of him. I really don't like this at all. He stops and turns to face the cameras at one point and I am not prepared for all the flashes and begin to stumble for a moment, but catch myself. He holds my arm to brace me and kisses my cheek whispering 'sorry' and reporters are asking who I am. He ignores them. We eventually make it inside and are met with a waiter carrying a tray of glasses and he takes two and hands me one.

"I think I need to sit." I say.

"Are you ok?" he asks with concern.

"I'm fine, I was just not prepared for all, all that." I wave my hands toward the doors that lead us in here.

He laughs. "Aww, I'm sorry. I think I'm so used to it that I forget you aren't." He says.

"Thank you for not telling them my name. I would prefer it that way. I am not a famous person, nor would I ever want to be." I point out.

We mingle, some people I recognize some I don't. Len introduces me to everyone and we enjoy ourselves. I ask someone to take a pic with my phone of the two of us. I think this is our first picture together. Well, besides the thousands taken outside.

We enjoy our meal and drinks continue to flow. Len accepts his award from the charity and has a nice speech. He returns to the table and kisses me on the cheek. We listen to the rest of the awards and eventually make our way back to his place. It's almost 11 by the time we get back. We sit by the fire on the balcony until I begin to fall asleep and I excuse myself to go to bed. I take a quick shower and fall asleep right away.

I wake up and look at my phone and see that its 8am. I get dressed and pack up my stuff and head to the kitchen to find Len with a cup of coffee and he offers me one. He is working on some scripts on the counter. "Sorry, these were sent over and I have to proof them all." He says.

"No worries, happens to me sometimes." I say.

"Ahh, just let me put them away now so I don't lose track of time and not take you to the airport." He says.

"Well, not sure on the traffic, but I should probably go soon." I look at the time.

Len puts my stuff in his car and we head to the airport. We talk about the awards and the weekend. He lets me know that he will be back in Connecticut in a few days. Soon enough we arrive at the airport. He drops me in the loading area and the trip is over.

I arrive back at Bradley and Rob and Scott are waiting for me to pick me up.
"How was your trip?" Scott asks.
"Highs and lows, same as always. Ohh, here is a pic." I pullout my phone and show him.
"You know, any time you need a guest, I can be available for you." He laughs.

Rob lets me know that the cops had to come to the bar for a fight, but Ty actually handled the situation professionally. He gives me the whole story beginning to end.
"Ehh, it happens." I say.

Rob and Scott drop me off at home and I begin doing the laundry from the trip and getting things ready for Monday morning. I eventually settle on the couch with a beer and send Lisa a pic of Len and I. 'good job on picking out the dress'

We text back and forth a few times, her asking about the night. Me telling her. Eventually I head to bed.

Chapter 37

Monday morning and things are back to normal again. The next few days are mundane, just the way that I like it. Tony is in the shop more as he is weaning himself off being at home so much. Mel and the baby are doing great. Len arrives back on Thursday and we begin to have lunch most days together.

Sunday afternoon, Rob and Scott are over to watch tv and my phone buzzes. I see that Nick is calling me.
"Hello, Nick, what's up?" I ask.

"Hey, I'm gonna be in New York City for something on Wednesday, wondering if you'll be free for dinner?" he asks.
"In the city?" I ask.

"No, I have a meeting at 11, I could drive out after." He offers.

"Uhhh, I guess. Send me a text with the details?" I ask.
"Sure. I'll talk to you then." He ends the call.
"Who was that?" Rob asks without taking his eyes off the tv.

"Nick is coming in and wants to have dinner." I say.

"Are you dating Nick Stone and Len Feldman?" Scott turns and asks.

"No!" I say. "Nick and I are just friends and Len and I are dating." I say.

"You have only known the social version of Rain, you realize that before you met her, it wasn't Rain, it was a continuous drought!" Rob laughs out loud.

"Rob! How dare you!" I say, jokingly. "Whatever, he is kinda right." I head out into the kitchen and put the leftover takeout away.

I get a text with a reminder from Nick that we will have dinner on Wednesday and the beginning of the week is same as always. Wednesday comes along and I start in the office till noon and then head to Tony's. I get all his work done and head home to get ready. Nick is waiting in the driveway in a rental car and he gets out as I pull into the garage.

"You know I find it absolutely absurd that you are in a rental car and you have a car in my garage as well." I point out.

"Well, I rented it in New York so it's not like you were coming to pick me up for dinner." He responds.

"You make reservations anywhere or are we flying by the seat of our pants tonight?" I ask.

"You're in a playful mood." He smiles at me.

"It's been so calm the last few weeks, drama free equals stress free." I smile back at him.

"I did not make any, where do you want to go? Anywhere you want." He says.

"How about a steakhouse? I could really go for a steak." I say.

"By choice? Are you sure you are feeling ok?" he puts his hand up to my forehead.

"Well, steak and salad." I sigh.

"That's better." He hugs me and we get into the Mercedes and head to the steakhouse.
We order and chat about life. I show him more pics of Don and Bella. I bring him up to date on Scott and Rob, the bar. Our food arrives and we are eating and enjoying ourselves.

"So, my parent's 50th wedding anniversary is coming up and I wanted to know if you want to go?" He asks.
"Uhh, your parents?" I ask.
"Yeah, go with me to the party." He says, looking straight at me.

"Why me?" I ask.
"Well, they both like you, they'd love to see you." He says.
"Do they think we are together?" I feel a bit anxious anticipating his answer.

"Well, no, but I'm not gonna lie, they want to see us together." He says.
"Nick, then I can't go, Jesus." I reply.

"Come on, Lisa and Tony will be there, you know Tony's parents and mine are close. Please? For me?" he asks.

"It's weird. Is that why you took me to dinner?" I ask.

"No, I was in New York, but I did want to ask you in person." He says.

"Cause you know you'll wear me down?" I ask.

"Kinda." He starts to smile. "Please? I will even bring you home after it's over, you don't even have to stay the night." He takes my hand from across the table. "Rain?"

"When is it?" I ask.
"Two Sundays from now, you won't even have to miss being at the bar. No missed work." He sounds happy. "I can even get a car service to pick you up and bring you."

"Fine, just send me the details." I sigh.
"I owe you one!" He kisses my hand.
We finish dinner and head back to my house. "You aren't driving back to New York tonight, are you?" I ask as I realize its 9pm when we arrive.

"You know, I really didn't think this through. I sorta did this without Doug." He says.
"Just stay in your room, it's fine." I say and head to the kitchen and make the coffee pot for the morning.

"I have my own room, I feel special!" he is trying to turn up the charm.

"You seem to have used it the most, so I guess it's yours." I smile at him. "I have to get up in the morning so I am heading to bed."

Chapter 38

I wake up and hop in the shower and begin to get ready to head downstairs and realize that Nick is already down there cooking breakfast.

"Coffee?" he hands me a cup when I walk in the kitchen.

"I do miss this sometimes." I say to him.

"What? Boyfriend doesn't make you breakfast?" He smirks.

"I actually don't really eat breakfast, and stop it." I say with a seriousness to my voice to let him know we are not talking about Len. "I will be in my office." I say and leave the kitchen.

I begin my work and wrap up pretty early and head back out to the living room and find Nick watching TV.

"Don't you have somewhere to be?" I sound more annoyed than I am and it causes him to abruptly stand up.

"Huh? I'm sorry, I can go." He says.

"No, sorry, I just wasn't sure you would even be here when I was done working. I actually have to head to Tony's is all." I try to sound a bit nicer.

"You can stay if you want, but I have to go. Don't forget to text me the details." I get my purse and head to the door, I stop and give him a quick hug on my way out and head to Tony's shop.

Len calls and says he has to go to California for the weekend and he will see me when he gets back. Looks like it will be a quiet weekend. I head from Tony's to the bar and then home. The following week and half go by without incident and things are really falling into a rhythm. I get a text from Nick that the car service will pick me up on Sunday at 9am to make the ride out. Well, at least I can sleep on the ride out there. I see Rob at the bar on Saturday night and let him know that I have to go to Jersey on Sunday. Scott looks disappointed and I offer to let them come over in my absence. I honestly have no idea if they will or not.

Sunday morning comes around and I opt for a sheath dress with a suitcoat to go over it and a pair of white heels. The car is here promptly at 9 and I ask if we can stop for a coffee before getting on the highway.

The ride is long and boring, I think I doze off a few times and feel awful when I finally arrive at the hotel. I send Nick a text that I'm there and he comes right down.

"How was the ride?" He asks and I just shrug my shoulders. "Dull, not a fan of riding by myself for that long all alone." I reply, stretching when I get out.

"Tony and Lisa will be down in a few minutes, we'll all ride over together." He replies.
A feeling of awkwardness comes over me as the two of us just stand in the parking lot together. Neither of us speaking to each other and waiting on Lisa and Tony. It is probably 5 minutes until they come down to the car, but feels like an hour.

"Hey, long time no see." Tony comes up and gives me a hug. "How ya been?"

"Good, long car ride." I say as I stretch my back out again.

"Well, just another half hour." Lisa joins in. "Right, Nick?"

"Yeah, about that. You all ready?" He asks and heads into the car.

I get in after him and Lisa and Tony follow.

"So, your parents are going to be there, too?" I ask, to break up the silence in the car.
"Yeah, they live a few streets away from Nick's. Haven't seen them since the wedding." He adds and back to silence. Why am I doing this I think to myself? To amuse his parents? We ride the rest of the way with idle chatter from Nick and Tony about the band and eventually the car pulls into a parking lot of a banquet hall. We head in and Nick's parents are there greeting people.
"Rain, you made it!" His father hugs me.
"Yeah, happy anniversary. 50 years is special. A long time." I say.
His mother kisses me and holds me at arm's length. "We should see more of you." I am becoming more uncomfortable with each passing moment and look to Nick who is engaged with other people around his parents' age. Tony and Lisa are speaking with his parents. We speak for a few more minutes and eventually have a seat at a table and more idle chatter. Tony's parents make their way over to the table.
"Rain, I am so sorry about your father. We didn't find out till after we got back home. Was wondering why you just disappeared from the wedding like that." His mother says.

"Oh, I am sorry I had to leave like that, but thank you for the kind words." I reply back.

"You've been through so much, but at least you're still keeping Nick in line." Tony's mother says and her statement confuses me. I need to talk to Nick.
"Nick? Want to join me outside for a cigarette?" I ask him.
"Uhh, sure." He says and we head outside.
"Whats the deal here?" I ask, getting right to the point, while I get a cigarette out of my purse.
"What do you mean?" He asks.
"Why am I here?" I ask him and he just looks at me. "I know you said your parents are fond of me, but come on, Nick. Tony's parents mention me still 'keeping you in line' your parents say they need to see me more. What gives?" I ask, looking right at him.

"Look, they know we aren't 'officially' back together, like engaged like we were, but maybe they think we are seeing each other?" He says and I wait for him to continue. "Look, I didn't lie to them, I just kinda stay away from discussing it with them." He says.

"Nick! And you brought me here, without even telling me?" I ask.
"Would you have come?" He asks.
"No!" I exclaim and realize. "That's fucked up. Jesus Christ, you're seeing someone, what's her name…Tandy!"

"I'm not seeing her, she's just…."

"You're an ass." I reply. "And.....I got to take a six hour fucking car ride by myself, which I get to repeat again tonight." I am mad.

"You want me to ride back with you?" He asks, as if that was going to make it better.

"Yeah, and you can drive the car back and this can be done!" I spit back.

He is really taken back by my statement. "Rain? Are you serious? Look, I'm sorry about all this, I think in my head I thought it would be different." He sounds sad.

"I can go back by myself, its fine." I say. "Let's go in and eat."

We head in and I see him head to Lisa and is talking with her. She then heads over to me.
"You really pissed at him?" she asks.
"How would you feel?" I ask her back.
"I wouldn't have put up with half the shit you have from him, but you already know that." She says matter of factly.

"He really doesn't know any better." She says, putting her hand on my shoulder.
"Big dumb animal, I know." And crack a small smile.

"Come on, let's get you a drink." She says.
We eat and then there are some speeches from friends and one heartfelt one from Nick. Tony's parents also speak. Dancing begins afterward. After watching Nicks parents have a dance to themselves, slowly other couples join the dance floor. I remain in my seat and play with my

phone, going through emails, checking on a few accounts I can access from the phone. I send Rob a text and ask if he went to my house.

"May I have this dance?" I hear Tony from behind me.

"Me? Shouldn't you be dancing with Lisa?" I smile.

"I think she would be ok with just one between us." He takes me out onto the dance floor.
"Well, at least someone asked me to dance." I say while we are dancing.
"Nick's scared of you right now." He replies.

"Good." I say.
"Rain, what's he supposed to do?" He asks me.
"Well, don't invite me to come see him and have his girlfriend with him. Don't lead his family to think we are together...especially when we are both seeing other people. Don't drag me 4 states away to ignore me....want me to continue?" I am flustered.
"No, I'm not saying I disagree with you, I'm saying I know Nick. And he's not doing it on purpose, is all."

"I know." I sigh. "But, he's done a lot of things he might not have meant to do, but it doesn't change the outcome for me." I finish. I see his expression change and he knows I'm right.
"Rain, all I can say, is he would never do anything to upset you, hurt you or anything like that. Just be careful with his feelings." He sighs as the song ends and he escorts me back to the table.

I have a drink at the table by myself and Nick comes to sit down. "Do I even get one dance?" I ask him.
"You want me to dance with you? Of course, come here." He takes my arm as I get up. We head out to the dance floor.

"Nick, I'm sorry." I say as we begin dancing.
"Shhh." He pulls me closer and I lay my head on his chest.
"I really didn't mean for it to turn out this way." He says.

"I know." I whisper.

"No, you don't. I never wanted 'us' to turn out this way, friends, like this." He says. "I just don't know what to do. I feel like I can't fix this."

"I know." I whisper again. "Sometimes I wish we just went back in time and met all over again, clean slate." I say. We dance the rest of the song in silence and head back to the table.
"Thank you for the dance." I say. I notice the crowd is starting to disperse.

"How long you want to stay for?" He asks me.
"Whenever, it's your parent's party." I say without emotion.

"Well, I'm ready, I'm sure Tony and Lisa are dying to get out of here. Let me go find them." He says and gets up.

We say our goodbyes and head out. I check my phone and no missed calls or texts, its 8:30pm.

"You want me to ride back with you?" Nick asks as the car heads to the hotel.

"Nah, then you'll just be stuck at my house. Its fine." I say.

"I will if you don't want to ride alone." He says again.

"No, its fine, I will probably fall asleep anyways." I sigh.

"Are you sure?" He asks again.

"She said she can take a car ride by herself." Tony replies from the other side of the car, sounding annoyed.

Nick gives Tony a dirty look. "Fine, but if you change your mind." He says to me.

We pull into the hotel and Tony and Lisa exit the car and head in. Nick is standing outside the car with me and pulls me close to him.

"I'm really glad you came out today." He says quietly.

"Its fine, Nick. It was good to see you all." I say.

"You aren't still mad at me?" He asks as he puts his hands on my shoulders.

"No, its fine. I'm good." I reply back as his hands slide down my sides and encompass my waist. "I should probably go, it's gonna be a long ride home." I reply.

"OK." He says and kisses the top of my head. He releases me and heads into the hotel as I get into the car to begin the ride home. I fall asleep before we are out of New Jersey. I awake upon arriving home. Straight to bed for me.

Chapter 39

I get up Monday morning late and head straight to Tony's shop, grabbing a coffee on the way.

The next week is busy. Halloween is coming up and the bar is having a huge costume party. I have lunch with Len a few times and dinner once. Friday afternoon my phone rings and its Nick.

"Whats up?" I ask.

"Next weekend? I was wondering if you wanted to come out? We've been working on some new songs and was gonna try them out at the club. Wanted to see if you wanted to come hear them?" He asks.

"I don't know, when is it?" I look at my calendar.

"Friday Night?" He replies with hopefulness in his voice.

"I'll see." I reply.

"I'll see means no. Say yes." He says.

"Nick, I really don't want to fly out there to go to a club, I have one out here to go to that I don't enjoy that much." I laugh.

"Rain, it's important to me." He is trying to sound convincing, but it's coming off as irritating and whiny.

"I said I would see. I'm not making any commitments I'm not gonna keep." I try to put some authority in my voice.

"Fine, but please? Just text me and I will take care of air and a place to stay and everything."

"Is that all you called for?" I try to change the subject.

"Yeah, kinda." He says.

"OK, well, I actually have to go. I will text you if I can make it." I say and hang up.

I get back to work and Rob and Scott appear at the door to the office at the bar.

"So what do you want to do for your birthday?" He asks.
"Uhh, it's November 5th. We aren't in November yet." I say, looking at the calendar.
"I know, but you made mine spectacular so I have to repay." He sits down. "

"Shit, So do I, I never would have met him if you didn't plan the party that got him the gift that led him to that club." Scott says. He is really odd sometimes.

"Uhh, ok?!" I reply and burst out laughing.

"I want a day of peace, where there are no cell phone, no bar, no calls. That would be bliss." I say leaning back in my chair.
"You wouldn't know what to do with yourself." Rob says in an accusatory voice.
"Try me!" I say.

"But seriously, what do you want to do?" He asks.
"Get my family together, you two and dinner? That would be fine." I say, being serious.

"I think I have enough connections to pull that off." He gives a maniacal laugh.

"I have to get back to work, you guys hanging around tonight?" I ask.

"Yeah, we will be out there." Rob replies.

"You are so lucky she is your best friend, we never have to pay for date night." Scott says.

"Huh?" I ask.

"It's like the coolest thing, to have a club, This Club, to go to and never get charged." He says, looking at me. "Honey, you are, the bartenders keep track...." He has this shocked expression. "It comes due if you ever break his heart." I laugh out loud and his look of fear turns to a smile.
"Never." He says and they head out of the office.

I take care of all the paperwork and eventually head out to the bar. Having a few drinks and Len comes in and finds me.
"Shocking seeing you here on a Friday night, what do I owe this pleasure?" I kiss him.

"Nothing much, just came to check out the talent." He sits at the bar next to me.
"Seriously? Want a table closer?" I ask.

"No, I just got a call from the network is all." He says.
"Ohh, good news? Bad News?" I ask.

"The season premiere is next weekend. They want me to be in Vegas for some viewing party, fans have entered contests to go. Wanted to see if you wanted to go with me?" he says.

"Vegas? Next weekend?" I ask.

"The party is Sunday, cast in costume, open buffet, 5 star deal all weekend." He says.

"I have to check my calendar." I say.

"Well, you can if you want. Kinda last minute." He says.
"Do you need an answer right now? I guess I could." I say.

"We can figure it out." He replies.

We watch the band and a bit before it's over he heads out. I see Scott and Rob block him and talk to him, following him outside, probably about whatever 'surprise' party they try to throw me. I close down the bar and head home.

Saturday morning and I head over to my mothers to help her clean out some stuff for winter. Ty and Tony are there as well. We help get the house ready for winter. Halloween is Wednesday. I promise Bella that I will be there to go trick or treating with her. Mostly in case Mel has to leave early with the baby. She is almost 5 and on a mission for candy. She loves her little brother, but has to have a contingency plan in case he cramps her style. She is adorable.
We get everything done and have pizza for dinner before I have to head for the bar.

I work the next few days and then head out trick or treating with Mel and Tony and the kids. Bella is having a blast and Lisa starts texting me.
'nick said he invited you, heavensent is playing Friday night you coming?'

'probably not, sorry'

'it's a big deal, you know, they are releasing songs off the new album you should really come'

'it never ends well at the storm, lol'

'come on for me?'

'I'll see'

'please? Let me know'

Eventually, I make it home from trick or treating. Mel and Tony manage to keep Don from fussing too much, thankfully, its warm out. If it was cold, I would probably have ended up with Bella on my own.
I head to the office Thursday and there is an email from Len's assistant about Vegas. I call Len.

"Hey, beautiful. Everything ok?" he asks.
"I just got an email from your assistant." I say. "I realize that I never got back to you about Vegas. I guess I can go. Do I respond to her or is letting you know ok?" I ask.

"I can take care of it. When do you want to fly out?" He asks.
"Let me check the calendar." I look and see the event at the storm on Friday night. "Actually, there is something else I was invited to, an album release for 'heavensent' on Friday. Maybe I could fly there for Friday night and fly to Vegas Saturday?" I am thinking out loud.
"That could work, I will be in L.A. on Saturday to fly out that afternoon. We could go together." He suggests.
"Ok, I will meet you in L.A?" I say.

"Let the network take care of it. You want to be in LA for Friday night? I will have my assistant send you the details. Do you have a place to stay? Stay here!" he suggests.
"That will be perfect." I say, thinking I will head to the storm and head straight to his house then fly to Vegas and then head home.

I call Rob to see if he can handle the bar for the weekend. He mentions that he is there more than anywhere else and maybe he should just take over the manager position. I mention that we can discuss it later.

I spend the rest of Thursday wrapping up details to head out Friday. It is really not the best idea ever to own a bar and enjoy going out on the weekends, I think to myself. How did my life become so complicated? I laugh to myself. I complete all the things I need to get done and head to bed.
I get up Friday night and pack. I head to my office and quickly get some work done and head to Tony's shop by 10am to wrap up everything there.
"Why you here so early?" Tony comes into the office.
"Ehh, hectic weekend. I'm seeing Nick release his album Friday night and heading to Vegas to see Len for the season opener of his show. Sounds exciting, but I'm honestly looking forward to sleeping in my own bed when I get home." I say. When you say it out loud, it sounds ridiculous?

"Anything else?! It sounds pretty boring to me." He says with sarcasm.

"You need anything special or specific from me? I gotta go." I say.

"Nah, take some pics. Sounds like you are gonna have a good time." He says and heads out of the office.
I wrap up all his stuff and head home to pack. My flight leaves at 6 pm and I should get to the bar at the perfect time. I just need to take my carry on with me. I figure I can leave it in Lisa's office while I'm there, realizing that I never actually texted them that I was coming. Ehh, it will be a surprise. They will love it.
I decide to wear some spandex jeans and a white lace up form fitting top with pirate type sleeves. I put on some thigh high leather boots with nice platform heels and head out. Scott is driving me to the airport since Rob is still at work.

I board my flight, first class. In my head, I have to remember to thanks Len for the nice seat when I get there.
I land at LAX and call a cab to the club. I arrive and it's pretty crowded for a Friday night. Probably because 'Heavensent' is headlining. I have a problem at the door with my carry-on. I don't recognize any of the security people. I text Lisa and she is at the door in a minute or less.

"It's fine." She tells the security guard. "Holy shit! What are you doing here!" she is in shock.
"Well, long story. But I'm here till tomorrow and then flying to Vegas. I meant to text you but got caught up in stuff." I say as she hugs me. She tells security to take my luggage to her office and we head in.

"Nick is gonna flip. You know this is the first time anyone is gonna hear the new music, right?" She says with excitement in her voice. "Shit, I haven't even heard it yet."

"He kinda made it seem important, that's why I'm here." I say.

"You do always come thru for him." She hugs me again. "Come on, Doug and Jen are here. Jen is not working tonight either." She laughs. She brings me to the table at the front of the stage and sits me down. Doug and Jen are shocked that I am there and I get thugs from both of them.

"They aren't going on for another hour or so, come on. I will tell him you are here!" Lisa seem excited.
"Actually, let him see me here when he comes out." I say.
"That's evil, I love it!" She exclaims. "I won't say a word." She says. "But I have a million things to do, so I promise I will be back." She adjusts her headset and takes off.

"Want a drink or something? I can get it for you!" Jen asks.
"Relax, it's your night off." I reply. "I'm sure there will be someone by shortly." She seems to always want to make everyone happy at a table.

"So why you out here?" Doug asks.
"I'm flying to Vegas for the premiere of 'Sentinnial'" I say.

"Oh, with Len?" Doug asks. "You happy?" He asks.
"Yes, for the first time in a long time." I say, looking from him to her. "It's really a great feeling."

"Then more power to ya, to happy relationships." He puts up his bottle of beer and realizes that I still don't have a drink.

"Jesus, service sucks in here, let me go get you something." Jen laughs. "Rum and coke? I will just bring back a 2 liter and a bottle." She exits shaking her head. She returns with 5 rum and cokes on a platter. "There!" she sits down with a sigh.

"Jesus! Thank you!" I am laughing at the platter. "To us." I lift up a glass and we all clink glasses and drink.

We catch up over the last few months and the bar and the stage goes dark. The band takes the stage and Lisa slips into a chair next to me. "I am so antsy, I can't wait to hear it. I promise I didn't say anything" She hugs me from the side.

The stage lights up and the place erupts into applause. Lights shine on each of the 4 members of the band and Nick has still not taken notice of me. Tony, however, looks down at Lisa and notices me sitting next to her. In the first song, he must have said something to Nick because it seems as if he pauses in the middle of the song as we make eye contact. He seems like a different person, energized almost, after he sees me and I'm glad that I came.

They play a few more songs and take a break, exiting off the stage. Someone comes out and announces a 15 minute intermission. Tony and Nick make their way out to our table.

"Oh, my god! You're here." Nick exclaims. Tony heads straight for Lisa and they begin making out.

"Only till tomorrow, but it sounded important to you so, here I am." I say as he hugs me. He smells of alcohol, but otherwise only seems tipsy.

"Thank you!" he says and sits down at the table. "I think I have time for a quick beer and then need to head back up there."

Fans try to get thru to the table. People are shouting for Nick and he just drinks his beer and ignores them, sitting next to me. He has one arm around me the entire time. He finishes his beer and kisses me on the top of my head as he gets up. "Hope you like the last song, it's for you." He says and he heads back stage.

"What's that all about?" I look over at Lisa.
"Not a clue, I told you, I haven't heard any of this. It's brand new to me, too." She says, tapping the seat next to her for me to move over. The band takes the stage again and begins to play about 3 more songs. A woman sits down at our table. She is tall and thin, hair and makeup like she is trying out for a video. Clothes to match.
"Can I help you?" Lisa says.
"Ohh, I'm with the band." The woman replies.

"Really! And you are?" I hear Lisa go on the defense.

"Tiffany." She replies, matter of factly.
"Never heard of you." Lisa throws back her beer when she finished speaking.
"And who are you?" Tiffany replies.
"Tony's fucking wife." I instinctively put my hand on her

arm. I don't know if Lisa has ever been in a fight, but I think this is what it would feel like.

"Ohh, don't worry, sweetie, I'm here with Nick." She smiles at the end.

I feel like I've just been kicked in the stomach. "What did you say?" I ask.
"I'm here with Nick." She smiles at me.

I look up at the stage and Nick is apparently blissfully unaware of his special guest's arrival. He is singing away. I lean over to Lisa, "I need a drink....now." I say.
"You and me both, what the fuck!" she signals for a waiter who comes right over. "Shots, line them up right here." She says as she motions between the two of us. Doug and Jen are still at the table and Jen engages in a more polite conversation with her.
"Hi, Im Jen. So you are with Nick?" She introduces herself.

"Yeah, I was with him the last couple of nights. He mentioned he was playing tonight and I wasn't gonna miss my man playing." She replies and Jen carefully makes eye contact with me to make sure I am paying attention.
"Oh, he didn't mention you were coming. Doug and I take care of vip stuff for these things." She is slick. I give her credit.
"Yeah, it's kinda a new relationship, but I wouldn't miss it." I can tell she is becoming more comfortable talking to Jen.
"Besides, I hear he calls his girlfriend up on stage and sings to her, so I wanted to be here." She finishes.
I grab a shot and suck it down. "I cannot actually believe I am hearing this shit." I say to Lisa.

"I'm telling her to leave, I'm gonna throw her out of here."
Lisa begins to stand up.
"No, I want to see how this plays out. I need to see." I
plead with her and pull on her arm to stay seated.

"Fine." She takes a shot. The band has stopped playing.
Nick walks up and the lights go dim. "This next song, well,
it's kind of my opus. It's been a long time coming and, well,
you know who you are." He looks down at the table.
Tiffany is beaming, thinking she is going up on stage. I take
another shot and feel this one in my core. I am becoming a
bit too tingly. The look on his face when he sees her is
priceless. He looks from her to me and I am disgusted. I
just shake my head at him and take another shot and sit
down. He is thrown off his game and Tony has to come
over and get him back on track.
"I think he was talking about you." Lisa leans over.
"I think I don't fucking care." I say and take another shot.
"Slow down, sweetie." She says and I look from Tiffany to
her. "Or not."

The song starts off acoustic and slow with some electric
bass in the background. The room is spinning but I can
make out the chours. We're gonna make it, Rain.

"Do you hear this?" Lisa is excited.
"Yes, I hear it, are you fucking kidding me?" I am pissed.

"Rain, come on. This is amazing." She is talking in my ear.
For a split second, I feel good and look back to the stage
and see Tiffany swaying back and forth with her hands
clasped like she is praying to him. I look to Jen and she
comes over.

"She is a skank, I don't know what to say." She shrugs her shoulders.

"Can you go get a few more shots for the table?" I ask her, seeing the empty glasses on the table.
The song ends and the place erupts into applause and the band heads backstage.

"Jen, stay here with us! I will get someone to get them." Lisa says.
"OK." Jen is shocked.

"Sit on the other side of Rain and don't get up." She orders her.

Tony and Nick make their way to the table. Tony kisses Lisa and she whispers something in his ear and he looks to Nick and me.
Nick heads over to me and asks to talk. "I don't think that's a good idea." I say as another tray of shots is delivered.

Tony takes the tray and passes one out to everyone at the table. "To the album." He lifts a glass and we all follow suit. I can handle this.
Tiffany speaks up. "And to Nick and I."
"That's it, I'm done." I say, standing up.
"Rain, wait!" Nick tries to block me.
"Oh, sorry, to you and Tiffany." I hold up my glass, then suck the shot down and slam the glass on the table. "Now I can go." I say and attempt to push him out of my way. I am a bit more wobbly than I thought.
"Tiffany, fucking leave, now!" Nick turns to her and

commands.

"But Nick?" she whines.

I slip away from the table and head out of the vip area and Lisa and Jen follow me. I hear Nick behind me. We stop in an open space near a hallway.

"Rain, I'm sorry. I didn't tell her to come, I wanted you here. Please wait. The song? What did you think?" He asks and I stop and turn to him.

"The song." My head is spinning, I only heard the chorus. We're gonna make it, Rain.

I feel my anxiety coupled with my buzz taking over. "It's fine, I just need to go." I say.

"Rain, wait, I want to talk to you." He says as his friend Tiffany comes up next to him and half wraps her leg around him and puts her arms around his neck.

"Come on, Nick, lets get out of here. We can go back to your place and make it rain again." She says.

"What the fuck did you just say!?" I shout as Nick and everyone else stands there in shock.

"I said that we could go back to his place and make it rain again!" This bitch literally said it again. I can feel my blood begin to boil.

"Fuck you and fuck even coming here." I say as Jen and Lisa move a bit closer to me.

"Get the fuck off me, leave!" Nick pushes Tiffany aside.

"What? Nick? You wrote it for me! Why are you so upset?" She is fawning at him.

"Are you that naive? This is Rain! You stupid bitch." Jen yells at her.

Everyone seems a bit shocked at Jen and I use this as my opportunity to quickly turn and begin to exit through the crowd of people. "Rain, stop!" I hear Nick shout. I hear Lisa yelling at him and Tiffany. "Security! Stop her!" I hear Nick yell a bit louder and I pick up the pace.
I feel a hand grab my hair and my head yanks back a bit. Instinctively, I make a fist and turn around swinging. The security guard is a bit taller than I anticipate and my balance is off and I connect with his throat. He immediately begins coughing and another security guard tackles me. I hit the cement floor of the club with a thud and my head smacks the floor. I have a flash of white and immediately have a throbbing from the back of my head.
"I got her!" I hear the security guard yell out.
"Get off me!" I begin kicking as Lisa is at my side yelling at him.
"What the fuck is wrong with you, get off her!" she is trying to help me up and I feel dizzy. I lift my head as Nick, Jen, Doug and Tony also make it to where I am on the floor.
Lisa helps me sit up and I put my hand to the back of my head and it feels warm and sticky. "Fucking gross." I say.

"Call 911, we need an ambulance." I hear Lisa shriek.
Nick leans down to help me up. "Don't fucking touch me." I spit at him.

"Rain, I'm sorry." He says.
"Here, let me help you." Jen shoves her way in. Tony and Doug are clearing people away from me.

Lisa comes back with some bar towels and ice and starts placing them at the back of my head. "Ambulance is on the way, just stay here. Hold this." She puts my hand on the towel with the ice.

"Rain, I'm sorry. I didn't mean for this...." Nick starts again, kneeling next to me.
"You're always sorry and I'm always fucked. I'm sick of this shit, I'm done." I say to him.
The police come in and clear the way for the emt people and start taking statements. I manage to get myself on to the stretcher and Nick stops at my side.

"Rain...." He tries to hold my hand.
"It's fine....Hey, at least I get to use my real name this time!" I snap at him and within moments everyone surrounding me understands. I am placed in the ambulance and everyone seems to be trying to go in it with me. The emt person stops and tells them that only one person is getting in. I close my eyes on the stretcher and the guy in there with me begins to explain that I'm not going to sleep.

"I just want to rest my eyes." I say.

"Have you had anything to drink tonight?" He asks with his clipboard.
"Yup, lots." I say. "Am I gonna make it?"
"Rain? Is that your name?" He asks and I start laughing. Laughing uncontrollably.
"Am I gonna make it Rain?" I say it out loud and begin to laugh even more. "Ohh, this is so fucked up." I say.

"Stop." I hear Nicks voice.

"Nick? Is that you?" I ask and he slides over to see me. My head is strapped to a board so I cannot turn.
"Yeah, I'm right here." He takes my hand.

"Sir, can you stop this thing?" I ask the guy on the other side of me.
"Why?" He asks.

"This guy here left his girlfriend back at the club." I begin to laugh again.
"Rain, stop." Nick says again.
"You don't get to tell me to stop, you don't get to speak to me. You did this." I say and close my eyes again.

"Nope, open those eyes back up, miss. No sleeping." The guy pokes me a bit.

We arrive at the hospital and Lisa and Tony are already there waiting. Lisa places my purse at my side and asks how I am.
"Why did he have to ride with me?" I look at her and she has no response.

"Want me to call anyone?" She asks me.

The nurses start cleaning the wound as I sit on a table.
"This is only gonna need 5 or 6 staples. You have such long hair, no one will ever know." She says, trying to be helpful.
"You will be outta here in 45 minutes or so." She smiles at me.

"Call Len, have him come get me? My phone is in my purse." I say and see Lisa and Tony look to Nick and then to each other. Nick looks hurt.

"I think I can do that out in the hallway. You guys ok in here?" She looks to Tony.
"Go, we're fine." Tony replies.
"The two security guards are getting fired tomorrow." Tony looks at me. "You got quite a right hook!" He is trying to make me smile. "And to aim for the throat? That's pretty sweet." I begin to smile. "Where did you learn to fight? Maybe Lisa should have you at security." He laughs.
"Two older brothers, I can take care of myself." I pause and look at Nick. "Most of the time." I finish. I see Nick sigh again as he hears my words.
"I love the new songs, the album sounds great." I say to Tony.
"You really do like it?" Nick joins in and I continue to ignore him.
"Did you write any of the lyrics?" I ask Tony seeing that the conversation is now making him uncomfortable.

"Nah, maybe one or two, but Nick always seems to do that just fine." He says, trying to put Nick in a better light.
"He's on his way." Lisa comes in and announces saying nothing more.

"Can I get a water or something? My stomach is upset." I ask.
"Let me go find a nurse or something." Lisa seems to jump at the chance to get out of the curtained room.
"Maybe I can help." Tony joins in and the both exit.
"Rain." Nick lifts his head and looks at me.

"Don't say anything." I say to him.

"None of this was supposed to happen like this." He says.

"Ya know, it's never supposed to happen like this, but it seems with you? It always does." I say flatly.

"What do you want me to do?" He asks.

"Nothing." I say back.

Len enters the room. "Rain! Are you ok? What happened?" He is concerned.

"Ehh, I got tackled." I say, hearing how ridiculous it sounds.

"I said I was sorry." Nick offers again.

"You did this to her?" Len asks in an accusatory tone.

"It wasn't supposed to happen like this, I yelled for security to stop her and they took it too far...." Nick replies.

"What the fuck, Man" Len is getting louder. "You could have killed her!" he is almost yelling.

I have Nick on one side of the bed and Len on the other. I really don't need any yelling.

"He didn't actually do it, he just set off a chain of events that led to it." I say calmly.

"Miss Brady?" The er doctor steps in. "Len Feldman? Nick Stone? Well, aren't you a lucky little lady. How does one end up with these two accompanying them to get their head stapled back shut?" He thinks he is funny and the three of us are staring at him. "Well, ok. Let's get this taken care of and on your way." He says and has me sit up to look.

"Rain, they don't want you to.....oh, the doctor is here already...and so is Len." Lisa says as she enters the room. "Well, if Len is here, we can take off. You all set?" She asks.

"Yeah, I guess." I say as the doctor is cleaning the wound.

"Call me tomorrow and let me know how you are? Nick, we can bring you home, let's go." She says.

Nick stands up and hesitates while looking at me as if he is going to say something and Tony tugs at his sleeve to leave with them.

About 15 minutes later I am all better, 6 staples down the back of my head. Great! The doctor writes me a script for some painkillers as he explains that I will probably have a massive headache for a few days. He goes over care instructions and asks if anything else is bothering me and we are out of there.

Len leads me to his car and we just sit.

"Fun night?" He asks me.

"Oh, my god. This trip was a bad idea. I just want to be home." I say.

"Well, Vegas tomorrow, it's not home, but it certainly ain't here." He replies. "I just have to swing by the house and get my bag. We have enough time to stop for some breakfast and then head to the airport."

We drive and get his stuff and go out to breakfast at some diner. We head to the airport. "Where is your bag?" He asks me. Oh, shit.

"Fuck, it's probably still in Lisa's office." I reply. "This is a sign, I really should just head home." I say, frustrated with just one more complication.

"Really? You really want to go home?" He asks.

"Len, I'm tired, I have a headache, no clothes. I'm gonna feel worse once I go to sleep and wake back up. It's probably best." I sigh.

"I have to go whether you go with me or not." He says.

"I know. I'll probably feel better when you get back to the east coast." I say, trying to sound hopeful.

"Well, let me take care of the tickets." He heads to the counter and is there for about 20 minutes and returns.

"Your flight leaves in an hour, mine in 20 minutes. It's direct to Bradley." He says.

We spend the next ten minutes with me trying to explain the events that led up to the incident while leaving out enough details about Nick and myself. He eventually says goodbye and heads for boarding.

I text Rob to see if he can pick me up from the airport. No response. I text again and get a separate text from Scott. Apparently, Rob is sick as a dog, but he says he will get me. I send him the details for the flight and head over to wait.

The flight back is uneventful. I ask the stewardess to wake me up if I fall asleep form more than 30 minutes. Dr's orders, I tell her. She is ok with it and brings me a cup of coffee. I land at Bradley and its 11am east coast time. Scott is waiting to get me.

"Where's your bag?" He asks.

"In a club in LA. Long story." I say.

"Is that paint all over your shirt?" He asks.

"No, blood." I say realizing how tired I sound.

"From where?" He is walking around me inspecting me

now.

"This!" I part my hair to reveal the staples in my head.

"Holy shit! That looks disgusting." He replies.

"Thanks, it's the look I was going for." I say.

"Rain, what happened?" He says as we reach his car.

The ride back to my house, I go over the story with him.

"I do kinda feel bad for him." Scott says.

"What?!?" I say.

"Rain, he tries so hard with you. He really does. It just never seems to work out for him. I mean, you aren't' wrong the way you feel, I just feel bad for him is all." He says.

We reach my house and he helps me in. "Want me to stay for a bit?" He asks. "Rob is sick anyways, his mom is trying to cure it with pasta and sauce." I laugh as that is exactly what I picture Corinne doing.

"Yeah, its fine. I think I'm just gonna chill on the couch." I say.

"Maybe a shower first? You still have all that blood…." He seems kind of put off by it.

"Ahh, your probably right, be down in a bit." I say and head to take a shower. I put on sweatpants and a tee-shirt and head back down to the couch.

"Want some soup?" He asks. "You have some in the cupboard."

"I am kinda hungry. Whatever you want. We can eat out here on the couch." I say and get a blanket to curl up with. He brings me a bowl of soup and I eat it right away and then doze off.

"The instructions say not to let you sleep for too long, you have to get up!" Scott is poking me.

I sit up for a bit and we watch tv. I dose off again and we repeat the process. "Ehh, I should text Lisa that I'm ok, can you find my phone?" I ask and he wanders around my house and returns with it.
Texts from Nick. 'im sorry' 'call me'

I send Lisa a quick text. 'im fine, head hurts, happy trails' and I get a text back quickly. 'glad your fine, fired security' I show it to Scott since I told him the whole story.

"So you ready for tomorrow?" he asks.
"Tomorrow? What's tomorrow?" I ask back.
"You're birthday! You actually forgot it's your own birthday? You really did get hit in the head." He laughs.

"Uhhh, maybe?" I say, counting days in my head. "I guess it is." I reply.

Rob calls the house and him and Scott talk for a bit, I hear Scott bring Rob up to speed on my adventures on the west coast. I doze back off while he is talking.

"Wake up!" He is poking me again.
"I am beginning to dislike you more and more." I say with a smile. "What the hell time is it anyways?" I ask.

"11pm. should I stay the night?" He asks. "I can wake you up at 3 and then in the morning." He suggests.
"Fine, can I go back to sleep now?" I ask.
"You might want to take one of those painkillers so you aren't grouchier when you wake up again." He prods at

the coffee table where there is a bottle of water next to my prescription.

I take the pill and fall back asleep. He wakes me up at 3ish and then again at 8am.

"Rain, its morning. You lived!" he is trying to cheer me up. "Hey, uhh." He sounds completely nervous.

"What?" I ask.

"You should look at this." He is holding his phone. "What!" I say as he hands me the phone. I look at the Hollywood news page and there is the headline. 'Len Feldman marries in Vegas'. What the fuck is this!!

"Rain, I'm confused." He says, staring at me blankly. "You think you are? Holy shit." I exclaim. "I read it, seems it was some old girlfriend, there were pictures of them at events from like a year ago." He says.

"Holy Shit! This is a fucking nightmare, I'm still asleep from hitting my head.....maybe I'm actually dead watching this all happen." I begin thinking out loud.

"Rain, calm down." Scott says. "What would be the appropriate reaction? Huh? My boyfriend got married and didn't invite me." I begin to nervously laugh. "I need a drink." I say. "Its 8 in the morning." Scott replies.

"My boyfriend got married last night!" I say it again. "Ehh, fine, what do you want?" He asks me. "Ehh, just coffee, can you bring it in the office? I need to get on the computer." I say and get up. My head begins to throb.

Scott brings in a cup of coffee a few minutes later as I am scrolling through google looking at the two of them. "See this shit?" I let him move in front of the screen.
"Hey, looks like Lisa texted you" He hands me my phone as I get up and let him sit.
'congrats. Please call me' and I text back 'that's not me' and my phone rings 30 seconds later.

"Lisa, I fucking flew home, I have no idea what the hell is happening." I say before even saying hello. We chat for a few minutes and I tell her I need to sort this shit out and I will call her back.

"Wow, this is fucked up, Nick's really gonna feel like shit when he sees this." Scott say absently as he is reading different posts.

I pick up the office phone and dial Nick.
"Wow, now you call me." He answers the phone.
"Nick!" I say and he interrupts me again.
"I get it, it's done. Why are you calling now?" He sounds depressed.

"Jesus Christ, I'm calling you from my house phone. I am not in Vegas, I did not get married." Any thought of sympathy immediately turns to annoyance talking to him on the phone.
"What?" He says.
"Jesus, Nick, I didn't get married. Not sure who the fuck he

did marry, but it was NOT me!" I yell.

"Rain! Are you sure?" Nick asks.

"Are you serious? 'Are you sure?' of course I'm fucking positive I did not get married. I had such a headache I flew home after I left the hospital. I am home, by myself, while my boyfriend is on his honeymoon." I say it and I begin to cry.

"Rain, don't cry, its ok." He says softly.

"Really? It's OK? Who is making that call? Who decides what's ok? This is so fucked up. Look, I just wanted to let you know, you know, that it wasn't me. Look, I gotta go, happy fucking birthday to me." I hang up the phone.

"Well, that sounded like it went well." Scott says.

"Oh my god." I begin to compose myself. "I guess I better call my family before they see it." I begin to call Tony and Ty and my mother. Over the next few hours, my house fills with everyone coming over.

Ty, Tony, Melissa and the baby, Rob, Scott, Bella and my mother are all over. We decide to order some pizzas and wings and I go thru the events of the last few days all over again.

"Rain, you really shouldn't have hit someone." My mother interjects.

"That's what you are taking away from all this?" I am shocked.

Tony pipes in "Jeeze, mom, she thought she was being attacked. Good for her."

The conversation flows, Ty and my mother head home eventually. Bella is bouncing around the house in her princess dress and I decide to talk to her instead of the conversation at hand.

"So you are the princess, which one?" I ask her.

"I'm not a princess, I am the fairy godmother, she gets a magic wand. Better than a princess." I laugh as Bella hits me with her magic wand. "Don't worry, auntie Rain, you will find your prince." She says to me and twirls away.

"And with that, I think it's time we get her home for bed." Mel gets up and starts gathering all the accessories you need to travel with a baby.

Mel and Tony and the children head home and I sit down on the couch with Rob and Scott and have a beer. There is a knock at the door.

"What the hell now?" I do not get up. Scott and Rob look at each other blankly.

"It's ok, I guess I can get the door." Scott heads over and opens it. "It's for you, Rain."

Nick walks in. "Rain." He says with a bouquet of roses in his hand.

"What the hell are you doing here?" I am in shock and do not move towards him.

"I think we should go." Rob says and gets up nudging Scott who is firmly planted in his seat already.

"No, I think you should make popcorn." He says while watching us intently.

"Well?" I look at him.

"Can I come in?" He is still standing at the door.

"Fine." I reply flatly.

"I just didn't want you to be alone." He says.
"I'm not alone." I splay my hands toward Rob and Scott.
"And like 6 and a half people just left." I huff.

"Did you call him? What did he say?" He asks me.
"No. Did I call him? For what? He got married, I'm assuming he's good with it. What am I gonna talk him out of it? Ha, did I call him. Jesus, Nick." I say as I sit back down on the couch.

"I feel like this is my fault." He says as he sits on the couch.
"Nope, a lot of things are your fault, but this one….Len getting married a few short hours after I got out of the hospital and came home….that is not your fault." I say.

"What are you gonna do?" he asks me.
"What am I supposed to do?!? I guess I could send a wedding gift." I laugh out loud. "What do you suggest I do? I don't think I understand the question." I look at him.
"Look, I'm just trying to help." He sounds flustered.

"Trying to help? Are you kidding me? Help how? By begging me to come to the release, making me feel bad enough to drop what I am doing and to only to have you flaunt your whore of the month in front of me?" I ask and Nicks jaw drops. "To then try to leave and not be a part of it to get tackled to the ground and have my head split open. But if that's not fucked up enough. I come home to find that the guy I'm dating got married." I begin to cry.
"You want me to stay or go?" Rob interrupts. "I've got work in the morning."

"Go, thanks for everything." I say, calming down a bit.
"No, problem. Her instructions are on the counter, she is kinda like a gremlin, don't get her wet, and don't feed her after midnight....you know." Scott interjects and starts laughing. He comes over and kisses my cheek. "You know I'm only playing, I love ya and will see you tomorrow."
Rob and Scott are gone.

"Instructions?" Nick is confused.
"Yeah, the staples, the concussion?" I say pointing at my head. "Want a beer?" I ask as I head into the kitchen.
"Sure." He says.
I come back with 2 beers and he opens them. "Where are you staying?" I look at him.
"I figured my room." He looks up. "I'm just here to take care of you."

"I think that's the problem. I am safer solo. Nothing happens." I sigh.

"Don't say that." He moves closer to me on the couch.
"I'm not kidding. I seem to only have control when I am single and alone." I say.

"That's no way to look at life." He says back.
"Really! Cause relationships for you end so well." I look at him.
"Well, that doesn't mean you stop trying." He says.

"You certainly are always trying....maybe I should be like you and just have random hook ups." I wait for his response.
"Don't be like that." He says.

"It's good enough for you." I look at him again and take a drink from my beer.

"The last few times I've been out there, Tandy, Tiffany...wait..are you just going thru the alphabet? You know it eventually comes to an end." I laugh.
"That's not funny." He looks irritated.
"Yes, actually it is." I laugh more.

"Well, if it amuses you, fine then." He smiles and puts his arm around me and I leave it there.

We sit quietly for a few minutes. "What the hell is wrong with me, Nick?" I ask.
"What do you mean? Wrong with you. Nothing is wrong with you." He replies.
"Obviously, there is. I mean, I try not to be clingy, I try not to be overbearing. I don't need constant attention. I can support myself, I acclimate to whatever and still, I get treated like shit in the end." I sigh and drink more from the bottle.

"You don't deserve that." He says, squeezing my shoulder. "You deserve better."

"Then why do you do it to me?" I ask and he sits forward and looks at me.
"I thought we were talking about Len?" He says.
"Why did you insist I come out there if you were with someone?" I ask him directly.
"She wasn't supposed to come there." He says.
"But you were sleeping with her when you were begging

me to go?" I am trying to figure out the timeline in my head.

"Rain, she meant nothing. I was bored." My face becomes deadpan looking at him. "That sounds awful, but she was just supposed to be a one-night stand. She just sort of kept coming over. I thought you weren't even coming to the show."

"Keep digging." I say.

"Look, no one will disagree that I am not perfect, I am who I am. You were with someone anyways." He says.
"But why was it so important that I be there?" I ask.
"The song, I've never written a song for anyone before, I wrote it about us. I wrote it for you." He takes my hands in his. "I thought if you heard it, it might change something between us, I don't know. Then she showed up and fucked it all up." He says with disgust. "Even without you coming, I didn't want her there."

"I need another beer." I announce and Nick gets up and retrieves one for me.

"You need to take it easy, your head and all." He opens it and hands it to me and I drink it down without really stopping. "Really?"

"I need another beer." I say again, partly to see how he reacts.
"No." He says.
"I can get up and get my own beer." I say and stumble a bit over the afghan on the floor.
"Sit, Jesus, I will get it for you if you slow down." He brings

339

back another beer and hesitates as he hands it to me. "Slow."

"Wanna hear something weird?" I ask him and he raises his eyebrows at me in anticipation. "It felt worse when Tiffany started telling me you two were together than when I read that Len was married." I say, not even sure why I told him that. It's the truth, but I never share things like that.

"What are you saying?" He asks.

"When Scott told me that Len got married, I was annoyed, pissed, but whatever. When I was at the bar and Tiffany said that you two were together it felt like I got kicked in the stomach, it was so much worse." I lean back on the couch realizing that, yet again, I have had too much to drink.

"So you are saying I still hurt you more....Rain, I can't say I'm sorry enough." He seems sad.

"I don't know what I'm saying. I'm just a bit tired and a bit tipsy. I shouldn't have told you. I'm sorry." I say and feel myself drifting to sleep.

"Rain, its 2am, why don't you head up to bed?" Nick is nudging me. "Ahh, I will carry you." He says and brings me to my room and places me in bed. "You want me to help you undress?" he asks.

"I can do it." I say half asleep, I slip off my bra and sweatpants and climb into bed with a t-shirt and panties on. "Stay?" I am already falling back asleep. I hear him take his pants and shirt off and climb under the covers and wrap around me.

Chapter 40

I wake up in the morning curled up with Nick. He seems to be awake. "How long have you been up for?" I ask.
"Ohh, maybe an hour?" He says.
"Just laying here?" I am surprised.
"Yeah, just enjoying it." He replies and stretches around me to kiss my forehead.

"Nick." I stop him before he gets any stupid ideas. "What time is it?" I ask him and he checks his phone.
"9:30"

"Oh, shit, I have to get going. I have to get everything done early." I say as I spring out of bed.
"Why?" He asks

"The dinner tonight?" I say.

"What dinner?" he says.
"With my family, for my birthday." I reply as I get in the shower.
"When is your birthday?" He asks following me into my bathroom.
"Today?" I say as I start to wash my hair.
"Today!" he seems shocked.
"November 5th every year." I say.
"Shit! How did I not know this?" he seems agitated.

"Its fine, Rob put together a nice dinner for me and my family and him and Scott." I say.
"Can I come?" He asks.
"Yeah, you can have Len's seat, I'm guessing he won't be showing up." I rinse and shut the water off. "Hand me a

341

towel?" I ask.

"That's not funny." He says, handing me a towel.

"If I can laugh about it, it's funny. I get to decide these things." I look at him with a towel wrapped around me. "Let me be? I have to get ready." I say and he heads out of the bedroom and downstairs. I put on a pair of jeans and a long sleeve blouse and head to my office. Nick comes in a few minutes later with a coffee.

"Thank you." I say.

"Hey, Doug did some digging. He has the backstory on Len's wedding if you're interested." He sits down.

I look up from my computer at him as he continues, "They were together for a long time and they broke up. I think you were just some rebound or to make her jealous."

"Stop, enough." I cut him off. "I really don't care anymore."

"Got it, can I get you anything for breakfast?" He asks.

"Nah, I kinda have a headache and think I might just head out to Tony's." I say.

"Did you take anything for the pain?" he looks concerned.

"No, but they make me lightheaded, I can't take then and drive." I say.

"I can drive you, it's the least that I can do. Let me go get ready. 5 minutes." He says and heads upstairs and comes back down ready to go.

He drives me to Tony's shop in the Mercedes. "Want me to stay here or will you be a while?" He asks.

"Yes." I reply.
"To what?"

"I'm gonna be a little bit, but I don't want to be waiting to go." I say with a sigh, knowing I'm being unreasonable.

"That's fine." He subsides.
I head into the office and he follows me. I think to myself that I might push my luck if I tell him to wait in the car. I sit down at the desk and take care of incoming and outgoing invoices and Ty comes in about to say something and pauses when he sees Nick.
"uhh, Hi Nick." He says slowly, looking over at me.
"Hi." Nick says back.

"Just checking on you from yesterday." Ty says to me.
"Thank you. Ty, a cup of coffee sounds awesome." I reply, not looking up from the desk.
"2 cups of coffee, coming right up." He returns with 3 cups, one for each of us. "How's the head?" He asks.

I take the bottle of pills out of my purse and shake them at him. "About to be a bit better."

"That's good." He looks over to Nick. "When did you get here?"

"Last night. I think right after you all left." He says.

Tony begins to walk into my office as well. "Mel wants to know what kind of ca....Hi Nick." Tony seems surprised as well that he is here. "You come out for Rain's birthday?" he asks.

"That's not why I came out, but I'm here for it so…."Nick trails off.

"Mel wants to know what kind of cake you want?" Tony looks back to me.

"Chocolate." He is staring at me trying to figure out the situation. "And tell Bella her fairy godmother wand is defective." I look back at him. I see him thinking and then begin to laugh out loud. "Ohh. Rain!" He smiles at me and heads out of the room.

"So, did you hear Len got married?" Ty asks and I choke on my coffee.

"Ty!" I blurt out.

"Yeah, he's an asshole." Nick replies.

"Yeah, but good for you, right?" Ty asks and I begin to get out of my chair and he shields himself. "Not the throat." And begins laughing hysterically.

"Get out of here, now!" I say and sit down at the desk. "I think I'm gonna be done sooner than I thought. I take the papers, flip through to see if there is anything that has to be done today and put them in a folder that I mark Monday on. "Let's go." I say to Nick.

"Headed out so soon?" Tony asks as I pass him in the hallway.

"Ask Ty." I reply without stopping.

We get in the car. "Whats Ty's deal?" he asks me.

"He's been getting weirder since he moved back with Mom. I think he resents us sometimes for him drawing the shortest straw." I say.

"Where are we off to now?" he asks me.

"Home? I just want to lay down." I say. "These pills take

the throbbing away, but they make me tired." We reach my house and I lay back down on the couch. I doze off and am awoken by the doorbell. Nick answers it and a gigantic bouquet of roses are delivered. He puts them on the coffee table and hands me the card.

"You?" I ask him.
"I didn't know it was even your birthday till a few hours ago, not me." He says as I open the card. I scan the card.
"Just throw them out." I say.
"Why?" he asks.
"They are from Len, shit you not." I say.
"Gone." He says and picks up the vase and puts it back outside on the stoop. "He didn't send them to you today. He probably ordered them a week ago or something."
"Whatever." I say and lay back down.

"You like flowers?" He asks me, sitting on the edge of the couch next to me.

"Have you ever even bought me flowers?" I look up. "I can't even remember." I say, sounding tired. "Oh, yeah, after I came home from your birthday...." I trail off, remembering sending them all back. "I think I just need to rest now." I say falling asleep.

"Rain, wake up. You slept for 3 hours, its 2." Nick is nudging me.

"Ohh. Ok." I say as I turn over on the couch.

"Look, I'll let you sleep for 30 more minutes, then you should really get up." He says and kisses my forehead and heads out of the room.

I lay there and decide I probably should just get up or I will never sleep tonight. I head to the kitchen and over hear him talking to Lisa. He seems to be asking about what to get me for my birthday. I walk in the room and he hangs up with her quickly.

"Eavesdropping?" He looks at me.
"Talking about me behind my back?" I smile back at him.
"Jesus, Rain, It's your birthday. I didn't even know. Everything this weekend, and I didn't even do anything." He is really annoyed about this. "Fuck, Len even got you flowers."

"Nick, stop, its fine." I say walking over to him. "A day without any drama. That's all I asked for. You can ask Rob, I told him that weeks ago when he asked what I wanted. I simply want a day where nothing goes wrong." I lean up to him and put my head on his chest and he instinctively puts his arms around me.
"Rain, I want this. This right here." He says softly.
"Taking my birthday wish, are we?" I smile at him.
"I'm being serious. Doesn't this feel right? This right here." He squeezes his arms around me a bit snugger.
"Friends, too much has happened." I say, sadly.

We sit on the couch and watch tv for a few hours. It feels weird just sitting and doing nothing but I don't think that my mind is strong enough to actually process doing anything. Rob and Scott arrive at my house to pick me up.
"Hey Nick, made it through the night, I see." Scott laughs.

Rob and Scott both hug me separately and wish me a happy birthday.

My mother and Ty arrive next. "Rain, most people put mums out on the stoop in the fall, those roses will be dead in 2 days." She says to me.

"I know, mother, they were from Len, I really didn't want them in the house." I reply with a sigh.
"Ohh, well, then that's the perfect place for them." She smiles at me,

Tony and Melissa arrive child-free. "Mel needed a night out so we hired a sitter. Bella is mad, but I promised her you would stop by to see her this week. OK?" Tony says as he comes in.
"Of course." I reply.
Tony gives Ty a weird look.
"I'm sorry for being an ass this morning." Ty looks to me and then to Tony.
"You are making him apologize?" I laugh.
"I know whatever he said was worse than the version I got, so, yeah. I am." Tony seems to be acting tough.
"25 years on this earth, and now, finally, this one time, you crossed the line, Ty." I laugh.

"Yup, only once. It won't happen ever, ever again." He is trying not to laugh himself.

We all head out to a restaurant and have a nice dinner. Everyone is having a great time. Melissa seems to de-stress a bit without the kids and eventually we have cake and some cards are handed to me and we head home.

"See," I say to Nick as he is driving. "Just a birthday, not a big deal. Never liked too much fanfare." I say.

"OK, I know." He leans over and pats my hand. "How is your head?" He asks.

"Ehh, not too bad." I say.

"Can I do anything for you tonight?" He asks me.

"Like what?" I ask.

"Whatever you want." He says.

"Give me options." I reply, almost giggling. "What are my choices?"

"It's only 8, we could go see a movie?" He suggests.

"No. Try again." I quickly respond.

"We could go find a bar and I could let you drink till I have to carry you out." He laughs.

"Ehh, maybe. We'll put that on the back burner for now." I laugh.

"I could run you a hot bath and get you a glass of wine and then when you are done, I just rub your back?" He looks to me quickly while he is driving.

"See, you do know me a little bit." I laugh.

"Consider it done, we get back to your house and wait on the couch." He says.

"I think I can manage that." We reach the house and Nick heads upstairs and I hear the water running.

"You can come up here now." I enter the bathroom and my tub is filled with bubbles. "Go ahead, I have to go get you a glass of wine. Do you want one of your pain pills with it?" he asks and I nod my head yes.

He returns with a glass of wine and a pill and hands it to me in the tub. I relax and drink my glass.

"You feel good?" He asks me.

"Yes, very good." I say, tilting my head back. I soak in the tub for about 20 minutes. Nick only stayed for about 5. I get out of the tub and put on a t-shirt and robe around that and head downstairs. I feel light headed along the way.

"Nick, I think I'm just gonna go to bed." I say not quite at the bottom of the stairs.

"What? You ok?" He asks.

"I just feel a little dizzy." I say.

"Well, I can come up and rub your back?" He asks.

"IF you really want to, not making any promises on how long I will be awake for." I head to my bedroom and get under the covers. I hear Nick enter the room.

"You want to lie on your stomach or just on your side." He says.

"I'm comfortable the way that I am." I say and he slides into bed next to me. He begins to rub my shoulders and works his way down my back. It all feels good and I begin to drift.

Chapter 41

I wake up Tuesday with him curled around me again.
"Nick, wake up." I nudge him.
"What? Ohh," He seems to not quite realize where he is at first. "Rain." He says and snuggles back next to me.
"Nick, I have to get up." I say and begin to slip out of his grip.

"Ok." He says, I look at him wanting to almost stay in bed. I skipped really doing any work yesterday so I really have to catch up today. I leave him and head to the closet to get dressed. I head to the kitchen and make coffee and head into my office to begin my day. An hour or so later Nick joins me with a cup of coffee.
"You didn't need to leave me to sleep." He says.
"I woke you up once, I had things to do. Besides, you must have been tired. I slept great." I say, actually feeling a lot better than the last few days.

"I'm glad you did. Hey, I have to head home later today. I have meetings with the label early in the morning tomorrow." He says, watching for my reaction.
"It's ok. I will manage without you." I actually don't want to be here alone right now. The whole thing with Len and all....

"I can come right back if you want me to." He says, seeing that it has affected me a bit.

"Nick, we both have to get back to what we do. It's fine." I feel depressed. "Besides there is probably a small group of women whose names start with the letter 'u' wondering where you are." I laugh at my joke.

"Rain. Why?" he does not find the same amusement as I do. "It's done, no more." He says.

"What's done?" I am confused.
"Those types of relationships. Done. No more." He says.
"For what? Nick the Rockstar becomes Nick the Celibate? Come on. That's not who you are." I say, trying to determine if he is serious.
"No, it's hurt you too many times." He says.

"Nick, getting tackled hurt, you...well that's just something that I have to get over." I say. "Friends, remember?" I look at him.

"It's my choice." He says.
"Look, I don't want to have this conversation again. It's actually been a nice visit. Can we just end on a good note?" I ask.

"You are absolutely right. Want to have lunch? Then maybe drop me at the airport?" He asks.
"Sure, we need to go now?" I ask.
"Probably, if you want lunch." He replies and I get up and gather my things.
We head out to lunch. He talks about the meeting and getting ready to release the album. A few meetings on Wednesday and then he is done. I tell him to keep in touch and see him off at the airport.

The next two weeks go by. I am getting back into my routine. Thanksgiving is next week and it will be the first without my father and I am dreading it. I think we all are, but we carry on and prepare. Melissa and Tony usually head to her family, but under the circumstances they are eating with our side this year. I got an invite from Lisa and Tony for dinner, but they also understand. Nick is heading to his parent's house and then plans on heading up Friday to see me at the bar.

Dinner is sad and feels forced. The kids were great and we cleaned up and watched football the rest of the afternoon. I head home and go to bed.
I get Tony's office work done pretty early as he gives everyone the day off and there is no one there but me. I head to the bar afterwards. I get some scheduling done and call Lisa to check in with her and chat about dinner. I also call Rob. His relationship has reached the point where him and his mother joined Scott's family for dinner. He said it was nice. His mother offered to host it for all of them next year.

The bar starts to pick up about 7ish and Nick stops in.
"Hey, how ya been?" He asks me with a hug.
"Good, Yesterday was a little depressing, but what are you gonna do?" I say with a sigh.

"I'm so sorry." He says and hugs me again. "Any plans for the weekend?"

"Just being here, maybe a little shopping for Christmas? I don't know, why?" I ask.
"Why don't you come out to LA? Relax a little?" He offers.
"There has never been a relaxing trip to LA." I say, laughing a little.

"Anywhere, where do you want to go?" He asks.
"I don't want to go anywhere." I say.

"OK, just offering." He says and backs off a bit.
"Want a drink?" I look to the bar.
"Sure, a beer will be good." He says. "Hey, want me to play tonight?" He looks out to the stage.
"That would be a question for the booked and, not me." I point out. "It's just a cover band, nothing too big, it's the day after Thanksgiving." I say. "They will probably love it, they are in the back, go see 'em." I say.
He heads back there and comes back a while later. "One song, that's all I'm playing."

"They only want you on one song?" this sounds odd.
"No, I'm gonna play a few with them. I am doing one solo song." He says.
"Ok." I have no idea what he is talking about and move along. I take a seat at the end of the bar as the band begins to play. They do a few songs and then take a break. They come back and play 2 more and then Nick joins them on stage and the place goes insane. Nick plays along with them for about 3 more songs and then they break again. A few minutes later, Nick comes out solo with a stool and an acoustic guitar. He announces that there is a new album coming out soon and that this is his favorite song on it. He plays 'make it rain' and it is beautiful. It seems heartfelt and I feel almost sick to my stomach it aches so bad. He finishes, the place gives the applause and cheers that it deserves and he turns the stage back to the cover band. He comes to find me at the end of the bar and is being bombarded by fans, some guys, some women throwing

themselves at him. He reaches me and I suggest we head to the office and we head directly there.

"Nick, that was amazing." I say, thinking that I did not recall most of it the first time I heard it that infamous night in LA.

"Rain, I love you." He says, moving closer to me.

"Nick, stop." I say.

"But why?" He asks.

"I can't go thru this again. Every time, Nick, every single time something else happens and it just makes it worse. We can't wipe the slate clean and too much has happened. I've been hurt too many times. I can't do it again." I say, feeling tears well in my eyes and try to compose myself. "Want to just go?" I ask.

"You want me to leave right now?" He asks, a bit shocked.

"No, not you, us, do you want to just go back to my house now? I don't want to be here anymore." I say.

"Sure" He says and I drive us back to my house.

"Want a coffee or something?" He asks me as we head in.

"Nick, I need to go to bed." I say and head to my room.

Chapter 42

I wake up in the morning and hop in the shower and dress and head down stairs. Nick is cooking breakfast and offers me a cup of coffee. "Can you take me to the airport? I have a flight home at noon." He says.

"Uhh, sure." I reply.

"Thanks." He says.

I check my phone and see some missed texts and check my emails from last night, Nick still isn't really talking to me.

"You ok?" I ask him.

"Something came up, I have to head back, it's all good." He says and cleans up after he eats and heads upstairs to get his luggage. He returns a few minutes later. "Whenever you're ready." He says.

"Uhh, sure, I can grab a coffee on the way." I reply and we head out to the airport. The ride is quiet with him mostly on his phone and we reach the unloading area.

"Hey, thanks for the ride." He says and gets his stuff and heads in. I sit there for a moment and watch him walk away. Did he finally get it last night? I begin to drive home and replay the evening. I told him I love the song, it was a much better reaction than the first time that I heard it. I told him the truth about us, nothing more, nothing less. I don't want to date anyone. Too complicated.

I stop off at the mall on the way home, 2 weeks till Christmas. I buy things till I can't carry any more bags and decide to head home. I get home at 4 with enough time to grab a bite to eat and head to the bar. I focus on the bar all night and push Nick out of my head. The next week goes by smoothly, no accidents, no tackles, no whore drama, no marriages. Just Christmas shopping and routine.

Friday afternoon, I get a text from Nick. He is at the guitar store and he wants me to come down
'I am wrapping presents'

'please, just come over'

'nick, I'm busy, I have to get this done and head to the bar. Stop by there'

I get another text from Doug. 'you really need to come down here'

Oh, what the hell now. Is he drunk? Is he back on drugs? I reply back to Doug 'be there in a few' and head out to my truck and drive to the guitar store. I get there and head in. There is a line formed to a table where Nick is sitting signing autographs. I am looking around the store and see that the line is getting shorter. I step toward the line and Doug heads over to me.

"Excuse me, Nick is wondering if you would like to have a drink with him on the bus." Doug is trying to not look at me.
"Hell will freeze over before I ever get on that bus with him." I am shocked he would even suggest something like that. I turn around to go look at pianos and Nick is by my side.
"Hey there, we don't have to have a drink on the bus, how about dinner?" I turn to look at him and see the line is gone and it's just the two of us.

"Nick?" I'm bewildered. "What is all this?" I ask realizing this is exactly how I met him.

"You said our only hope was to start fresh, clean slate." He looks at me. "Dinner? Just the two of us?" He asks.

The End.

Book 3, the final Rain book coming soon.

Find me on Facebook @ Rain: Rachel Ann

For contact info email @ rain.rachelann@gmail.com

www.ingramcontent.com/pod-product-compliance
Lightning Source LLC
Chambersburg PA
CBHW021438240626
47153CB00001B/206